THE RECOGNITION RUN

Recognition Series Book 1

HENRY VOGEL

Published in the United States of America by Rampant Loon Press, an imprint of Rampant Loon Media LLC, P.O. Box 111, Lake Elmo, Minnesota 55042. "Rampant Loon Press" and the Rampant Loon colophon are trademarks of Rampant Loon Media LLC.

www.rampantloonmedia.com

Cover design by www.ebooklaunch.com

ISBN: 978-1-938834-98-1 (ebook)

ISBN: 978-1-938834-99-8 (print)

First publication: July 2017

RECOGNITION CEREMONY

Olivia

I watched my older brother with pride shining in my eyes. Robert Kahn succeeded where all of our ancestors failed. No one else in the history of our family ever came close to matching Robert's victory. Centuries of futility—until Robert assumed the dukedom, that is.

He terrified the Wilkinson family.

He targeted them, driving the family heirs into hiding.

He killed the heirs off one-by-one, until none was left.

He eliminated the family without once leaving evidence of his deeds.

He brought down our ancestral foe.

Of course, His Majesty and the heads of the other Houses *knew* Robert was behind the destruction of House Wilkinson. House Kahn wanted it no other way. What is the point of destroying political and familial enemies if no one knows you've done it? But knowing it and proving it are not the same thing.

As a result of Robert's brilliant campaign, Neert, the largest duchy in the Star Kingdom, was simply sitting there ripe for plucking by the first family willing to lay claim to the title and establish Recognition. Yes, there was still the dowager Duchess, but Lady Evelyn was a Wilkinson by marriage, not blood. She held her title only until the completion of today's Recognition ceremony.

As if on cue, Her Grace the Duchess of Neert Evelyn Wilkinson entered the Recognition chamber. Conversation stopped as all heads swiveled toward the woman. The Duchess scanned the gathered crowd, ignoring the stares turned toward her with a haughty disdain worthy of any noble present. Though I hate to admit it, even to myself—she was still a Wilkinson, even if only by marriage—I admired the woman's style and composure.

Then Lady Evelyn's eyes locked on me. Despite my hatred and all of my carefully trained court composure, my breath caught when the Duchess glided toward me. Murmurs rose from the gathered nobles, no doubt speculating what Lady Evelyn had in mind for me, a much younger woman. For my part, I forced myself to breathe evenly and kept my eyes firmly locked on the approaching woman.

"Hello, Olivia," Lady Evelyn said, after stopping well inside my personal space. I knew the dowager Duchess enjoyed making people uncomfortable in that way and consciously stopped myself from stepping away from her. In an even, measured tone, Lady Evelyn continued, "You're looking as beautiful as ever, I see. Your blonde hair and pale complexion provide a striking contrast to your black gown. Alas, the effect is marred by your cold, blue eyes."

"Greetings, Lady Evelyn," I responded, struggling to match the older woman's tone and bearing. "I cannot begin to tell you how sorry I am at the death of your youngest son, Charles."

"You're very kind, Olivia, though not kind enough to stop your brother from killing him." Lady Evelyn maintained her even tone, but I saw the anger and anguish burning in her eyes. Good, I'd scored the first hit.

I shook my head in mock disapproval. "You surprise me, Lady Evelyn. I never thought you would be one to listen to court gossip! Surely, His Majesty would have Robert in chains were there any evidence supporting this outlandish claim."

"Just as surely, His Majesty has no desire to attract Robert the Butcher's attention," Lady Evelyn countered.

I felt anger flare at the name some uncouth members of the court gave to my brother. Score a return hit for Lady Evelyn. "You mean Robert the *Smith*—the nickname given to my brother because he is strong and has a will forged from steel."

"I meant exactly what I said, Olivia. You're an intelligent young woman, surely you've noticed the line of bodies your brother leaves in his wake." Lady Evelyn's lips turned up in a cold and cruel smile. "After all, your own parents are among those slaughtered by Robert."

"*That is a lie!*" My shout cut through the low conversations in the Recognition Chamber, drawing all eyes our way. Damn this woman for bypassing my defenses so easily!

"Come now, dear, even someone as remarkably biased as you simply cannot deny the similarities between your parents' accident and the one that claimed my Lord Arthur's life." Lady Evelyn shook her head, dismay at my supposed naivety written plainly on her face. "Then there was the death of your last suitor. Bizarre though his demise was, the similarities between his 'accident' and the others are quite remarkable—unless you consider who arranged those deaths."

"I will not listen to such slander against my brother," I insisted. "I know the real reason you're so upset—you don't want to lose your position to Robert."

"I never even wanted my position, dear." Lady Evelyn's cold smile broadened. "But if I were you, I wouldn't be so sure I was about to lose it."

What did she mean by that? My mind whirled, searching for a proper response, but before I could think of one the royal fanfare sounded. Conversation halted abruptly as everyone turned toward the dais at the other end of the room.

A herald banged his staff on the floor three times before announcing, "His Royal Majesty Bernard the Second, king by the grace of God. All present, give obeisance due to His Majesty!"

As one, we took a knee and bowed our heads as King Bernard entered and climbed the dais. Several seconds later, the herald called, "All may rise!"

The king's gaze swept over the nobles present before coming to rest on a powerful man standing apart from the others. "It appears your show is very popular among Our aristocracy, my Lord Robert."

Robert clicked his heels together and bowed to his king. "You honor me with your presence, Sire, as do my fellow members of the aristocracy."

"Yes, quite," Bernard said lazily. In formal tones, he continued, "For the record, please inform the Court of your intentions, Lord Robert."

"I have come before Your Majesty and these assembled nobles to stake claim to the Duchy of Neert," my brother proclaimed, his voice filling the large chamber. "As Lord Arthur and all of his children are dead, I shall place my hand upon the Star Stone and request Recognition as the new Lord of Neert."

"This is in accordance with the laws and customs of Our kingdom," Bernard stated. "The Star Stone will only grant Recognition if Lord Arthur has no other living children. You are aware of this and of the consequences should an heir still live?"

"I am, Your Majesty."

"Does any member of Our court wish to challenge Lord Robert for the right to request Recognition?" Bernard's gaze swept the nobles a second time. When no one stepped forward, his eyes returned to Robert. "As none challenge your right of Recognition and as you are aware of the risks inherent in this course of action, we accede to your request."

Robert bowed once again to King Bernard and approached the Star Stone. The huge, multifaceted gem sparkled scarlet. To my eyes, the stone's color deepened as if it anticipated its role in the ceremony. Robert gave me one quick glance, his usual confident smile flashing for my benefit.

Pulling the glove off of his right hand, Robert laid his bare hand on the Star Stone. In a strong, clear voice, he declared, "I, Robert Kahn, Lord of Gaunner and loyal vassal of His Royal Majesty Bernard the Second, request Recognition as the new Lord of Neert."

The Star Stone pulsed once and then bright scarlet light enveloped Robert. He had time for one startled cry before the light blazed so brightly that we all were blinded for a second. When the spots faded from my eyes and I could see again, all that was left of my brother was a cloud of ashes settling to the floor next to the Star Stone.

Stunned silence filled the chamber, so we all heard when Lady Evelyn, dowager Duchess of Neert clapped her hands, gave a delighted laugh, and said, "What wonderful entertainment! Lady Olivia, I believe your brother must now be called Lord Ro*burnt*!"

THE OLD MAN

Drake

Three years later and 102 light years away

"Can you spare a few credits, sir?"

The voice was thin with a quaver of age and infirmity that was almost undetectable. It drew my eyes to a collection of oversized clothes and the old man wearing them. His white hair was wispy and equally white stubble covered a dark, lined face. The old man kept his deep brown eyes downcast, but I was certain those eyes missed little of what was going on around him.

Today, that meant a busy day at the open market just outside of Thinda's largest spaceport. Locals hawked everything from fresh vegetables to crafts—supposedly handmade, authentic planetary folk culture that made perfect gifts for spouses and children back home—and from narcotics to prostitutes. I had seen dozens of these markets on dozens of different worlds and knew how they really worked. Instead of growing the vegetables themselves, the vendors usually bought them at stores far away from the port, marked the prices way up, and then sold them to spacers short on time for shopping. Most of the folk crafts were mass-produced in factories that probably weren't even on this planet. The narcotics and prostitutes were real enough, though, as were the dangers anyone faced if they partook of the promised pleasures from either of them.

One thing that was missing was anybody willing to toss a few coins into the old man's hat. No one besides me even gave the man a single glance. I dug a few coins out of my pocket and dropped them into the man's hat.

The old man smiled broadly at me. "I thank you and my belly thanks you, good sir!"

"Hungry, are you?" I asked, drawn to this man for some reason I couldn't quite identify. I squatted down next to the man and tried looking him in the eyes.

The old man's eyes darted away from mine, but he bobbed his head. "A bit, sir. Just a bit."

"Then perhaps you could do me a favor, sir. I'm newly arrived in port and am hungry for something other than shipboard rations. I'm also starved for conversation. If you would agree to help me with the conversation, I'd happily pay for the meal." I rose and extended a hand to help the old man stand up. "I realize it's an imposition and I'm taking shameless advantage of you, but I hope you'll accept."

The old man took my proffered hand, his grip surprisingly strong, and cackled, "You're a right smooth one, young man. I'll try not to bore you too much."

Prepared for boredom, I was pleasantly surprised at Jared's—for that was the name the old man gave me—breadth of knowledge and his collection of improbable stories. He kept me laughing —honest laughter, not feigned out of politeness—throughout the meal, and left me wondering just how this man ended up in his dire situation. I was so distracted, I didn't even notice the girl at the bar until Jared pointed her out at the end of the meal. Considering how long I'd been without the company of a woman, that's saying a lot.

"I think you've wasted enough time with an old man like me, Drake. There's a right pretty girl over at the bar who's been looking over here whenever she thinks no one is paying attention. I know it's not *me* she's interested in!"

I glanced at the bar, not sure what to expect, but once my eyes locked on the girl they stayed there drinking in the sight. The woman was lovely, with pale skin and flame-red hair. She was seated, but I was sure she was built tall and slender—exactly the type of woman I've always found attractive. My eyes met her bright blue ones for just a second as she glanced toward the table and then, her cheeks coloring slightly, looked away. Damn, but her combination of looks and innocence was incredibly alluring—especially for someone like me who'd spent the last few weeks alone on a spaceship. And that's when my mental alarm bells began ringing.

Turning away from the woman at the bar, I glared at the old man. "I may not be as old as you, sir, but this isn't my first port of call. How much are you hoping to extort from me when this is all over?"

Jared drew himself up, indignation written on his face. "I have no extortion plans for you, young man. I am simply trying to give two rather lonely young people the pleasure of each other's company."

"And just how do you know she's lonely if you don't know her?" I challenged.

"I never said I didn't know her, Drake. I said I wasn't planning any extortion against you." All during lunch Jared never looked me in the eye. Now, his eyes suddenly captured mine. They blazed intently as he continued, "Jeanine has been known to help me out from time to time. She probably came in here to make sure I was okay, but she's mostly been looking at *you*."

I drew back slightly from Jared's intensity, then leaned in again and studied his expression. If he was lying, he was too good at it for me to catch him. After a few more seconds, I nodded. "Sorry if I offended you, but I've had lots of men try that trick on me in ports all around the kingdom and a few places outside of it."

Jared broke eye contact and waved off my apology. "Nah, you've got a good point, Drake. I shouldn't have gone off on you like that.

It's just that Jeanine does a lot for me and I like to repay my debts. You're a good man and I know you and she could have a good time together. I'm sure the two of you would find more interesting stuff to talk about than you have with an old man like me!"

I grinned, "Even if part of our conversation involves me saying 'Good morning, sleepyhead' to her?"

The old man cackled with good humor. "It would do her good to get properly laid. Do you good, too, I'll bet!"

I couldn't help but laugh. "You're one dirty old man!"

"Ain't that the truth, lad," Jared responded. "Now, why don't you go talk to her. Tell Jeanine I said you were okay."

ARGENTA PROTOCOL

Jeanine

Drake and I talked for an hour and a half after he introduced himself. I hate to say it, but I never even noticed when Grandfather left the tavern. We made arrangements to meet for dinner and I gave Drake a quick peck on the lips in parting. He took it for what it was and didn't try for anything more—definitely a good sign—and I sauntered away. Certain Drake was still watching me, I worked my hips just a bit. I wasn't sure just how far things would go after dinner, but it never hurts to let a man know what might be in store if he behaves himself.

I reached the alley from which I was certain Grandfather was watching us. Without looking, I pointed into the alley and crooked my finger in summons. Grandfather scurried right out and joined me.

I gave him my best glare, which only drew a smile in response. Then my grandfather said, "You and the dashing Drake appear to have hit it off rather well."

"Did you really tell him it would do me good to get laid?" I demanded.

"Of course not," he responded. "I said it would do you good to get *properly* laid. And if I'm any judge of character, that young man will put your pleasure ahead of his own."

"Gah!" I growled. Lowering my head, I massaged my temples as if dispelling a bad headache.

"Jeanine, dear, you're a healthy woman who is just short of her twenty-fifth birthday. Sexual desire is—"

"Natural," I interrupted. "Yes, I know. I'm not exactly a virgin, after all."

"Technically, you're correct, though I don't think fumbling around with that inexperienced boy six years ago really counts. In all definitions of 'virgin' beyond the strictly biological one, I'd say you still qualify."

"This conversation is over and we will never, *ever* resume it. Is that clear?" I said as forcefully as I could manage.

"I suppose that means you don't want my advice on what to wear tonight?" Grandfather asked, unable to suppress a grin.

"I neither want nor need your advice!" God knows that was true. My grandfather had no fashion sense at all.

After we got back to our apartment, I spent much of the afternoon sorting through my small collection of clothes looking for just the right thing to wear. I must have tried dozens of combinations before settling on a pair of black pants and a matching black shirt. Relenting to Grandfather's curiosity, I modeled the outfit for him.

"What do you think?"

"You're lovely, as always, Jeanine. You've always looked beautiful in black. And, of course, that color makes it much easier for you to disappear into the shadows. Do your legs have sufficient range of motion in those pants?"

Rather than answer, I snapped off a kick that ended with my foot several centimeters above my head. Then I transitioned into a spin kick with my other leg before dropping into a deep crouch. Rising, I said, "Satisfied?"

Grandfather nodded and asked, "Weapons?"

"Daggers strapped to my wrists and one on my back. I've got my blaster in my bag."

"That's my girl!" Grandfather beamed.

I picked up my bag, felt the reassuring weight of the blaster inside it, and kissed Grandfather on the cheek. "Don't wait up."

He patted my hand fondly. "Have fun and if you find yourself tempted tonight, give into the temptation!"

Then, with a roar, the apartment's door blew in.

With the instincts forged through two decades of training, I dropped to the floor. In my peripheral vision, I saw my grandfather do the same. The door to our little apartment tumbled over us. Despite the noise from the blast, I heard a surprised grunt come from the balcony as the door crashed into someone coming in the back way. I rolled away from the line of sight from the doorway, triggering the catch for the dagger strapped to my right wrist. It slid neatly into my hand as I rose into a crouch.

"Balcony," I said, my right arm already in motion.

With the flick of a wrist, I released the dagger. It spun toward a man partially covered by the door. He spotted the whirling blade a split second before it buried itself in his throat. His hands rose in a futile attempt to staunch the blood spurting from his throat as a second man leapt over the railing and onto the balcony. With professional detachment, the new man did not even spare a glance at the plight of his fellow. He should have taken a quick look. The man's right foot landed in the spreading pool of blood and the foot slid a few inches. It wasn't much of a slip, but it distracted the man and kept him motionless for just a tick too long. The dagger from my left wrist plunged into his right eye.

There was no one else coming over the balcony railing, so I spun toward the front door. Three men sprawled on the floor, already dead, as my grandfather broke the neck of a fourth.

"Clear," I said, amazed that my voice remained calm and even. Lord knows I was anything but calm on the inside.

From the hall, I heard the sound of a single person walking toward the doorway, the footfalls too heavy for a woman. I found its measured pace frightening as if an implacable and unstoppable enemy was after me.

My grandfather looked over his shoulder at me. "Argenta protocol."

I gasped, my fear rising toward terror. Argenta protocol was simple—I ran for my life while my grandfather fought on alone. I never thought I'd hear Grandfather speak the words except as part of a training exercise.

Turning away from me, he did a second thing I never thought I'd see—he took his ceremonial sword off the wall and drew it from its scabbard. The blade I'd never before seen slid free, its brightly polished metal glowing in the late afternoon light streaming in from the balcony.

"Go!" Grandfather ordered, his eyes on the doorway. In a low voice only I could hear, he added, "Don't forget your date tonight."

I ran for the balcony, grabbing the bag with my blaster as I went.

A strong, pleasant voice filled the room. "It's been a very long time, Jared."

"Not nearly long enough, Phillip," my grandfather snarled in reply.

I vaulted the railing of the balcony and dropped toward the street two stories below. Behind me, metal struck metal, ringing with the sound you only get from superbly forged steel. I fell past a third man huddled below the balcony, hit the awning for the shop on the ground floor—one reason my grandfather selected this apartment—rolled over the edge of the awning, and dropped lightly to the street below.

My sudden arrival startled everyone around the shop, all of them drawing back from me and the blade I drew from my back. When the third man rolled off the awning and dropped to the street in front of me, the pedestrians recoiled even more. So you can imagine how they reacted when I drove the dagger up under the man's ribcage and into his heart. Looks of fear turned into screams of panic as people ran from me. Their terror served my purposes. If these mysterious attackers had allies on the street, they would have to fight the stampede to reach me, and that would give away their identities. Either there were no allies or, far more likely, they didn't want to make targets of themselves. Whatever the reason, I had no trouble blending into the running crowd and then slipping into the second darkened alley I came to.

As I'd known since Grandfather and I moved into this apartment, there was a fire escape in the alley two buildings down from ours. I quickly ascended several floors until I found an open window at the end of a hallway. Slipping through it, I walked quickly and quietly down the hallway toward the stairs. Most of the residents no doubt used the drop chute, but those things can be death traps. You're a sitting duck if pursuers shoot at you, or a dead one if they simply turn off the grav unit. Besides, I needed a minute to brush dust from my clothes and straighten my hair.

Five minutes later, I walked boldly out of the building's main entrance. I smiled and held the door for an elderly woman carrying a package, completing the illusion I was simply a resident on my way out.

The woman smiled her thanks and said, "I hope your young man appreciates just how lucky he is."

"Pardon?" I asked, my mind still on the events at the apartment.

"A pretty girl like you all dressed up like that?" the woman replied. "It'd be a downright shame if there wasn't a young man waiting for you."

I forced a smile, hoping it didn't look ghoulish. "That's so kind of you to say, ma'am. Yes, there is a young man waiting for me."

The woman nodded sagely. "First date jitters, dear?"

I guess my smile wasn't as genuine as I'd hoped. "Yes, ma'am."

"Just be yourself, dear, and try to have fun. That always worked for me." She waggled a couple of fingers at me in farewell and I released the door.

I forced myself to walk casually down the sidewalk, just a girl heading out on the town. I kept my eyes sweeping the area, watching for anyone paying too much attention to me. I caught a few men eying me, but their eyes focused on my breasts and butt instead of my face. I'm used to that reaction and sometimes even appreciate the glances. Killers aren't so easily distracted, so I knew the men checking me out were just men being men.

When I reached a shopping district, I ducked into a clothing store, selected a far more daring outfit than I usually wear from the catalog, and slipped into a fitting and fabrication unit. A few minutes later, I emerged wearing a skirt barely long enough to cover my backside and a midriff-baring top that showed a lot of cleavage. I didn't have time to change my hair color, but I'd put my hair up and covered it with a hat. Anyone looking for a redhead in black pants and shirt would look right over me—I hoped.

Twenty minutes later, I rounded a street corner and saw the tavern where Drake and I were meeting. Drake was standing outside, just as he said he'd be. He caught sight of me and his smile of greeting quickly widened as he took in my outfit. Still working hard to look casual, I sauntered up and gave him a kiss on the lips. It wasn't a long kiss, but it lingered just enough to build his hopes for an interesting evening.

"Hello, there," Drake said, his arm snaking around my waist. "Are you hungry?"

"Mmm hmm," I purred, "but why don't we pick something up and take it back to your ship?"

"Just like that?" he asked.

"Just like that," I replied. "After all, you heard what my grandfather said I needed."

"He's your *grandfather*? And he suggested I, um, you know?"

"Yes, he is." I desperately hoped that was still a true statement. "And yes, he did. Are you going to take his advice or not?"

We grabbed take-out from a food vendor on the corner. Then Drake flagged down a passing cab and we were on our way to the spaceport. I was one step closer to getting off this planet, just as my grandfather ordered me to do.

Drake

Jeanine leaned against me during the ride to the spaceport, squirming up under my arm and putting her head on my shoulder. Her warm breath tickled my throat, and she was trembling ever so slightly.

The trembling gave me pause. Maybe she was just anticipating what was to come when we got to my ship, but somehow I didn't think so. In our short time together, Jeanine struck me as the kind of girl who committed herself with reluctance, but didn't suffer from second thoughts once she was committed. I found myself wondering just how much Jeanine wanted to get 'properly laid.' As much as I enjoy a good romp in the sheets—or in the shower or against the nearest bulkhead—I want a willing and interested partner. I definitely did *not* want a girl who was only doing it because her grandfather said she should.

I was still trying to figure out what was running through the girl's head when I paid off the cab. Holding our take-out dinner with one hand and Jeanine with the other, I led her the final few hundred meters through the maze of docking bays until we reached mine. I keyed us through the door, wondering for the umpteenth time why something without a roof had a locked door, and motioned Jeanine inside. The lights came on automatically, illuminating my pride and joy.

"This is my ship, the *Rising Star*," I said, my tone formal.

"You've got a Helldiver blockade runner!" Jeanine gasped. She ran down to the *Star's* tail section. "And she even has the Class III star drive!" In an undertone, she added, "This is perfect."

Jeanine bent over and stuck her head between the three main thrusters and it was my turn to gasp. Seeing this girl from behind when she bent over would have been a real treat for any man, but seeing her bent over while wearing that incredibly short skirt was... Let's just say I was so distracted, I missed her next question. When I didn't respond, she pulled her head out of the engine. Only after she straightened, did I suddenly discover the ability to think and talk again.

"I'm sorry, what did you ask?" I said.

She turned to face me, apparently unaware of the effect she'd had on me. "I asked if you modified the engine yourself. What do you get, an extra five percent thrust from the mods?"

"About that, yeah. A friend of mine made the changes for me," I responded. "You sure know a lot about starships and space drives."

"For a girl, you mean?" she asked, arching an eyebrow.

"No, for anybody. Most people learn everything they know about starships watching adventure vids." As Jeanine's eyebrow came down, mine rose. "What did you mean when you said 'this is perfect'?"

"Hm? Oh, that was nothing." She might have fooled a lot of people, but I realized Jeanine was temporizing while she came up with an answer. "My grandfather flew one of these back in the Siruul Uprising. He was one of the pilots who helped defeat the blockade of the Chychie home world."

Jeanine flashed a wide smile that didn't quite make it to her eyes, then she bounced on her feet as if in excitement. I knew she was using her jiggling breasts to distract me from further questions, but

I'm still a man and it had been far too long since I enjoyed the company of a woman. In other words, her distraction worked. Taking my arm, she led me to the *Star's* main hatch. I held still while the biometric scanner verified my identity and then identified Jeanine as a guest. That designation told the *Star's* security systems that I wasn't under duress and restricted Jeanine's access to the living area.

I immediately started setting our dinner out on the small dining table and shortly we were tucking into the food. Jeanine was everything a perfect date should be—attentive, playful, happily offering bites of her dish and accepting bites of mine, and she gave just the right amount of coquettish flirting. And she asked me about the *Rising Star*.

"Did you inherit the *Star*, Drake?" Having a mouthful of food, I shook my head. She cocked her head and asked, "You bought her?"

Jeanine scored major points with me by referring to the *Star* by name and in feminine terms. Most people refer to my baby as 'the ship' or 'it' or something similar. Jeanine never did that even once. Despite all the flirting, it was this trait I found the most appealing.

"I found her abandoned and neglected in the back corner of a sales lot. The salesman wasn't too thrilled I ignored the nicer—and much more expensive—ships in the front to waste time with an old war relic he'd almost forgotten was even on the lot. I basically got her for the cost of moving her off the lot."

"How long did it take you to fix her up? It must have been a while since she looks practically brand new now."

"Less than a year. I wasn't working a regular job and had...come into some money...but she needed a lot of work on her outer hull. On the inside, she mostly just needed regular maintenance. I had some friends who helped a lot, all in exchange for food and alcohol. They didn't ask for anything else, but I told each of them that I owed them a big favor sometime in the future."

"Did any of them call in your favor?" When I nodded, Jeanine asked, "Were any of the favors interesting?"

"I took one friend and his new wife on their honeymoon. They had enough money to afford a week in a pleasure station, but couldn't afford the space flight to the station. On their wedding night, they asked me to cut the gravity so they could try sex in zero-G." I grinned at the memory. "Their stomachs didn't react well and within ten minutes they were begging for me to turn the gravity on again. It took me an hour to clean up after them."

Jeanine laughed at the story though it sounded a bit forced—sort of like this entire evening with the sole exception of her enthusiasm over the *Star*. "What about the friend who modified your engines—what was his favor? Ooooh, wait, let me guess. He wanted you to smuggle something for him?"

I gave the girl a long, careful look before nodding once. Her eyebrows shot up and something I couldn't quite figure out flashed in her eyes. She looked down and said, "I'm sorry, I didn't mean to pry."

I waved away her apology. "No, I'm willing to talk about it—at least just between you and me. My engine-fixing friend had a cousin who was about to come of military age on Voskiri." From Jeanine's expression, she obviously didn't recognize the name. "It's a planet in the Duchy of Gaunner. Anyway, this was a few years ago when House Kahn was still waging its non-war against House Wilkinson. My friend and I flew in with a load of normal trade goods and flew out with her uncle, aunt, and all of their children. We got away cleanly, but as a precaution I've stayed clear of Gaunner space ever since."

With a nod, Jeanine's expression turned thoughtful. She nibbled at the food, too, but obviously wasn't really hungry anymore.

I leaned back, openly giving the girl an appraising stare. Her eyes darted up to meet mine a couple of times. Then, with her eyes on the plate in front of her, she asked, "So, would you like to...you know?"

"No."

Jeanine's eyes widened and her head shot up. She met and held my gaze. "Oh... Do you want me to leave?"

"I want you to be honest with me." I sighed and tried for a

friendly smile. "Something has been bothering you since you showed up at the tavern this evening."

"I've been looking forward to our night together," Jeanine said.

"If you'd told me that earlier, when your grandfather sent me over to talk to you, I might have believed you. Something has happened since then, but I don't know what it is."

Before Jeanine could respond, the ship's comm system buzzed. The signal indicated someone was at the docking bay entrance. I wasn't expecting any deliveries and I hadn't done anything illegal—not on this run, anyway. Also, Jeanine just about jumped out of her skin when the comm sounded.

Acting on instinct, I motioned Jeanine away from the comm's vid pickup. Once she was clear, I keyed the comm on. Two men stood outside the docking bay, one wore a customs uniform while the other wore the uniform of Thinda Planetary Security.

I gave the men my best smile. "Isn't it a bit late for inspections?"

"You are Drake Haral, owner of the *Rising Star?*" the customs official asked.

"I am."

The security officer said, "We're searching for a young woman and we believe she's onboard your ship."

Across from me, Jeanine's eyes widened in surprise and fear. Then her eyes began darting around the small room as if searching for something—a hiding place, I assumed.

"You're mistaken, officers," I replied, settling into the slightly bored tone of voice I always use with government officials. "I'm the only one on the ship."

Most freight haulers in the galaxy fall into exactly the same tone when they find themselves dealing with bureaucrats. It's what bureaucrats expect to hear, too, so it tends to put them at ease. That's especially useful on those occasions when I actually do have something to hide—like now.

The security officer said, "So you haven't had a woman with you tonight?"

"I didn't say that," I replied, trying to inject a little puzzlement into my voice. "I had a very attractive woman in here not that long ago."

"Describe her," the security officer demanded.

Assuming they had access to security vids, I gave a superficially accurate description of Jeanine, putting emphasis on her long legs, barely covered butt, and pushed-up breasts. The officers exchanged a glance as I wrapped up the description, both giving a fractional nod.

"And why did this young woman leave?" the security officer asked.

"I assume her, ah, business manager had another customer lined up."

"You're saying the woman is a prostitute?"

"Yeah, and a good one." Jeanine's eyes narrowed in what I hoped was amusement at that, but I couldn't risk looking directly at her to make sure. "I paid her, she relieved my...tensions...most admirably, and then she left."

A third voice spoke from off screen. It was pitched too low for me to understand the words, but there was no doubt the owner of that voice was issuing orders to the officers. Jeanine heard the voice, too, and she went very still and deathly pale at the sound of it.

The customs officer spoke next. "I'm afraid we're going to have to search your ship, Captain Haral."

"Oh, hell, did you guys outlaw prostitution since I was here last?"

"No, Captain Haral, we did not," the security officer said. "But we still must search your ship."

"Have you got a warrant?" I asked, aiming for confused belligerence in my voice. "I don't have to let you in unless you have a legal warrant."

A hand came in from off-screen holding a ducal badge. The third voice, now perfectly clear, said, "Yes, Captain Haral, you *do* have to let us in. Now stop wasting my time and do as you're told."

There was only one possible answer to such a demand, and I gave it. "Of course, sir. I'll be right out."

The vid winked out, and I tossed the screen on the table in disgust. Jeanine spoke for the first time since the comm buzzed. In a trembling voice, she said, "You can't give me to them. That man will kill me."

"Not if I can help it," I growled, standing. "Come on, we don't have much time."

I led Jeanine into my sleeping cabin. Dropping to one knee, I ran my hand over the deck beneath my desk. I found a minor depression most people wouldn't even notice, fitted my thumb into it, and then lined the rest of my fingers up next to my thumb. Sensors hidden in the deck read the prints from all five fingers. A soft whoosh sounded from the middle of the room as one of the deck plates slid aside, revealing a small compartment.

"It'll be a tight fit and I really hope you don't suffer from claustrophobia, but you'll be safe in here," I said, guiding Jeanine toward the compartment.

She eyed the hole with understandable trepidation. "What if they have hand scanners?"

"The compartment is shielded. They shouldn't find this unless they get really serious and start tearing up deck plates." I helped her down into the compartment and pointed to a recessed button. "If something happens to me, this button will open the deck plate."

Nodding and shivering, Jeanine sank into the compartment. She brought her knees up under her chin, gave me one last look, and said, "Close it."

Seconds later, I dashed out of the *Star* and across the docking bay to the door. I took just a second to compose myself, then keyed the door open. A team of customs inspectors streamed past me, led by the security officer. Then the customs officer entered, followed by a solidly built man who simply exuded power and competence. He could be none other than the owner of the third voice.

The customs officer said, "Captain Haral, may I present Sir Phillip of Reimund, Knight of the Realm and Royal Enforcer of His Majesty's Law."

My heels snapped together with an audible click and I bowed deeply to the knight. "It is an honor, Sir Phillip."

"Rise," Sir Phillip said. "I must say you're rather well-mannered for a tramp freighter captain. Did you serve in your lord's military?"

"I did not have that honor, sir," I replied, skirting around the truth only slightly. "Instead, I had parents who were—and still are—sticklers for proper manners."

"When next you see your parents, convey my approval of their parenting," the knight said, striding past me and toward the *Star*. "Commoners who truly understand their place in the galaxy are far too rare."

Fixing a smile on my face, I trailed after Sir Phillip. "They will be honored, sir, as am I in their stead."

The three of us entered the *Star*. Shock stopped me just inside the hatch. One member of the customs team was running a hand scanner meticulously over every square centimeter of the deck while a second did the same with the bulkheads. I'd sort of expected something like that, but the rest of the team was methodically destroying everything in the ship. Three of my cushions had already been slashed open and the woman responsible was about to slice open a fourth. A man dumped drawers from my desk, smashed the drawers, and then sifted through the pieces. The rest of the team was out of sight, but from the sounds echoing through my ship, they weren't treating my possessions with any more care than these two.

Surging toward the woman with the cushions, I yelled, "What are you doing? There's no way a woman could hide inside a cushion!"

Sir Phillip's left hand caught my arm in a vise-like grip. "They act under *my* orders, Captain Haral."

Since I don't have a death wish, I didn't struggle against the knight's grip. Bitterness evident in my tone, I asked, "When you don't find anything, Sir Phillip, may I assume the crown will reimburse me for these damages?"

"Of course, Captain Haral." Sir Phillip might have been discussing the weather for all the feeling his voice held. "Simply present an itemized list to the proper agency on Xapreathea. In person."

"In other words, all I have to do is fly one hundred light years to the capital planet of the Star Kingdom—"

"One hundred and two light years, to be precise, Captain," Sir Phillip said.

"Okay. And once there, present an itemized list to the proper agency. I don't suppose you could tell me the name of this agency?"

"Alas, Captain, I do not bother with such details. Oh, and you must remain available to answer any questions the agency may have. I'm told it only takes a few weeks."

"Of course…" I turned and looked the knight in the eyes. "If I may be so bold, Sir Phillip, why didn't you simply say 'no' in response to my question?"

The man barked a hearty laugh. To my surprise, the humor reached the knight's eyes. "Well said, Captain. Your directness is refreshing for a man who spends far too much time among courtiers and politicians." Then the humor drained from Sir Phillip's eyes. "Do not be so bold again."

I nodded and returned to watching the destruction of my ship's interior. An hour and a half later, the team gathered before the knight and the security officer said, "There's no sign of the woman, Sir Phillip. Scans are negative and we found no evidence of wrongdoing against Captain Haral. However, the scans were also negative for indications of sexual intercourse in Captain Haral's bed."

The knight turned to me, his face impassive. "Would you explain that, Captain?"

"We began with dinner—the remains of which you can see scattered all over the floor. As I told the officers, I've been in space for a long time and I decided I couldn't wait until we finished eating." I looked down, feigning embarrassment. "She bent over the table and, well...you know."

"Yes," the knight replied dryly. "It appears the inspectors should scan you, now."

I shrugged, "They won't find anything. Any spacer who's not an idiot knows you thoroughly clean yourself after spending time with a prostitute. Disease, you know."

Since this had the advantage of being the absolute truth and was one of the first things taught to new spacers, I was on solid ground here. The knight simply raised an eyebrow. "That's a lot to pack into one hour, Captain Haral."

"I spent a month alone in space," I said. "It doesn't take very long to release that much pent-up tension, Sir Phillip."

The knight stared at me for a few seconds as the inspection team struggled to keep from laughing at my response. Without another word to me, the knight turned and left my ship. The inspectors and two officers trailed after him.

Before he turned away, the security officer said, "Don't leave the planet, Captain Haral. Sir Phillip may have more questions for you."

Looking at the ruined interior of the *Rising Star,* two questions dominated my thoughts. Who was Jeanine and what had she dragged me into?

LUCKY ME

Jeanine

My first few minutes in the smuggler's compartment weren't too bad. I didn't have a lot of space, but Grandfather's training regimen kept me limber enough that I wasn't really uncomfortable. A cushion beneath my backside would have been nice, but at least my neck and shoulders weren't hunched. And then the commotion began above me.

Feet pounded over my head as one—no, two—people entered the Captain's cabin. They stamped around overhead doing Lord knows what in the cabin, and I found myself ducking every time they approached the sliding deck plate. Since the deck plate was part of the small area of open floor space in the cabin, they stomped right over me a lot. Every time they did, I caught my breath, waiting for the plate to slide aside and leave me revealed and helpless before whoever was searching the room.

I initially thought I'd get used to the tromping overhead and no longer feel a stab of fear every time someone crossed the plate. I never did. Worse, my body's fight-or-flight reaction pumped adrenaline into my bloodstream with every crossing. I was jittery with excess energy by the time the two people finally left the cabin. Sweat trickled down my face and between my shoulder blades, adding to my discomfort.

Even when the two people searching the Captain's cabin left, I found relaxation impossible. Though muffled by distance and the deck plate, I heard lots of other banging and stomping inside the *Star*. Could my little compartment be the only smuggler's hold in the ship? Of course not. I remembered Drake's casual tale of smuggling an entire family out from under House Kahn's noses, so there were bound to be several more compartments hidden throughout the ship. If those searching found just one of those other hiding places, I felt certain the man in charge—the man Grandfather called 'Phillip'—would have the *Star* torn apart until he discovered every compartment.

And me.

Then I would die just like Grandfather had.

That's when the fear I'd held at bay, the one thought I'd refused to acknowledge, broke through my willful ignorance and occupied my mind. Grandfather was dead. He had to be. There was something in the way this Phillip and Grandfather spoke to each other, some long-past undercurrents that made me certain their fight had been to the death. Besides, I knew Grandfather would die to protect me. He told me as much all the time while hammering into me the understanding that I must not waste his death, that I must use the seconds he bought to run away.

Growing up, I assumed Grandfather was using this melodrama to make me take my training seriously. Even if there *was* some strange secret foe chasing Grandfather, I assured myself that I would stay and fight with Grandfather when the foe appeared. And having me fighting at his side would tip the balance of the fight in his favor. In my dreams, we'd vanquish the enemy and, pride shining in his eyes, Grandfather would tell me how I had saved his life and helped bring down some intergalactic criminal.

When the all-too-real foe came through our doorway, I didn't hesitate. The second Grandfather said 'Argenta protocol' all of my childhood determination went by the wayside and I ran. I abandoned him without a second thought. I left my grandfather to die.

Filled with shame and remorse and sorrow, I found myself

blinking back tears. Only the tears couldn't be blinked back. They overflowed my eyes and streamed down my cheeks. Then the dam broke, and I had to stuff my fist in my mouth to muffle my sobs as my entire body shook, racked with grief.

Finally, emotions spent, I subsided into quiet mourning for the man who raised me. I have no idea how long my grief consumed me, but the racket from the search no longer had any effect on me. I just sat in my little hole and waited for whatever would come next.

It grew stuffy and hot in the smuggler's compartment as my body heat raised the temperature in the small space. Soon my sweat-soaked top and the short skirt were plastered to my skin and my hair stuck to my neck. When sweat rolled into my eyes and stung them, I looked straight down so the sweat dripped onto my lap instead.

I was so miserable from grief and discomfort that I didn't notice when all the banging around the ship ended and feet tromped off the *Star*. Only when a single pair of feet entered the cabin did I realize how quiet it was. I resisted the temptation to find and press the button that opened the deck plate, assuming the feet belonged to Drake and that he'd open the compartment soon. Then I heard a single voice raised above me. I couldn't make out the words nor could I imagine who Drake was talking to, but I desperately wished whoever was out there would leave so Drake could let me out.

I felt the stab of bright light and the blissful rush of cool air as the deck plate suddenly slid aside. Drake looked down at me with concern written on his face. "Are you okay, Jeanine?"

I raised my face and let the wonderful fresh air blow across me and nodded. "Are you alone? I heard you talking to someone."

"I was quoting a few choice local laws, just in case Sir Phillip had the inspection team plant a few video and audio bugs on board. It's a pretty common practice with customs officers and, in this duchy, completely illegal unless they have a warrant of some kind." Drake held up a small device. "This thing sends out a pulse signal that overloads the receptors for any bugs they left behind. I always quote the laws before triggering it so they'll know it would be a waste of time to come back."

"How do you know they didn't have a warrant?" I asked.

"Because someone like Sir Phillip would have done a whole lot more than trash the furniture if he had any authorization beyond his badge." Drake extended a hand to me. "Come on, let's get you out of there and into a shower."

I accepted the help gratefully, groaning as protesting joints and muscles uncoiled. Wondering if Drake planned on joining me in the shower and also wondering how I'd react if he did, I let him help me to the bathroom.

"Do you have any other clothes besides what you're wearing?" he asked, stopping outside the bathroom.

I patted my bag. "Yes, thank you."

"Good. Toss your sweat-soaked clothes out here and I'll run them through the cleaner while you're bathing." Leaving me at the door, he added, "The *Star* is hooked up to the city's water system, so take as long as you need in there."

I did exactly as Drake instructed. The clothes I'd been wearing slapped wetly on the deck when I tossed them out of the bathroom. More importantly, the water didn't shut off after two minutes like it would if we were in space. I luxuriated under the hot water, scrubbing myself all over twice before I felt clean. Then I just stood under the shower and let the water cascade over me. My brain tried to think about what I was going to do next, but I simply couldn't concentrate. Grandfather always said I shouldn't force myself to think about something unless it was a life or death situation. My overall situation *did* fit that description, but the threat wasn't imminent any more. I told my brain to shut up and just let myself relax. And grieve some more for my grandfather.

Eventually, the hot water lost its appeal, and I shut it off. I emerged from the steamy bathroom a few minutes later, dressed in the black outfit I'd planned on wearing for our date. Drake hadn't been idle while I was showering, either. He'd cleaned up the little living area where we'd eaten our dinner a few hours ago. Drake had even managed repairs of a sort to some of the cushions.

He gave me an appraising look. "How are you feeling?"

"Clean," I said. "Sad. Scared."

"You've already figured out your grandfather is dead?"

I nodded. "That damned knight would be dead if Grandfather was still alive. Did you find some kind of news report about it?"

"Yeah. The report blamed it on criminals, of course." Drake waved me over to a chair with one of the repaired cushions. "You need to tell me what's going on, Jeanine. Why is Sir Phillip out to get you?"

I flopped into the chair and gave Drake a look with far too much desperation in it. "God's truth, Drake, I have absolutely no idea."

Drake gave me a long appraising look. I'm used to getting those looks from men. I'm *not* used to having the look focused entirely on my eyes. In fact, most of the appraising looks I get never move farther north than my breasts. I know how to deal with that kind of casually sexual appraisal, but Drake's look was different. His wasn't a superficial physical judgement. No, it was as if Drake was looking beyond my eyes and judging my soul.

After what felt like forever but couldn't have been more than a few seconds, Drake said, "All right, Jeanine... Ah, is Jeanine your real name?"

I forced myself to meet Drake's gaze, willing the truth to shine through my eyes. "Yes. That's the only name I've ever known, anyway."

He nodded absently. "Maybe I'm crazy, but I believe you. Since you don't know why that knight is out to get you why don't you tell me what you do know. Tell me who your parents are and what happened to them. Tell me about when your grandfather took over raising you and how you ended up here. Then tell me about what happened between the time you left me this afternoon and when we met again this evening."

I let my head fall back and stared up at the ceiling. "I wish I could tell you about my parents, but I don't even remember them. Grandfather told me they died in an accident when I was less than a year old." Remembering Drake's intent gaze, I brought my head up and met his eyes again. "As far back as I can remember he's been the only family I've ever had. And now I don't even have him."

Tears welled up in my eyes again and Drake looked away, giving me a moment to compose myself. "I know this is painful, Jeanine, but your life depends on figuring out what's going on. Mine probably does, too."

Wiping at my eyes and sniffing back tears, I said, "I'm sorry I dragged you into this. I just didn't know where else to go. Grandfather always told me to get off-planet as fast as possible if anything ever happened to him."

"So, am I nothing more than your interstellar taxi driver, Jeanine?" Drake's voice was calm and level, as if he was talking sports scores or something.

"No—I really was looking forward to our date tonight! And the last thing Grandfather told me was not to forget about it—and that was while that knight was walking toward our apartment door."

"Why me?" Drake asked. "I mean, it's not like Jared really knew me very well."

"He knew you well enough to be sure you'd treat me well and be gentle and considerate if we...you know." Despite my grief, I found myself smiling. "Grandfather always said you could see a person's true character in the way they responded to powerless people when there wasn't an audience to see and judge their actions."

"That's why he was begging in the market?"

I nodded. "He went begging a few days each week. He had several arrangements in place for dropping out of sight and getting off-planet, but he was paranoid about having those plans derailed. Begging near the spaceport gave him a chance to size up ship captains who were just passing through."

"And out of all the captains in port, he picked me?"

"No, Drake, you picked yourself. You gave Grandfather money and then even treated him to lunch. You weren't trying to impress anyone and no one in the market would have given it a second thought if you'd just ignored Grandfather—everyone else did." It was my turn to give Drake an appraising look. "Why did you do that?"

Drake looked away for a couple of seconds. In a flat tone, he said, "We aren't talking about me right now, Jeanine."

"Sorry, I didn't mean to pry," I said. "Anyway, after Grandfather spent lunch talking to you, I guess he decided you could be trusted more than any of the people he had made arrangements with."

"Lucky me," Drake muttered.

I don't know if it was the grief or the stress or what, but something inside of me snapped. Standing, I said, "You know what, Drake, you're right. You didn't ask for this and I've caused you more than enough trouble." I dug a credit stick out of my bag—I had several for emergencies, all of them with hefty balances on them—and tossed it to Drake. "That ought to cover the damages to your ship. I can see myself out."

Drake ignored the credit stick and jumped to his feet. Reaching for my arm, he said, "Wait, Jeanine."

Drake was off balance from his sudden leap up from the chair. I caught his reaching arm, pulled it past me and tripped him with an outstretched leg. As the man sprawled to the floor, I resumed my march toward the airlock. Drake was quicker than I'd imagined. He spun his body around in midair, landing on his back rather than his chin. He swept my legs out from under me, caught me before my head hit the deck, and then rolled up to straddle me.

I thrust my left hand, fingers spread, at his eyes while my right hand dug into my bag for the blaster. Drake dodged the hand aimed at his eyes. A fingernail raked his cheek, drawing a thin line of blood. That was fine since the attack to his face was just a distraction for drawing my weapon. But Drake's left hand clamped down on my right wrist, immobilizing my hand, while he used his right forearm to push my left arm down to the deck.

Our faces ended up centimeters from each other, our eyes blazing. I waited for him to force a kiss on me and wondered if he would expect me to react like the women in the vids—resisting at first before giving in with such ferocious passion that the scene could only end in rough and energetic sex. He had a huge disappointment in store if that's what he expected. I'd bite his lip, free one of my legs and—

"Will you please calm down, Jeanine?" Drake asked, pulling his face away from mine. "I'm going to get off of you now. Please do not attack me again."

So much for my action-vid drama scene. My rage slowly drained away. "Okay."

True to his word, Drake released my arms, carefully climbed off of me, and stood up. Then he extended a hand and helped me stand as well. Once I was on my feet, he held his hands out, palms toward me. "I'm sorry I made such a thoughtless comment—especially considering everything you've been through today—but the last few hours haven't exactly been all sweetness and light for me, either. Will you please sit down again?"

I took a moment to look around the interior of the *Rising Star*, this time paying much better attention to the damage done to it. This ship was how Drake earned his living, but I was sure she was also something much more to him. When I looked at the situation in that light, his reaction was more understandable. The last of my anger faded away. I nodded, suddenly more emotionally drained than I'd ever been. I fell into my seat and dropped my head into my hands.

"You know, we can have this talk tomorrow after you've had a chance to rest. While you were in the shower, I cleaned up the bedroom, too." Without asking, Drake bent over and scooped me up in his arms. "In fact, I think that's the right thing to do. I'm putting you to bed now."

A few steps later, Drake gently laid me on the bed and pulled a light blanket up over me. "Goodnight, Jeanine. I'll be on the sofa. Just call if you need anything."

After he shut the door, I pulled off my pants, rolled onto my side, and then curled up into a ball. I waited for sleep to claim me, but it wouldn't come. My mind played the events in the apartment over and over. When it got tired of that scene, it created new and disturbing images of what would happen to me if Sir Phillip ever got his hands on me. I tried to turn my brain off, but it simply kept spinning.

If only Grandfather were here, maybe he could tell me how to stop thinking. But he wasn't here and never would be again. I tried to imagine what advice he'd give to me and that's when I realized he already *had* given me his advice.

I got out of the bed and padded out to the living area. Drake was on his back, staring at the ceiling. As the door slid open, he looked my way and his eyes widened.

"Please sleep with me, Drake."

Propping himself up on an elbow, Drake's eyes started at my feet and swept up the length of my body before capturing my eyes. "Are you sure? I don't want to take advantage—"

I began unbuttoning my shirt. "I'm very sure."

Grandfather was right. Drake was gentle and considerate. As his mouth and hands explored my body, my mind stopped spinning, and I lived in the moment. Much later, he held me as I drifted off to sleep.

SIR PHILLIP'S REPORT

Olivia

Listening to the steady sound of my assistant's approaching footsteps, I assumed an expression of dispassionate concentration as my eyes drifted over the reports arrayed on the screens in front of me. I wanted nothing more than to jump to my feet and rush to meet the man approaching my private office, but I forced myself to stay seated. I wanted to twirl my hair around my finger in a nervous manner, but I held my hands still. I wanted to stare at the door in anticipation, but I kept my eyes firmly locked on my screens even though I couldn't focus on the information. In other words, I wanted to act like a typical nervous young woman in her late twenties waiting for life-changing news.

The office door swung open and my assistant took two steps into the room. "My lady?"

I drew a deep breath and released it, willing my voice to be calm. "One moment, Colin."

To my ears, my voice sounded properly composed and disinterested, exactly what I'd been aiming for. But Colin had served as the personal assistant for two Dukes of Gaunner and continued in that capacity for me, the family's first duchess in two centuries. He'd been a solid and dependable presence in House Kahn my entire life and knew me better than anyone.

When my father was too busy to attend to my needs, Colin was there. He bandaged my scraped knees and elbows from childhood and soothed my bruised pride and emotions from puberty. He even defended my honor, taking it upon himself to personally thrash the son of a baron who was telling anyone who would listen—and since I'm of House Kahn, that was a lot of people—that he had claimed my maidenhead. When, red-faced, I had admitted the boy was telling the truth, Colin told me, "I know he was, my lady, but the truth is no excuse for such disrespectful behavior toward a lady of House Kahn. Better he learns that lesson from my fists today than from your brother's blade in the future."

In other words, I'm sure Colin knew exactly how tightly wound my nerves were and heard subtle emotional undercurrents in my voice that I didn't even know were there. After all, he was the man who taught me the Duchess of Gaunner should never appear anything but calm and in control. So I let Colin wait for a full minute and then added an extra ten seconds just for show.

At last, I looked up. Colin stood patiently in the doorway, looking as if he was prepared to wait there for hours if it suited my whim. I had no doubts that he was prepared to do exactly that.

"Yes?" I asked.

"You have a subspace call from Sir Phillip, my lady."

I rose and walked toward the office door. "Did you speak with him, Colin?"

"Of course, my lady," Colin said. "I believe he brings mixed news. His expression is not sufficiently contrite for complete failure nor is it sufficiently prideful for complete success."

I mulled that over as we strode toward the subspace comm array. "Do you think Sir Phillip found the missing Wilkinson bastard?"

"I believe so, my lady, but I doubt Sir Phillip captured him."

Colin opened the door for me when we reached the subspace relay room and assumed his usual attentive posture outside of the room. He never entered the room without my invitation even though I always issued one.

Waving my hand, I said, "Join me. I may want your advice, Colin."

I settled myself in front of the vid and activated the call. Sir Phillip's face filled the screen, and I noted his bland expression. Like Colin, the knight appeared quite ready to wait patiently until I chose to take his call. He would be frothing at the mouth if he was paying for this call, but he appeared happy to wait as long as House Kahn was footing the bill.

"My lady," the knight said and even gave a respectful bow of his head.

"Sir Phillip," I said. "Colin tells me you have news?"

"I have found the Wilkinson bastard, my lady," Sir Phillip replied. "I must also report she has slipped through my fingers, though only for the moment."

She? That was an unexpected development. "What makes you think this woman is the bastard and how did she slip through your fingers?"

"She was in the company of Jared, the Recognized Knight of House Wilkinson. Sir Jared has been missing for twenty-five years and his disappearance has always been a mystery. Some claimed his courage failed him and he ran away. Others said he spurned his oath for a woman. Those who knew him assumed he died. I was one of the latter, my lady." Sir Phillip's attention turned inward. "He and I fought together during the Toduk Uprising. Sir Jared was many things knights are not supposed to be—earthy, crudely humored, and generally unfit for the company of nobility—but where it truly counted he was everything a knight should be. I knew he would never willingly gainsay his oath."

"You admired him?" I asked.

"For his abilities, I did, my lady."

I hardened my tone. "Is that why the bastard slipped through your fingers, Sir Phillip? Did your admiration slow your sword arm?"

The knight's eyebrows lowered, and I watched him fight to keep his temper in check. Good. While Sir Phillip concentrated on concealing his anger, he would let other emotions slip through. After a few seconds, he brought a sword into view.

"*Nothing* slowed my arm, my lady. This is Sir Jared's sword, which I shall return to the Hall of Warriors so it may be displayed as part of a properly respectful memorial to him."

My eyebrows rose in surprise. "You killed Sir Jared in single combat?" At Sir Phillip's nod, I continued, "Then how did the bastard get away from you? Surely you had a team with you to ensure her capture!"

"A seven-man team, my lady. Four of them came through the front door ahead of me and three covered the second-floor balcony. All of those men are dead—three at the hands of the bastard."

I glanced back at Colin. "What do you think?"

"If Sir Jared raised the girl, it's likely he gave her extensive training in the martial arts. I've no doubt that this woman is quite dangerous, especially if her opponents underestimated her." Colin turned his attention to the screen. "Sir Phillip, did you and your men see the bastard before you engaged her and Sir Jared?"

Sir Phillip nodded. "She's tall, slender, graceful, and quite attractive. The men I hired made jests about the fun they were going to have with her once they caught her."

"Why did you not reign in such talk, Sir Phillip?" I asked, the rebuke obvious in my tone.

"My lady, that is how men such as those behave before a fight. They came highly recommended by people I trust, so I saw no reason to interfere with their banter."

In my peripheral vision, Colin nodded in agreement with Sir Phillip's explanation. Damn men and their ways and damn the Wilkinson bastard for making me tread this path instead of my brother.

"Very well, Sir Phillip. I assume you will use this debacle as an example for the next team you employ?"

"Most assuredly, my lady."

"Good," I said. "Now tell me everything that has happened since you found the bastard and leave nothing out."

For the next thirty minutes, the knight gave a precise rundown of his search, his discoveries, the duel with Sir Jared, and the aftermath of the fight. One part in particular caught my attention.

"This pilot the woman was seen with intrigues me," I said. "Are you certain the bastard wasn't on board his ship?"

"On the contrary, my lady, I believe she *was* on board during the entire search. The pilot is probably a smuggler of some kind with cleverly concealed compartments in the ship. That is where I suspect she was hidden."

"If that is the case, why did you not tear the ship to pieces until you found her?" I demanded.

"This planet belongs to House Lockridge, my lady," the knight replied. "I cannot act with the same impunity I would have within your holdings. I was granted some leeway due to my badge of office, but will require a proper warrant from a local judge to do more than I have done."

"At least tell me you bugged the ship," I spat, my temper fraying a bit more.

"Of course, my lady, but Captain Haral had a device that overloaded their video and audio receptors. He quoted the precise laws Lockridge enacted pertaining to the situation before activating it, too."

It irritated me to get so close and then be stymied by typical Lockridge bleeding-heart foolishness. I resisted the temptation to rub my temples. "I understand, Sir Phillip. Is there anything else you can tell me? Any impressions that might help us track the bastard down?"

Sir Phillip considered my question for several seconds. "I don't think Sir Jared told the girl of her true heritage."

I couldn't see how that would be useful, but kept my expression neutral. "Thank you, Sir Phillip. I'll be in touch." As the screen snapped off, I leaned back and then *did* rub my temples. "At least we know the bastard is a woman and what she looks like."

"We know rather more than that, my lady," Colin said. "If she doesn't know who she is, she's bound to be wondering why Sir Phillip is pursuing her."

"So?" I hated that I sounded petulant.

"So, she will seek answers to the mystery of her identity—and the easiest way to do that is with a simple DNA examination. Every examination must access the Royal Genealogical Database." Colin bestowed a rare smile on me. "She'll be the only person in the galaxy with a fifty percent match to Arthur Wilkinson. If the examination office delays her for as little as twenty minutes, we can have the local police pick her up."

"Do you think the examination office will cooperate?" I asked.

"If we have one of our slicers attach a warrant for the results her test will produce, the office will be duty-bound to report it." Colin extended a hand and helped me to my feet. "If you'll sign a warrant from House Kahn, I'll ensure it is properly inserted into the database."

I smiled as I stood. At last, revenge for Robert was close at hand.

NEW CREW MEMBER

Drake

I awoke slowly, my mind drifting up from pleasant sleep and pleasant dreams, only to discover the waking world held pleasures, too. Jeanine faced away from me, her body curled up against mine and her head cradled in the crook of my right arm. My left arm was draped over her, gently holding her close while my hand cupped one of her breasts.

As soon as my mind recognized the situation, my body reacted to it. Jeanine stirred in my arms and found a way to turn over without pulling away from me or whacking me with an elbow. Levitation, maybe? A sleepy smile appeared through the red hair falling over her face and her heavy-lidded blue eyes reflected the smile. I carefully brushed the hair away from her face and she gave me a languorous kiss.

In a low voice she asked, "Is that a blaster in your pocket or are you really happy to see me?"

I returned the kiss with a bit more vigor. "I don't have any pockets. Or pants, for that matter."

Jeanine's sleepy smile widened into a wicked grin. "Yeah, I noticed. Did you notice I'm not wearing any pants, either?"

I lowered my head to one of her breasts. "That *is* convenient."

Later, we shared a shower where we discovered, yet again, that neither one of us was wearing pants. Afterward, I fixed breakfast while Jeanine fussed with her hair. We ate, not saying much of anything and definitely nothing of any consequence. Unfortunately, breakfast ended, and we were both wearing pants by then.

"It's time to face reality again, isn't it?" Jeanine asked.

"I'm afraid so." I gathered up the remains of our breakfast and tossed them into the scrubber. "Are you up to telling me about life with your grandfather?"

For the next thirty minutes, Jeanine described a life spent moving and training. It was a life with few friends, none of whom were ever particularly close, and with a subtle sense of dread hanging over it.

"Grandfather told me we had to keep moving because people were out to get us. As a little girl, I concocted a romantic story of my heroic grandfather keeping me safe from foul villains who wanted me for a nefarious—and nebulous—scheme of some kind." Jeanine gave an embarrassed smile. "Typical kid stuff. When I was a teenager, I decided Grandfather was the nefarious one, a heinous criminal wanted in every system in the Star Kingdom. That story was still a bit romantic because I decided Grandfather chose to go straight once he found himself raising me. That happened because my parents, also members of his criminal gang, were killed by a rival gang."

"You were young," I said, remembering some of my childhood flights of fantasy.

"For the last several years, though, I'd come to the conclusion Grandfather was just sort of crazy. It was a lovable, harmless sort of insanity, but we'd been running and training for my entire life and we'd never even had a close brush with the foe he claimed was after us." Jeanine blinked her eyes rapidly. When she continued, her voice was thick with emotion. "And then yesterday I found out he was right. Someone was after us. Or maybe just after me. I don't know which and I can't ask him because Grandfather is dead."

Thinking back over all the stories I'd read as a kid, I asked,

"Did he tell you to go somewhere or do something in particular if anything happened to him?"

"Just get off planet and lie low," she responded.

"What about gifts—a locket that belonged to your mother or something like that?"

Jeanine gave me a surprised look. "It sounds like we read a lot of the same books growing up. No, his gifts were always practical. Like that." She waved toward her bag. Then her eyes widened. "Maybe he hid a message in the bag's lining or something!"

That sounded reasonable to me, proving beyond all doubt that Jeanine and I did read a lot of the same books. She emptied the bag's contents onto the table and we both studied the bag for any differences in stitching or feel—and found nothing. At Jeanine's insistence, we sliced open several seams and, once again, found nothing. Defeated, Jeanine slumped back in her chair.

"I'm at a complete loss, Drake. I don't know why Grandfather was attacked or why that knight is looking for me. And I don't know what to do."

"Do what your grandfather told you to do—get off planet." I sat down across from Jeanine. Putting a finger under her chin, I lifted her head up until her eyes met mine. "You can stay with me on the *Star* until you decide what you want to do. I've been thinking about taking on a crew member, anyway."

"You're just hoping to get me out of my pants again," she said. At least she smiled when she said it.

"You do have certain...qualities...anyone else will be hard-pressed to match," I admitted. "But I'm also part of your story now and I have got to stick around and see how it all plays out."

"Even if it turns out to be dangerous?" Jeanine asked.

"Especially if it turns out to be dangerous," I said. "You're not the only one with training, Jeanine."

"House military?" she asked.

"Partially," I said, but didn't elaborate.

"And you don't want to talk about it?"

"No," I said, then amended that. "At least, not yet. It's not that I don't trust you, it's that I have a hard time talking about it."

"It was that bad?" Jeanine asked, her voice soft.

"It was worse." I forced some false joviality into my voice and changed the subject. "But we were talking about you. Are you going to stay with the *Star*?"

"For now," she said. "Until we get to another planet, at least. Meanwhile, can we do some research into Sir Phillip? Maybe we can find a connection to Grandfather."

"No. I'm hooked up to the planetary net right now and the local officials are probably watching every net search coming from the *Star*. If we're not careful, we might give your presence away. Let's postpone net searches until we reach another planet."

"Didn't you tell me the customs official told you to stay here?" Jeanine asked.

"He did, but it's an order without much backing. If I have legitimate cargo to transport, they'll have to serve me with legal papers or release me." I walked over to the comm console. "I put the word out that I was looking for cargo and promised fast delivery time. Let's see what inquiries I've got."

I had several, one of which was absolutely perfect for my needs and paid well above the going rate. Without even discussing it between ourselves, Jeanine and I agreed that job was too good. Surely Sir Phillip placed the offer, hoping to steer me to a particular planet. As a precaution, I ignored the second best offer, too, and called the person who placed the third best offer of the bunch.

An hour later, we had a contract and scheduled freight loading for the afternoon. My next call went to the customs office. As I predicted, my contract overrode the unofficial request of a knight. We were cleared for an evening departure even before the cargo arrived.

A NOBLE SCHEME

Olivia

"It went as you predicted, my lady," Colin told me. "Captain Haral dismissed the obviously planted cargo and ignored the second best, also. He accepted the contract to the Bragua system though. I thought it was very thorough of you to submit five contract offers to the good captain."

"Do I detect just the slightest hint of approval in your tone, Colin?" I asked, allowing myself a slight smile.

"You do, my lady," Colin said, returning my smile. "If I may be so bold, your grandfather could not have done better."

I wanted to laugh with delight at the comparison, but carefully maintained my slight smile. Inclining my head a few centimeters, I said, "You honor me, Colin. And what of the warrant—will it come up along with the bastard's DNA scan?"

"It will, my lady."

"Excellent, Colin," I purred. "Once the bastard is out of the way, there will be no one to stop my Recognition as the new Duchess of Neert!"

ONE WARRIOR TO ANOTHER

Drake

Once the cargo delivery was scheduled and our departure clearance arranged, I spent the next half hour keying the locks to the *Star's* smuggling compartments to Jeanine's fingerprints and the ship's main locks to her retinal scan. We spent another half hour making sure she knew the location of each of the compartments large enough to hold her as well as how to find the camouflaged fingerprint readers for each of them. She was a very quick study—no doubt something she picked up from all the training her grandfather put her through—and I never had to repeat myself.

Helping Jeanine out of the last of the hidden compartments—she tested hiding in each one—I said, "If you feel safe in the *Star*, I'm going to go out and pick up a few supplies for our trip. Is there anything I can get for you without raising any red flags with the locals or Sir Phillip?"

Brushing absently at the dust clinging to her black pants and shirt, Jeanine said, "I'd love some new clothes, but there's no way you can pick up women's clothes without arousing suspicion. I can make do with most of the toiletries you've already got. How long is the trip to Bragua?"

"We'll have to make two hyperspace jumps, but neither of

them is particularly long." I ran the numbers in my head. "As long as it's an uneventful trip, we'll be there in five days. Why?"

"There are certain feminine products I'll need eventually, but not in the next five days." She laughed at the look on my face as comprehension dawned on me. Patting me on the cheek, she said, "Yes, Drake, women are more complicated than men—and in far more ways than you guys ever figure out, until you live with one of us for a while."

I fought very hard to keep my face impassive after Jeanine's teasing. She had no way of knowing my secrets and I wasn't ready to tell her, yet. I didn't quite keep a straight face, but she misinterpreted my expression.

Jeanine cocked her head and regarded me for a few seconds. "I'm the first girl you've had stay with you on the *Star*, aren't I?"

"Of course not! I've had women on board for breakfast before you."

"But that was it—no just-waking love-making, no shower-for-two—just breakfast, a quick peck goodbye, and then they were off the *Star*. Tell me I'm wrong." I shrugged acquiescence, and she got a curious look on her face. "In all the years you've been flying the *Star*, why have you never asked a woman to stay another night, much less travel with you?"

"None of them had a knight of the realm after them, Jeanine."

"Granted, and I'm sure you'd have helped any innocent woman in trouble, but there's more to it than just helping me. I just don't know what it is."

I hadn't given the idea conscious thought, but I realized Jeanine was right. There was something different about her that went beyond the old damsel-in-distress bit. As I examined my feelings, Jeanine waited patiently. Once the feelings coalesced, I wondered why it took her prompting before I put it all together.

"It's because you understand my relationship with my one true love."

"The *Rising Star*? Of course I do. She's your home and your livelihood and you brought her back to life with your own hands."

Her next statement completely floored me. "There's something else, too, but I can't quite put my finger on it. But the bottom line is the *Star* is part of you in a way no one or nothing else ever can be."

"See? You understand her." Then I remembered how this whole conversation began and turned back to the subject of supplies. "Okay, so we agree I can't buy you clothes and you don't need any... feminine...supplies right now. What about favorite foods?"

"Does dark chocolate count?"

"It doesn't even count as edible to me, but I know that makes me the strange one," I replied. "I'll make sure we're well supplied with the stuff."

Moments later, a cab dropped me off at the market where I'd first met Jared and Jeanine. I wandered through temporary stalls and permanent shops, grabbing some of my favorite foods, several staple foods I was low on, spices and, yes, even several varieties of dark chocolate. I didn't realize I was being watched until the chocolate merchant agreed to my lowball offer without haggling. Following the merchant's gaze, I saw Sir Phillip glaring at me from five meters away.

Taking shameless advantage of the merchant's nervousness, I doubled my purchase but only increased my offer by half. Once again, the merchant agreed without any complaint. I was tempted to clean the man out just because I could, but he probably had a family to support—though almost certainly not one with a sickly wife and a crippled child, as he insisted to the customer just before me—so I paid for the chocolate and turned away.

Rather than avoid the knight, I walked right up to him. "Good morning, Sir Phillip. What brings you out so early? You were up so late trashing my ship, I was sure you'd sleep in today."

"I know you've got the girl on your ship, Haral," the knight growled.

"I do?" I widened my eyes and raised my eyebrows in false surprise. "Surely your crack team of customs investigators would have found her if I did. They found—and wrecked—everything else on my ship."

"You had her hidden somewhere, probably in a smuggler's hold of some kind."

"I am offended even at the *thought* that I would consider breaking His Majesty's laws, Sir Phillip."

"All of you tramp freighter types are the same. Lawbreakers, every one of you." Sir Phillip obviously hoped to provoke me with the accusation. Since it was pretty much true, his attempted insult didn't bother me.

"Unlike you fine, upstanding knights who would never, ever break any laws?" I shot back. "Like, say, placing illegal audio and video recorders on my ship?"

I tried playing his game, hoping to trick an admission from the knight that I could use to file a complaint against him. Like me, he didn't fall for it. "Turn the girl over to me, Haral, and I will reward you handsomely."

Now that just pissed me off in the extreme. "I have no doubt you've looked up my public records." When the knight nodded, I continued, "Then you know I wouldn't take that offer even if I did have this girl you're looking for."

"I do, but my superiors insisted I try." The knight locked gazes with me. "Let me give you a warning, one warrior to another. You're going to find that girl far more trouble than she's worth, Captain Haral. Do yourself a favor and part ways with her sooner rather than later."

For the first time this morning, I found myself believing Sir Phillip's sincerity. Something big was going on behind the scenes and he knew what it was. Hoping I could use his 'one warrior to another' sense of honor, I asked, "Maybe I could help you if I knew more about this mystery girl you're after? Who is she?"

"I have said all I can say, Captain Haral. Heed my warning or you risk getting caught up in events well above your station." His voice hardened. "Despite my respect for your service record, I will not stay my hand should we meet on the field of battle."

My mind whirled at the implications of the knight's final warnings. "Your concern for my well-being is touching, Sir Phillip. Now, I must be going."

The knight stood in the market and watched me walk away. All the way back to the *Star*, I wondered whether the man unintentionally gave something away or whether the seeming slip on his part was purposeful. Either way, the simple phrase 'well above your station' told me Jeanine's problems originated among the great houses of the kingdom.

Our original plan when we reached Bragua was an extensive search of the net to find out about Jared and Sir Phillip and, if possible, Jeanine. We'd still perform those searches, but I realized we needed to go further than that. We needed to find out more about Jeanine's family and any possible connection to the great houses. Public records could lie—any slicer worth his hardware could modify those—but DNA never lies.

I decided right then that I would take Jeanine for a full DNA scan as soon as we reached Bragua.

The five-day trip to Bragua was just what I needed to regain my mental bearings. I had time to truly grieve for Grandfather.

Time to simply sit and remember the man who raised me.

Time to reflect on all he had taught me.

Time to evaluate everything I had done since the door to our apartment blew in.

Time to realize I couldn't have saved Grandfather.

Time to consider and choose my own future.

Time to consider and reject the cold logic of running and hiding.

Time to consider and embrace the hot emotional path of vengeance.

During all of this—from my sullen silences to sudden mood swings—Drake gave me the time and space I needed. He sparred with me when I needed to burn off energy. He stayed quiet when I needed solitude. He listened when I needed to vent. He held me when I needed to cry. He made love to me when I needed intimacy.

Entwined in each other's arms on the last night of the journey,

I realized something about Drake. "You know, you've responded exactly how I needed you to respond to every one of my moods."

"I hope it helped," he murmured.

"It did, more than I can say. It's like you know exactly what I've been going through." I gave him a gentle squeeze. "You *do* know, don't you? Because you've been where I am now."

I felt Drake tense. "Yes, I have."

"I can tell you're not ready to talk about it," I said. "After the space you've given me, surely you know I won't press you for details?"

The tension slowly ebbed from Drake's body. "Thank you. No one else has ever done that before—not the doctors who put me back together, nor my friends, nor my family. They all insisted I'd feel better after I let everything out. I never felt better, and they always felt worse when they heard...what had happened. What I'd done."

"That's when you bought the *Rising Star* and fixed her up?"

"Yes. The friends who helped restore her were crewmates of mine." A slight tremor ran through Drake's body. "They already knew what happened and what I did."

Drake fell silent, and I waited quietly in case he had more to say. He did, but he didn't use words.

While waiting for me to come to grips with everything, Drake tried coaxing information out of the limited version of the net the *Star* could store in her databanks. He found some information on Sir Phillip—properly titled Sir Phillip Ormon of Reimund, Knight of the Realm, Royal Enforcer of His Majesty's Laws, Order of St. George, along with half-a-dozen other titles and honors—but couldn't find much more than that about the man who killed my grandfather. And he didn't find anything at all about my grandfather.

"That's not much of a surprise," Drake told me. "The portable version of the net only has a tiny fraction of the information a planetary databank can hold. Maybe we'll find something more when we land and connect to the Bragua net."

We learned a lot more when we connected to the planetary net. Well, I did, anyway. Drake was busy overseeing the unloading of our freight. By the time he was finished, I had a lot of information and a lot more questions. Drake noticed my change in attitude the moment he came in after the freight was offloaded.

"Do you feel like telling me what you found and why it's bothering you?" he asked.

Sighing, I nodded. "You'll need to know all of this stuff, anyway, and it's best to get it out in the open now, in case you decide to just wash your hands of me and all the trouble I've caused."

"Even if all of this trouble centers around you, you haven't caused any of it," Drake said.

"Maybe not, but-," I broke off and decided to start again. "Just listen to what I have to say. Then if you decide you don't want to be involved any more, I'll leave."

"You know that's not likely. I can be pretty stubborn when I want to," he responded.

"Noted," I said, giving him a ghost of a smile. "Let's start with Sir Phillip. There's a lot more stuff about him on the net, but it mostly recounts his valorous deeds in service to the crown and his house—House Kahn."

"Oh hell, he's a knight of *that* house?" Drake spat. "Yeah, I guess that does make sense."

"I don't know much about the great houses. My, uh...grandfather," my voice broke on that word, earning a questioning glance from Drake, "...never taught me much about them."

"They're the assholes of the galaxy, as far as most of us commoners are concerned." A transformation came over Drake as he spoke, his face reddening and undertones of fury lacing his voice. "House Kahn is power-hungry, vengeful, and more than willing to crush anyone who gets in their way, no matter how young and innocent."

I waited to see if Drake would say more than that. It was obvious his past demons were tied to House Kahn in some way, but he just fumed silently for a bit then visibly mastered his emotions. "That explains why Sir Phillip didn't identify his house when he spoke to me in the market back on Thinda. Could you learn why a sworn knight of House Kahn was after you?"

Drawing a breath, I steeled myself for Drake's reaction to my next announcement. "Sir Phillip is not a sworn knight of the house. He's the *Recognized* Knight of House Kahn."

Drake stared at me for what seemed like an eternity while I waited for him to order me off the *Rising Star*. It's bad enough to go up against any knight of the realm, but it's something totally different finding out you have one of the kingdom's dozen Recognized Knights opposing you.

Instead of the expected outburst, Drake simply said, "I guess we're going to have to be even more careful than I thought."

"There's more," I said.

"There always is." Drake smiled when he said it, taking any sting out of the words. "Shoot."

"My grandfather...wasn't my grandfather."

This time, I completely lost it. Tears filled my eyes and streamed down my cheeks. I buried my face in my hands and my shoulders heaved as I grieved all over again, this time for a relationship and a family that never existed. Drake let me purge the emotions, waiting quietly for me to continue. Finally, I wiped my eyes and drew in a deep breath.

"Do you need more time, Jeanine?"

"Probably, but I don't think I can afford it."

"Who was Jared?"

Releasing the deep breath I'd drawn earlier, I said, "He was Sir Jared Wymark of Ascides, Recognized Knight of House Wilkinson. He vanished shortly before the death of Lord Arthur Wilkinson, Duke of Neert."

Drake whistled. "Those are a couple of serious enemies, but you're too young to be mixed up in the whole Kahn-Wilkinson feud."

I shrugged. "I don't know that much about the feud, other

than the odd vid drama I've watched. But I can tell you one more thing about Sir Jared's disappearance."

"What's that?" Drake asked.

"His last public appearance was the day before I was born."

I didn't really mean to speak my next thought aloud, but I blurted, "Why would House Wilkinson's Recognized knight disappear and spend the rest of his life guarding me?"

"I can think of one very good reason," Drake said, his voice low. When I looked at him, Drake's face was an expressionless mask and his eyes were devoid of all emotion. When he spoke again, his voice was as cold as I could imagine a voice could be. "What I don't know is whether *you* already know what I suspect."

The words stung, but the sheer menace suddenly radiating from Drake was more frightening than anything else that had happened to me in the last week. All the warmth and compassion I'd seen and felt from Drake was gone, replaced by someone I didn't know and didn't want to know.

With difficulty, I met his gaze and did my best to throw open the windows to my soul. I willed every last bit of my confusion, innocence, and pain into my eyes and waited for him to decide whether he believed me or not.

With an inarticulate growl, Drake broke our eye-lock. "All of a sudden, I don't know what to believe."

I threw up my hands. "If you can say that after everything we've been through—the tears and silence and especially the intimacy—then there's not a damned thing I can say now to change your mind."

Spinning on my heel, I went to the little bedroom we had shared during the spaceflight. In a numb daze, I packed what little I owned in my bag. The blaster went in last, right after I checked its charge, just as Grandfather—no, Sir Jared, *not* Grandfather—taught me to do.

Drake was still standing where I'd left him, staring at the deck. I stopped at the data screen and called up the location of the nearest office capable of doing a DNA scan. Noting they accepted walk-ins, I went to the ship's hatch. As the hatch cycled open, I pulled a random credit stick out of my bag and tossed it on the deck.

"That ought to cover the damages done by Sir Phillip and the cost of my passage from Thinda to Bragua." I ran my hand gently over the bulkhead as I exited the *Rising Star* and whispered, "Thank you for bringing me safely to this system, *Star*. Take good care of Drake."

The hatch slid shut behind me and I walked quickly away, blinking back tears. A quarter kilometer away from the docking bays, I found a taxi stand and took the first cab in line. I dictated the address of the DNA clinic to the robo-driver, inserted a credit stick to cover the charge, and spent the rest of the trip trying to figure out what went wrong between Drake and me. Nothing occurred to me during the twenty-minute ride, so I tried putting the man out of my mind and concentrated on finding my way into a very uncertain future.

I rode the lift tube to the eighty-third floor and found the right office. Inside, the clinic was comfortable in a detached and professional manner. Business must be good because the office had a human receptionist. She gave me a warm smile as I approached. "Welcome to Murray and Mize. How may I help you?"

"I, um...I want to get a DNA scan. I might be getting married, you see, and..." I trailed off, completely failing at my attempt to return the woman's warmth.

The woman's smile remained warm, but now compassion flowed into it. "Oh, honey, did he leave you?"

I wiped at my eyes and took control of my voice. "No. I left him."

"Good for you, honey," the woman replied. "But why do you still want to go through with the scan?"

"Because I planned to get one today and I'm not going to let some asshole ex-boyfriend make me change my plans." I thought I sounded pretty convincing.

Apparently, the receptionist did, too. Handing a pad and stylus to me, she said, "That's the spirit! Just fill this out and we can get you scanned."

Five minutes later, the receptionist turned me over to one of their scanner techs. She led me back to a small room furnished with two comfortable chairs and a data pad. Offering a perfunctory smile, the tech waved me into one of the chairs as she brought up my file on the pad.

"Let's see what we've got here, Jeanine," the tech said, peering at the information on the screen. Absently, she added, "Do you mind if I use your given name or would you prefer a more formal address?"

"Jeanine is fine," I said.

"Thank you," she said, turning to face me. The tech pulled a small device from one pocket of her lab coat. "Could you hold out one of your middle fingers?"

I did as instructed and the tech slid the device over my finger. "Don't worry, you won't feel a thing."

She tapped a button on the device. A second later it beeped and, a second after that, the device glowed green. The tech slid the device off of my finger. She was right—I hadn't felt a thing.

"I'm going to go analyze this, then Doctor Murray will read the results. He'll be in to talk to you after that." She stood and turned toward the door.

"How long will this take?" I asked, checking my chrono.

"Fifteen minutes, tops," she said, keying the door open. "Just relax and you'll be done here in no time."

The door slid shut and, once again, I was alone with my thoughts. I played through everything that transpired between Drake and me earlier, looking for something I'd said or done to put him on edge. No matter how many times I ran through our conversation, I came up blank. Could Grandfather—dammit, I had to get out of the habit of referring to the man who'd raised me as Grandfather. Could *Sir Jared* have misread Drake so badly? After all the intimacy between us, could *I* have misread him so badly? I couldn't believe that either of us was wrong about Drake, but that still didn't explain the cold shoulder he gave me.

Sighing, I stilled my whirling thoughts and tried to relax. Shouldn't the doctor have come in by now? I glanced at my chrono, wondering if my time sense was as confused as the rest of me. It wasn't. Twenty-three minutes had passed since the tech left the room. What was taking so long? I didn't have any pressing appointments, but like most people I hate waiting longer than I have to.

Sighing in frustration, I got up to go find out what was causing the delay. I keyed the door open—and nothing happened. I keyed again, this time paying close attention to what I was doing. The door didn't budge.

Instantly suspicious, I put my ear to the door. Muffled sounds came to me—quietly commanding voices, quietly shrill voices, and the sound of a lot of people hurrying toward the reception area.

Damn, damn, *damn*! I'd wasted my time worrying about Drake and let my guard down. I hadn't even heard anything when they locked the door. There must have been something in my DNA scan that set off alarms, but what could it be? I quickly abandoned that line of thought and turned my attention to getting out of this situation alive and free.

I drew my blaster, made sure it was not set to stun, and stepped as far back from the door as I could in the small room. I aimed carefully at the locking mechanism and fired. It was a simple office door and my one shot blasted a big hole where the lock used to be. From beyond the door, several people screamed.

"She's armed! Repeat, the woman is armed!" a man bellowed. "Clear the civilians out of here!"

Several more voices responded, all of them with the tone of voice you expect from professionals. Then the first man spoke again.

"This is the police. All of the exits are blocked and you cannot escape. Surrender is your only option."

I still had no idea why this was happening, but I was certain of one thing. If the police captured me, they would turn me over to Sir Phillip. And if Sir Phillip ever got his hands on me, I was as good as dead.

NIGHTMARE PAST

Drake

Jeanine spun away from me and strode to the bedroom. Everything in her walk screamed of hurt and anger. I knew I needed to say something, to take back the stupid words that had tumbled, unbidden, from my mouth. But then the memory that drove my reaction rose unbidden from the dark recesses of my mind and, as it always did, overwhelmed me.

I piloted our patrol cruiser easily through the asteroid field. The space around me was like my backyard, familiar and safe. I sat with my feet propped up on the co-pilot's seat, handling the controls with one hand and joking with the rest of the crew. We'd been out on patrol for a week, checking in with the other mining settlements in our district. We'd heard rumors of early pirate activity and extended our patrol by two days while we poked around some of the more remote corners of the asteroid field. When we didn't find anything, we headed home.

Coming within sight of our home asteroid, I sat up straight and brought both hands to the controls. I've landed at home at least a hundred times. It was no longer particularly challenging, but a smart pilot never takes chances. Heads turned as my crew waited for their first look at the home dome in the last seven days. I can't speak for others, but part of my mind was already planning a romantic dinner with Heather, assuming Candice cooperated and went to bed on time.

The settlement dome came into view and our relaxed chatter cut off abruptly. There was a jagged hole where the top of the dome should have been. For several seconds, our minds were unable to comprehend what we saw. Then my training took over.

"Dome breach protocol! Secure helmets and prepare for an emergency landing," I ordered. "I'm going to set down in the square. You all know your assignments in a situation like this."

"Drake, I can't—my house isn't in my assigned sector!" Zach said, his voice thick with emotion.

"And my house isn't in my sector, so I truly understand, Zach. Sticking to the drill will give all of our families their best chance for survival. Is that clear?" I asked. When no one responded, I barked, "I said, is that clear?"

"Yes, sir!" the crew barked as the tone of command in my voice pushed past their all-too-understandable concerns.

A minute later, I swooped through the hole in the dome going far faster than the regulations recommended in such situations. Even as I spun the cruiser for landing, I said, "Kelly, scan the edge of the dome. What caused the breach?"

"I don't need a scan, Captain," she replied. "The edges are slagged, not cracked. The dome was breached from the outside."

The ship set down hard and we all spilled out of it. The crew fanned out, properly sticking to protocol. I'd been prepared for one or two of them to break for their homes, but no one did. That they stuck with their assignments for the next thirty minutes was even more surprising.

The bodies of friends and neighbors were scattered outside of the buildings, people obviously caught unprepared for the breach. Some of them had emergency oxygen with them, but most people didn't bother carting those around unless they were going far from airtight buildings. Those wearing breathing masks had a different cause of death—they had all been killed by blaster fire. The same blasters were turned on the buildings, opening them to the vacuum.

We found a few pirate bodies, men and women shot by settlers defending their homes and loved ones. The pirates wore armor, which explained why there were so few dead pirates. It took a very skilled or very lucky shot to kill an armored man with a hand blaster.

One by one, the crew reached the home of one of their fellow crew members. One by one, each person's worst fears were confirmed. I was resigned to receiving the worst news imaginable, but that doesn't mean I was prepared for it.

"Skipper?" Kelly's voice was barely audible. "I'm at your house and... and..."

"They're dead?" My voice was a dry croak.

"Yes, sir." Kelly was silent for a bit, then added, "Heather took out two of the bastards before they got her. Candice was right next to her."

I leaned against a wall, my eyes closed as I tried to find a way to keep going, to keep living. In my mind, I imagined one of the pirates in my gun sights and that's when the rage blossomed.

"Finish the sweep, make sure there aren't any survivors, then return to the ship," I ordered. "We're going pirate hunting."

Two hours later, we took a moment to offer up a prayer for our dead. Then, riding on a column of fiery rage, our cruiser rose from the ruins of our lives on a quest for vengeance.

I forced my mind away from the memory, slowly pulling myself free from the horror that came with it. As was always the case when the dead came back to haunt me, I was appalled by what I'd said and done just before falling into the past. Worse, as always, I had no memory of anything that happened after my personal nightmare claimed me.

"Jeanine?"

My voice echoed around the ship with no answer. I hurried to the bedroom and immediately saw that Jeanine's bag was missing. A quick look around showed that everything she owned was gone, too. Hurrying back to the living area, I spotted something on the data pad screen—directions to a nearby DNA scanning clinic.

My foot kicked a credit stick as I stepped closer to the screen. I quickly transferred the directions to my personal pad and then retrieved the stick from the deck. Heading for the *Star's* hatch, I brought up the credit stick's balance and nearly tripped over my own feet when it displayed six figures. The first figure was a one, but it was still more money than I'd ever held in my entire life.

Rather than wonder how Jeanine got the money, I took it as further proof that my suspicions about Jeanine's background were right. That realization magnified my worries for her and made me all the more certain that Sir Phillip's little 'well above your station' slip wasn't a slip at all. I felt sure the knight *wanted* us to scan Jeanine's DNA—and anything he wanted was something I wanted to avoid.

Stuffing the credit stick in my pocket, I grabbed a concealable blaster and ran to the closest taxi stand. Of course, there were no cabs waiting for passengers. Setting off for the next closest taxi stand, I looked around hoping to see some faster way to get to the clinic's address.

I was so intent on moving quickly, I almost missed it when opportunity knocked. Something registered out of the corner of my eye, though, and I backtracked a few steps and looked into a big freight hauler's docking bay. A flitter dealer was overseeing the offloading of eight high-end sports flitters. The dealer gave me an odd look as I ran up to him. One hand dipped into a pocket, no doubt readying a weapon in case I tried anything.

Still breathing hard, I asked, "How much is one of these babies?"

The suspicion faded from the man's face and he turned back to his data pad. "More than you can afford, pal."

"Humor me," I said and this time there was an edge to my voice. I pointed to a convertible model I knew was fast. "How much is that one?"

The suspicion returned, but I wasn't threatening him or even standing too close, so he didn't reach into his pocket again. "Eighty thousand. Look, buddy, I'm really busy so—"

I pulled out the credit stick and showed the dealer the balance. "You can keep the change if you'll sell it to me *now*."

The man gave the credit stick a bored look. His eyes widened, and he reflexively reached for it. "Are you serious, sir?"

In other circumstances, I'd have laughed at the sudden change in the man's attitude. "I am very late for an appointment. If I don't get there in time, it will cost me a lot more than what's on that credit stick. Will you sell me the flitter?"

"Uh, sure. Let me just take care of—"

Tossing the credit stick to the man, I said, "I'll come back for the paperwork after my appointment. Don't worry, I know how to key the ignition to my retina print."

Hopping into the flitter, I wasted several precious seconds registering the ignition to my retina. As the system completed its processing, I checked the flitter's charge. It was just over fifty percent, a lot better than I'd hoped.

"Uh, do you have a flitter license, sir?"

The system initialization completed, and I fired up the engines. "Of course!"

I turned the flitters nose up and gunned it straight up and out of the freighter's docking bay. The flitter turned out to be just as fast and nimble as the manufacturer said it was. Any other day and I'd be having the time of my life. Today, I felt worry gnawing at me as I rose above the towers of the city. Ignoring the flying lanes, I accelerated straight toward the address of the clinic.

As I closed in on the building, I realized my worries were well-founded. Five police flitters were on the building's roof, their lights flashing but with no sign of any officers around them. I rolled the flitter, taking a quick look at the ground. Another dozen police ground cars surrounded the building.

My roiling gut told me the police were here for Jeanine, but how could I help her escape if I couldn't get inside?

ADVENTURE VID SILLINESS

Jeanine

I decided to play for time. Maybe I'd get lucky and come up with a plan that didn't involve me dying in a hail of blaster bolts or getting captured and turned over to the people who wanted me dead.

"I don't know why you're after me, but I didn't do anything illegal," I called.

"Then surrender, Miss Webb," the policeman replied, using the name I'd entered on the clinic's form. "If you're innocent, you can trust His Majesty's courts to find out and rule in your favor."

"If I thought I'd live to have my day in court, I'd happily take you up on your offer." God above, that sounded incredibly paranoid.

"Come now, Jeanine—do you mind if I use your given name?" the officer said.

"Sure, why not, officer-?" Two could play at the name game and the cops wouldn't mount a charge on my position as long as they thought they had a chance of talking me into giving up.

"Stewart—Larry Stewart."

"Considering the circumstances, Officer Stewart," I replied, "I hope you won't be offended if I don't tell you how pleased I am to meet you?"

Officer Stewart gave a false laugh. "I suppose that's one way of looking at it. Another is that you've been given a golden opportunity to clear up this misunderstanding between you and the legal system. And please, call me Larry."

My mind raced, trying to figure out how to get out of this situation. In an adventure vid, I'd keep good old Officer Stewart talking while I wriggled into the air ducts or improvised an explosive out of office supplies and blasted a hole down to the eighty-first floor. The air vent into this room wasn't more than ten centimeters across and the only office supplies were a couple of reading pads and a pen.

Instead of returning to finding an escape plan, my mind remained stuck on vid plot devices. I doubted there was a hidden or rarely used exit from the office. If there was, surely someone who worked in the clinic already told the police about it. That left my personal favorite bit of vid silliness—the flying car that shows up outside the window at just the right moment. Without giving it conscious thought, I glanced at the row of windows across the hallway from my waiting room. I stared, slack-jawed as Drake piloted an expensive sports flitter into view.

I couldn't move for several seconds. All the while Drake frantically waved at me. I finally regained control of myself and pointed down the hallway toward the police gathered down there. From the way Officer Stewart—excuse me, *Larry*—was still droning on with his attempt to bore me into surrendering, none of the officers had seen the flitter yet. Drake pulled out a small blaster, mimicked shooting the window out, and motioned for me to move back. Backing as far away as the room allowed, I signaled I was ready.

The first shot was barely audible through the window, but the *crack* of the second and third shots carried easily through the widening hole in the window. Good old officer Larry stopped rambling on about whatever it was he was saying and started shouting to the other officers to take cover. By then, I was already sprinting for the window.

I dove through the big hole and got a gut-wrenching glance at the street hundreds of meters below me. Then I landed half-in and half-out of the flitter's backseat. The little craft dipped down, and I scrabbled for a handhold of some kind as I slowly slid out of the flitter. Then Drake fed power to the left side repulsers and my slide reversed. As I tumbled into the backseat, Drake gunned the flitter down and away from the window.

"Strap in, Jeanine," he called. "I think we're in for a bumpy ride."

I took a quick look around us. A couple of police ground cars broke away from the building and tore down a street in the same direction we were flying, but none of the police flitters were after us yet.

"There's no pursuit yet, Drake. Keep the flitter level for a few seconds," I said. "I'm coming up front."

He did as I instructed and shortly I was strapped into the front seat next to him. I began scanning for pursuit as soon as I was secured in the seat. "Two police flitters are coming after us from the roof. Make that three. Now four. Five... Come on, how many cars did the police send to get me?"

"Those five flitters and a dozen ground cars," Drake replied. "Now that I know about those guys, watch ahead of us and to the sides for more flitters joining the chase."

I followed Drake's instructions, and we flew in silence for a few seconds. Then I said, "Thank you for getting me out of there."

"You're not out of it, yet," he replied, "but you don't need to thank me. I do hope you'll forgive me, though."

"Two flitters are coming in from the left. It looks like they're trying to get above us," I said. "I'll forgive you when I know why you acted like that in the first place."

"Fair enough," he said. "Hang on, we're diving."

Drake pushed the flitter's nose down, and we rocketed toward the street below. We also got down among the buildings, making it more difficult for the police to spot us. Leveling off about fifty meters above the street, Drake immediately banked hard to the left and cut down a new street. The buildings around us flashed by, but I still got the occasional glance at people with shocked expressions watching us zip past.

Drake glanced at the rearview screen. "Hold on again."

The flitter banked hard to the right, leveled off for a split second, then banked hard to the left. The buildings pressed in closer on either side and a lot less light reached us, making it seem as if dusk was upon us. Despite having little room for error, Drake didn't slow down.

"I've got a comm in my right pocket," he said, his eyes never leaving the narrow path ahead of us. "Can you get it out and look up something for me?"

My fingers dipped into the pocket and fished out the comm. "What are you looking for?"

"Find a public parking garage somewhere nearby and preferably ahead of us. We need to get rid of this car."

I turned an incredulous stare on Drake. "Please tell me you didn't steal it. God, Drake—"

"I bought it with the credit stick you left on the *Star*," he replied. "Please just do as I asked."

"Right. Sorry," I said and called up the unit's mapping program.

Drake made another turn. "No need to apologize. We've both had a rough day so far."

I told the program what I wanted. A couple of seconds later, it issued directions.

Drake followed them until we were nearly to the garage and then said, "Disconnect and then toss the comm. After that, watch above us and let me know if you see any police vehicles."

I did as instructed. As soon as the comm was gone, Drake took another quick turn while I kept watching above and around us for pursuit. I saw two police flitters fly by far above us, but I doubt they could see us in the deep shadows. Still, I told Drake and he immediately changed course.

Two minutes and a couple of more course changes later, Drake swung into a residential district, immediately slowed to an appropriate speed, and brought the flitter down to ground level. The expensive flitter drew admiring and envious looks from the few people out on the street, but no one appeared shocked that someone drove one down their street.

A couple of hundred meters after he slowed down, Drake turned into a parking garage. He settled the flitter into an open space on the lowest level and then took a few seconds to clear his retina scan from the ignition.

"You know anyone who wants it can just take the flitter, right?" I asked.

"I not only know it, it's what I'm hoping for," he replied. "So let's get out of the way and let the next owner get on with it."

Taking my hand, Drake led me to a lift tube. We rode the tube to street level where Drake flagged down a passing taxi. Settling into the cab, he ordered it to take us to the spaceport.

"Where are we—"

Drake put a finger to my lips, silencing me. With false joviality, he said, "It's a surprise. Just sit back and enjoy the ride."

I eyed him for a few seconds, doubt written all over my face. Drake met my gaze and mouthed, "Trust me."

I stared into his dark eyes a bit longer before nodding. Settling back in the seat, I wondered what life would throw at me next.

The cab dropped us off at the very busy public entrance to the spaceport. Drake paid the fee with actual credits rather than a credit stick. As the taxi rolled to join the line of other cabs waiting for passengers, Drake wrapped an arm around my shoulder and pulled me close.

Pretending to kiss my cheek, he whispered, "Act like we're a tourist couple heading back to our space liner after a visit on Bragua."

"Okay," I whispered, returning his pretend kiss, "but once we're in the clear, you'd damned well better explain your behavior earlier and why you think all of this is happening to me."

"I will." Drake steered me into one of the tourist shops just inside the spaceport and up to a rack of caps. He grabbed a blue one with 'Lovers love Bragua' written on it. "Isn't this cap great? Pile your hair up and let's see how it looks on you."

It didn't take a genius to figure out that Drake wanted to hide my hair from surveillance cams. That wouldn't do any good if the police already had my face loaded into their facial recognition software, but bureaucracies rarely move that quickly. I gathered up my hair and pulled on the cap.

"What do you think?"

"I love it!" He went to the checkout and slid credits into the payment slot. "We'll take the cap."

The robo-cashier noted the cost of the cap as the credits dropped into its slot. The cashier gave Drake his change with a mechanically cheerful, "Thank you!"

Outside, Drake pulled me close again and said in a caring voice, "If you're tired, honey, you can rest your head on my shoulder."

That would also partially hide my face from the security cams. I leaned on his shoulder, sliding my own arm around his waist. I stayed that way for the next several minutes, trusting Drake to steer us around security cams and the rare human guards. For about five minutes, everything went swimmingly. Then Drake made a sudden left turn, all but dragging me behind him as his pace picked up.

"Hey, all of a sudden I'm starving," he said, "and you know how the liner is about their food schedule. They won't feed us for hours yet."

The door slid shut behind us and the light dimmed as it blocked the late afternoon sun. We were in a cheap diner, the kind patronized by spaceport workers more than by tourists. At this hour, the place wasn't too crowded, but we still attracted more than our share of curious looks. Drake kept up his act, playing to the crowd.

"Now, *this* looks like authentic Braguan food—not like all those expensive places the tour directors said we should go to!" He grinned at a table of four men. "Am I right? Yeah, I can tell I'm right."

"It's food, and it comes from Bragua, if that's authentic enough for you," one of the men answered.

Even though he was talking to Drake, his eyes were on my chest—as were the eyes of his friends. Out of habit, I lowered my eyes and saw that my shirt was unbuttoned halfway to my navel. What the hell? Without thinking, my hands rose to fasten two or three of the buttons. Catching both of my hands in his, Drake swung me around to face him. His eyes flicked to my open shirt, and he gave a slight shake of his head.

I wasn't sure when—or how—the man found a way to unbutton my shirt without me noticing, but he had a reason for it. Then it hit me. This was yet another way Drake was keeping people from paying attention to my face. I smiled in acknowledgement and let Drake lead me toward the restrooms in the back.

As soon as we ducked out of sight of those eating, Drake said, "Don't panic, but I came into the diner because I saw a ship bearing the Kahn coat of arms sitting in a docking bay down the street. I was hoping we could work our way casually to the *Star*, but that's not an option any more. We're going out the back of this diner and then we're going to run for the ship."

"Won't that attract attention?" I asked.

"Yeah, but if that ship belongs to Sir Phillip you can bet he already knows where the *Star* is docked. House Kahn must have been behind more of those cargo contracts offered to us than I thought." Drake pulled up at the rear exit and surprised me by buttoning up my shirt. He gave me a tight smile. "We can't have you falling out of your shirt when we're running. That would attract even more attention than simply making a run for it."

"I promise I will do my best to keep my clothes on while we run," I said, smiling in return.

"Are you ready?"

I nodded and Drake cautiously opened the door. He gave a quick look in both directions and then we bolted. We drew a lot of attention running through the spaceport, but Drake played off of it as much as possible. He kept looking at his chrono, cursing, and then urging me to run faster or we'd miss our shuttle. People moved out of our path, some of them even wishing us luck making it to the shuttle in time. All in all, things were going very smoothly —until suddenly they weren't.

We rounded a corner and saw the *Star's* docking bay no more than fifty meters away. Loitering at the docking bay door were three big men. Their attention swung to us right after we came into view. Two of them started our way, their hands dropping into pockets. The third man pulled out a comm unit and spoke into it. We couldn't hear what the man said, but we didn't really need to. The men obviously worked for Sir Phillip *and* they were blocking us from our ship.

Drake

None of the men blocking our way into the *Star's* docking bay drew weapons—at least not yet. I didn't doubt they would do so the second Jeanine or I looked as if we were even thinking about pulling out weapons of our own. Whatever else happened, I did not want to get into a gun fight with these men. Sir Phillip wouldn't hire low-class thugs, so I assumed the men knew their business and could hold us at bay until the knight and his men arrived. Besides, there were too many innocent people wandering around to risk that kind of battle.

"Act scared, like someone is after you," I said to Jeanine.

"Someone *is* after me," she replied between breaths.

"Act like that someone is right behind us. Look back over your shoulder, that sort of thing," I said, picking up the pace. "We also need to appear relieved to see those three men."

"Uh, what?"

I waved my free hand over my head as if trying to get the attention of Sir Phillip's men. "Just play along."

The two men walking toward us stopped and exchanged confused glances. Behind them, the man with the comm stared at us for a couple of seconds. He briefly spoke into the comm and then put it away. As we approached, he sauntered up to join his friends.

"Oh, thank God we found you!" I drew in exaggerated gasps of breath and put my hands on my knees as if I wasn't used to running fast or far. Jeanine played along, leaning on me.

The man who had been on the comm spoke first. "And why is that?"

"You're port security aren't you?" I put a little confusion into my voice and darted my eyes around as if in fear.

Comm man straightened a bit and his voice deepened. "Yes, sir. That's us. What can we do for you two?"

The man might be great with combat and tactics, but his attempt at playing the heroic security guard was pathetic. Trying not to laugh at the man, I pointed back the way we came and said, "A man and a woman threatened us. They said they'd shoot us if we didn't run this way as fast as we could! The man showed me his gun, so I believed him!"

Jeanine said, "And the woman pulled a couple of knives from somewhere and then put them away again so fast I couldn't even tell you where they came from!"

"Can you describe them?" comm man asked.

I pointed at Jeanine. "The woman sort of looked like Beth."

Jeanine nodded enthusiastically, "And the man sort of looked like George, except he was in better shape." She gave me an apologetic look. "Sorry, hon."

I waved off her comment. "You've got to protect us from them! They said they'd be right behind us."

That's when we finally caught the break I was looking for. All three men looked up and focused on the corner Jeanine and I ran around just a few seconds before. I popped my concealable blaster out of its wrist sheath and thumbed it to stun. I hit the man on my left with the best uppercut I could manage with my off hand. As the attention of the other two men snapped back to me, I put my blaster against the second man's head and fired.

Comm man raised his gun even before his stunned

companion hit the ground. I tried to bring my little blaster around for a head shot, but I wasn't going to make it. Then a blaster pistol cracked from my right. The bolt splashed against comm man's head. I dropped to the ground as his trigger finger twitched. The bolt flashed over my head and through the people wandering the street behind us. Jeanine's blaster barked a second time. The man I'd slugged under the chin pitched backward and lay still.

Panicked screams rose behind us as Jeanine and I ran to the docking bay. She scanned the crowd behind us as I keyed the door open.

"Real security guards just came around the corner, Drake," she said.

The docking bay door slid open. I grabbed Jeanine's hand and pulled her along behind me. Inside, I slapped the button to close the door and gently pushed Jeanine toward the *Rising Star*.

"Open her up and get to the pilot's compartment. I'll be right behind you."

Without a question, she sprinted toward the ship's hatch. I thumbed my blaster to full power and blasted the door's locking mechanism twice. Then I turned from the slagged control panel and sprinted after Jeanine.

As she neared the ship, Jeanine called, "Emergency access override epsilon delta one three alpha tango."

The *Rising Star's* hatch popped open. Without breaking her stride, Jeanine ran into the ship. I followed a few seconds later. Just inside the ship, I stopped and closed the door.

"Emergency seal, *Star*," I said and looked into the retinal scanner.

Light flashed into my eye and then I heard the subtle clang as bars shot into the outer hatch. Once the Emergency Seal light turned green, I dashed after Jeanine.

I found her in the co-pilot's seat, already running the *Star* through the emergency startup routine. Plopping into the pilot's seat, I took over from Jeanine. Being far more familiar with the controls and the procedure, we both knew I could have the *Star* on her way to space before Jeanine could complete the process.

"We're being hailed by space control," Jeanine told me.

"Do you think you can play for time?" I asked. "Maybe make up a dire emergency that's forcing us to lift off?"

As an answer, Jeanine keyed on the comm. "This is the *Rising Star* responding. Please be quick as we are in the process of making an emergency lift off."

"Negative, *Rising Star*," a woman said. "You are not cleared for departure. Power down and prepare for an official inspection."

"Can't do that, Control," Jeanine said, her voice sounded properly harried. "We have a runaway reactor core. If we can't get the *Star* into orbit, you're going to have a smoking crater where this part of the space port used to be."

"Nice try, *Rising Star*, but modern reactor cores don't explode any more," Control responded.

"Control, is there someone with brains I can talk to?" The woman spluttered as Jeanine kept talking. "The *Rising Star* is a Helldiver blockade runner with all of the original equipment. That includes a reactor core manufactured before the current safeguards were developed."

There was a brief silence from the comm and then Control, her voice tentative, said, "Are you sure about that, *Star*?"

"No, I just made it up on the spot." Which is exactly what she had done, gambling that Control wouldn't know it. "Look it up if you want, but this ship is lifting off with or without your permission."

"Uh, roger that, *Rising Star*," Control said. "Hold one minute while I-"

The engine ready lights turned green—well, the most important ones did, anyway—and I shoved the throttle all the way forward. Jeanine and I sank into our acceleration couches as the *Star* roared into the late afternoon sky.

The woman from Space Control said, "*Rising Star*, I've been informed Helldiver reactors have all of the modern safety equipment. You have no emergency and you are making an unauthorized ascent. Cease acceleration immediately and return to the ground!"

In a dry voice, Jeanine said, "Control, if we cease acceleration now, we *will* return to the ground, but I don't think you're going to like the big, fiery explosion that comes with it."

Control blew out her breath in exasperation. "*Rising Star*, I obviously meant that you should make a controlled return to the ground."

"Oh, well that's completely different, Control!" Jeanine's tone was chipper as she responded. "Of course, we still can't do what you're asking."

"Willfully ignoring the instructions of Space Command carries a very stiff fine, *Rising Star*," Control said. "If you do not return to your docking bay immediately, I will personally make sure you pay the maximum fine for your actions. No plea deal will be accepted in traffic court nor will you be allowed landing permission on any of House Musgrave's planets while the fine is unpaid."

"So noted, Control," Jeanine replied. "Exactly how much is the maximum fine?"

"It's..." Control paused for dramatic effect and tried deepening her voice when she continued, "...five thousand credits."

Jeanine ruined Control's little drama by responding, "Gotcha. Are you set up to accept payment via electronic transfer?"

"Um, what was that, *Rising Star*?"

"Can I pay you directly by electronic transfer? Right now?" Jeanine enunciated carefully, just in case Control was having trouble hearing her. "I'd prefer to clear this up now rather than deal with it next time we land on one of Lord Musgrave's planets."

"S-sure, *Rising Star*, we can take your payment. Does this mean you are entering a plea of guilty to the charge of making an unauthorized ascent?"

"Yes, ma'am, we are guilty as charged," Jeanine sang out. "We are prepared to pay the fine now and clear this off our record. Just tell me where to send it."

Control rattled off routing information, which Jeanine dutifully entered into her console. Then she pulled one of her credit sticks from her bag, inserted it into the console, and sent five thousand credits. "There you go, Space Control. Are we all squared away now?"

"It appears so, *Rising Star*, but be advised you will not get off so lightly should you attempt a stunt like this in the future." Control's voice gained strength as she issued the threat. "Do you understand?"

"Loud and clear, ma'am," Jeanine responded.

That's when a new voice joined the conversation.

"Bragua Space Control, this is Sir Phillip of Reimund, Recognized Knight of House Kahn and Royal Enforcer of His Majesty's laws. The ship *Rising Star* carries a fugitive from my Lady Olivia's justice. In her name and the name of our king, I demand you stop that ship and place all of its passengers in my custody."

"Sir Phillip, we have received your credentials and they check out," Control said, her voice suddenly nervous, "but you know I cannot hold a ship simply on your word. Do you have a warrant or some other document authorizing this action?"

"Space Control, be advised that my shuttle is performing an emergency ascent effective immediately. Clear our flight path of all traffic," the knight ordered.

"Yes, Sir Phillip. I'm rerouting all traffic now." Control said.

Obviously unable to stop herself, Jeanine joined the conversation. In the most innocent of tones, she asked, "Gosh, Space Control, why didn't you tell me all I had to do was order you to clear the way for us?"

"Do not answer the woman, Space Control," Sir Phillip said. "She is the fugitive I seek."

That's when it dawned on me that letting Jeanine talk with Space Control hadn't been a good idea. From the look on her face, it just occurred to Jeanine, too. Dammit, I let myself get too wrapped up in getting away fast and forgot about getting away cleanly. Sir Phillip already suspected Jeanine was on board, but now he knew it and hoped to use it to turn House Musgrave against us.

"I'll admit he seeks me, Space Control, but not because I'm a fugitive," Jeanine said. Her voice took on a quaver as she continued, "It's not well-publicized, but Lady Olivia has...well, you *know* how she is, right?"

"What are you talking about, *Rising Star*?" Space Control asked, a hint of fascination in her voice.

"Lady Olivia has brought back the ancient practice of Prima Nocta." Sir Phillip spluttered when Jeanine said that, but she ignored him. "When she tried invoking it on me, my husband managed to get me to his ship and out of Kahn space. We thought that would be it, but she sent Sir Phillip to bring me back to her. Compare his flight plans with ours. We were on Thinda and he tried using their customs inspectors to find me. Do you think it's a coincidence he ended up on Bragua mere hours after we landed?"

Sir Phillip finally found his voice. "This woman spews vile and baseless lies against my Lady Olivia. I *demand* you stop that ship and turn its occupants over to me!"

"Hm..." Control said. After a few seconds, she continued, "Both ships *did* come here from Thinda."

"Of course, both ships came here from Thinda, Control," Sir Phillip said, his voice tight. "I am following them in an attempt to capture a wanted fugitive."

"And I'm still waiting for documents that back your claim, Sir Phillip," Control responded.

"What other reason would I have to pursue this woman so vigorously?" the knight asked.

Someone in the background at Space Control said, "Maybe she's hot, and he gets sloppy seconds?"

Control snorted, struggling not to laugh at the comment, and said, "Cut it out back there."

Jeanine injected a little fear into her voice. "Control, you don't think that's true, do you? Oh, God. Oh, God!"

Sir Phillip spluttered some more before shouting, "I will *not* tolerate this disrespect! Who made that comment? I will have his name so I can challenge him to single combat!"

Yet another voice joined the conversation, this one deep and calm. "That's enough, Phillip. You know it's illegal for a knight to challenge a commoner. You're letting a little rough humor override your common sense."

Jeanine glanced at me in surprise before saying, "Um, who are you?"

"Sir Gilbert, sworn knight of Lord Musgrave. My ship is on approach to Bragua. My pilot told me of this little...disagreement... and patched me into the discussion." The man sounded older than Sir Phillip, perhaps even as old as Sir Jared. "Phillip, why are you after this young woman?"

"She has been a fugitive from my lady's justice for decades. I finally tracked her down on Thinda and, when she fled to Bragua, followed her. This is a house matter, Gilbert. Have her turned over to me and I will be out of your jurisdiction quickly."

"She sounds rather young to have been on the run for decades," Sir Gilbert said. "Young woman, would you please tell me just how old you are?"

"I'm not quite twenty-five, Sir Gilbert," Jeanine replied.

"We'll run a voice print analysis, of course, but I'm inclined to believe you," Sir Gilbert mused. "Phillip, please accept my private comm so I can discuss this with you knight to knight."

The comm went silent and Jeanine muted her mic. "What do you think they're talking about, Drake?"

"You," I said. "And whether Sir Phillip can convince Sir Gilbert to intercept the *Star* for him."

"Can we get away if Sir Gilbert comes after us?" she asked.

"Maybe. I've found his ship on scanners and he's in a very good position relative to us. It will all come down to how good his pilot is." I checked the scanners a second time. "By the time Sir Phillip's shuttle docks with his ship, we'll be too far away for the ship to cut us off before we can jump into hyperspace."

We waited in silence for a tense thirty seconds before Sir Gilbert's voice returned to the comm. "Space Control, the *Rising*

Star has offered a guilty plea for an unauthorized ascent and paid their fine in full. Is this correct?"

"It is, Sir Gilbert," Control responded.

"Very well. I have not been given what I consider sufficient reasons to hold them or intercept the ship. On my authority, the *Rising Star* is free to go."

"You're making a big mistake, Gilbert," Sir Phillip growled.

"It wouldn't be the first time, Phillip," Sir Gilbert chuckled.

"Thank you, Sir Gilbert," Jeanine said.

"There is no need to thank me, young woman," Sir Gilbert replied. "I am but doing my duty."

Free from Bragua's atmosphere and free from immediate pursuit, I gave the *Star* full throttle and we blasted away from the planet. With luck, we would be in hyperspace before Sir Phillip's ship even cleared the planet's gravity well. Jeanine was safe—at least for the moment.

A ROYAL REQUEST

Olivia

Colin stood to my left, silently watching me as I listened to Sir Phillip's report. I struggled to maintain a passive expression as the knight described the debacle at Bragua.

"Had Sir Gilbert accepted my claims, Bragua's space patrol forces could have stopped Captain Haral's ship from leaving the system." Sir Phillip looked me in the eye. "I was insufficiently convincing, my lady, and my mission failed."

"What evidence did you present to Lord Musgrave's knight?" I asked.

"I presented the circumstantial evidence from Thinda tying the bastard to Captain Haral and the captain's behavior on Bragua, none of which was consistent with that of an innocent freighter captain."

No wonder the other knight refused to have the ship stopped. Had some knight of the realm presented such flimsy evidence to me, I wouldn't have accepted it, either. I *might* have acted on it anyway, but only if I saw some political benefit to doing so. Obviously, Sir Gilbert saw no such benefit.

"You didn't tell the other knight of the alarm triggered by the bastard's DNA scan?" I asked, again struggling to keep frustration from my voice. "I rather expect that information would have drawn the knight into the affair."

"I weighed that option very carefully, my lady, and rejected it for several reasons," Sir Phillip said.

"Such as?" This time, I couldn't keep a note of impatience from entering my voice.

"I landed on Bragua at the same time Captain Haral and the bastard were fighting their way past the men I hired to guard the docking bay. My shuttle made an emergency lift-off mere minutes after setting down. Sir Gilbert would have asked how I knew of the alarm triggered by the DNA scan."

"The alarm says she's wanted by House Kahn, Sir Phillip," I said, giving into the urge to cross my arms and glare at the knight. "It strikes me as perfectly reasonable that the Recognized Knight of House Kahn would check for such alarms upon arrival on a planet."

"That *is* my standard procedure, my lady—but I contact your embassy, not the planetary police."

"Why don't you simply go straight to the locals, Sir Phillip?"

"Ignoring the proper channels causes problems with both the locals and your ambassadorial representatives, my lady, and hinders cooperation from the planetary police."

The knight maintained the calm and reasonable tone of voice he'd used throughout the conversation, but I detected a narrowing of his eyes. Having his actions questioned in such detail apparently annoyed him. I felt a flash of irrational satisfaction at that.

Sir Phillip continued, "Had I brought up the alarm and the pursuit of the bastard, it is extremely likely Sir Gilbert would have taken a deeper interest in the matter. Neither he nor Lord Musgrave are fools. They would have recognized the girl's heritage and might have requested an investigation into the warrant tied to her DNA. I doubt you want the bastard under the control of one of your political rivals, nor do you want anyone looking too closely at the warrant."

The petulant part of my mind wanted to damn the man for

figuring all of this out before I did. It wanted to throw something against the wall and curse at the knight even if he was right. I took a few seconds to get control of that part of my brain. Then I drew a deep breath and slowly released it. Calm once again, I met Sir Phillip's eyes on the screen.

"My apologies for questioning your reasoning, Sir Phillip. You worked through the ramifications of the situation much more quickly than I would have." I smiled warmly at the knight, willing some of that warmth into my eyes as well. "As always, I thank God my father chose you as his Recognized Knight."

Sir Phillip's eyebrows rose just a fraction, the only indication my words caught him by surprise. He smiled and ducked his head in pleased response. Apparently, I'd successfully warmed my eyes. I decided to soothe the knight a bit more and, perhaps, strengthen his emotional bond to his duchess.

"Now that the bastard has slipped through our fingers, we'll need to start our search again. Please return to me here on Gaunner with all haste. Your counsel in this matter will be invaluable."

"At once, my lady!"

I slumped back in the chair as the screen went blank. Looking at Colin, I said, "Well, that could have gone better."

"The action on Bragua could most certainly have gone better, my lady," Colin said. "On the other hand, your handling of Sir Phillip was quite well done. Your apology and compliments were so good I almost believed them, myself."

I allowed myself a moment to bask in the praise. "Thank you, Colin. Now—"

The comm came to life. "Pardon the interruption, my lady, but you have another subspace call. It's—"

Irritation flared inside me and I let it out. "I do not care who it is, technician. You *do not* speak until I give you leave to do so! Is that clear?"

The technician responded meekly, "Yes, my lady."

I could tell he wanted to say something else. He probably

wanted to offer an explanation or apology, neither of which I was in the mood to hear. "That will be all."

I reached to mute the comm entirely, but Colin chose to speak. "Technician, who is calling Lady Olivia?"

"The man placing the call wears royal livery, sir," the technician responded. "Her Majesty, Queen Charlotte wishes to speak with Lady Olivia."

I turned wide eyes on Colin and was less than reassured to find him staring at me with an equally surprised expression. I cocked my head, silently asking if Colin had any idea why the queen was calling me. He gave me an apologetic shrug.

"Thank you, technician. You were quite correct to contact me *and* to speak without first receiving leave from me," I said. "Route the call to me and then disconnect your console from the subspace relay entirely."

"I understand and will do as you order, my lady," the technician responded.

A second later, the screen lit with the image of one of the many royal attendants. He gave me a nod of respect and said, "Please hold for Her Majesty the Queen."

The man's image faded from the screen and I waited with considerable apprehension for the queen. She and I have spoken, of course, as you'd expect from women in our lofty positions, but never in private and never at her behest. While my mind was still whirling, the screen cleared, and I looked upon Queen Charlotte.

The queen smiled at me and said, "Thank you for accepting my call, Lady Olivia. I know how busy you must be and am grateful to you for taking the time to speak with me."

"I can think of nothing more important than accepting a call from Your Majesty and am truly honored to receive it." For once, I didn't have to act sincere. Every last word I said was God's own truth. "How may I be of assistance?"

"May we speak in complete privacy, Lady Olivia?" Queen Charlotte asked.

"Of course." Though Colin wasn't in the video pickup, most

people knew he listened to all of my conversations. My curiosity piqued even more than before, I waved my assistant away. "That will be all, Colin."

When the door slid shut behind the man, I said, "The room is clear, Your Majesty."

"Excellent. First, let us continue on a more familiar basis. Please simply call me Charlotte," she said, settling back into her seat. "May I use your given name?"

This was a completely unexpected turn of events and my mind whirled even faster. "Of course, Your Ma- Charlotte. I would be honored."

"Thank you, Olivia," the queen said. She regarded me candidly for a few seconds. "You truly are a beautiful young woman, Olivia, every inch your mother's daughter."

To my horror, I actually blushed at the compliment. It is not one I hear very often. "I...thank you, Charlotte. Only my father and people who wanted something from me have said as much, prior to you."

"I suspect some of that was due to your brother. Robert was very...enthusiastic...about protecting you from any men who showed any sexual interest. But you also inherited your father's intelligence, which no doubt dissuaded the shallow young males among the nobles of the court."

I grimaced, all too familiar with that lot. "Alas, Charlotte, that describes every eligible young man in the court." Too late, I remembered the crown prince was among those young men. "I, um, don't mean Prince William, of course!"

"Yes, you do—and you're right to put him there. I love the boy dearly, but even I recognize William is a pretty package with very little substance within." The queen sighed, "He's quite like his father in that respect, Olivia."

That was an unexpected revelation. Everyone knows the queen is the real force behind the throne, but I never expected her to admit it—especially not to me.

The queen smiled at me. "You're surprised I said that aloud, aren't you, Olivia?"

"I am, Charlotte. It's not a secret, of course, but no one dares say as much." All of a sudden, my mind stopped whirling, and I found my bearings. I still didn't know what the queen wanted, but this was obviously a woman-to-woman talk, not a queen-to-subject chat. "Why did you really call me? It certainly isn't to swap court gossip."

The queen actually laughed, true humor sparkling in her eyes. "I've always liked you, Olivia. I may not have shown it, but I've watched you with considerable interest for many years. Truly, you rather remind me of myself at your age."

"I'm flattered, Charlotte, but you didn't answer my question."

"I'm coming to that, Olivia...It has come to my attention that you have a problem that has you rather distracted of late—the search for the illegitimate offspring of a certain late duke. Unless I miss my guess, you'd like this bastard to join her father in the hereafter."

That got my attention. I thought we'd kept our search well hidden from court scrutiny. "You're...remarkably well informed, Charlotte."

"I am the queen, dear. That means I have a *lot* of manpower simply waiting to do my bidding. I told you I've been watching you and that I like what I've seen. I believe I can help you find and eliminate your bastard." The queen leaned toward the screen. "And you, my dear, can help me with my pressing problem."

"What problem is that, Charlotte?"

"Much as I hate to say it, I won't live forever. When the time comes, I want to leave the kingdom in capable hands." The queen's eyes bored into mine. "I want those hands to be yours, Olivia. Would you be interested in reigning as queen when I am gone?"

"Only a princess of the realm may take the throne, Charlotte, and only then if she's the eldest child. I'm neither of those."

"True, my dear, but I was neither of those, myself. I am, however, the wife of the king."

My eyes widened. "Are you suggesting what I think you are?"

"Yes, Olivia. Please tell me you'll agree to marry Prince William?"

KNOW YOUR ENEMY

Jeanine

Normal space vanished as the *Rising Star* made the jump into hyperspace. Drake heaved a sigh of relief and leaned back from the ship's controls.

"Based on our last sensor readings, Sir Phillip's ship won't be clear of Bragua's gravity well for at least another thirty minutes," he said. "If they want to chase us, the best they can do is guess our destination based on our vector when we entered hyperspace."

"Are they likely to guess right?" I asked.

"Not a chance. There's a heavily populated system along our vector, but we're not going there."

"Where are we going?"

"About two light years out into open space," Drake replied. "Then I'll calculate a new course and we'll head off on a totally different vector than the one we're on now. The crew of Sir Phillip's ship will probably guess that's our plan, so they may not even bother following us."

"How much time do we have before we return to normal space?"

"Long enough for me to tell you why I faded out back on Bragua and what I think this is all about," Drake said.

"Good." I spun the copilot's seat around to face Drake. "Tell it in whatever order you think is best, but don't stop until you've told me everything. I'm tired of being in the dark."

Drake nodded and then leaned his head back. He stared at the ceiling for a short while, obviously gathering his thoughts. I willed my suddenly racing heart to slow down and did my best to cultivate the patience Sir Jared worked so hard to instill in me.

Drake finally looked at me and said, "Shortly after we first met, I told you I received training in my lord's house military, but I didn't say much more."

"I remember. It was when you offered to let me stay on the *Star*."

"I got all of the training that house military gets and took it alongside new recruits, but I was in my lord's Space Patrol," Drake told me. "The Patrol is part of the military, but our main job involves working with civilians. I was good at my job, too. Within a few years, I was given command of a patrol ship and posted to a system without any colonized planets, but with quite a few mining settlements in the asteroid belt. It was a big step up for me, so I gathered up my family and moved to one of the settlements."

"Family? You have a *family*?" I couldn't keep the anger from my voice as I looked away from Drake. I'd never have slept with him if I'd known about his family.

"I *had* a family." Drake gently caught my chin. He raised my head, and I saw unshed tears in his eyes. "My wife and daughter have been dead for seven years."

I felt my face redden in shame. "I'm so sorry, Drake—both for those you lost and for thinking you'd cheat on your wife."

He waved off my apology. "It's no worse than me thinking you might be using me when we were on Bragua."

Drake told me how he and his crew found their settlement destroyed and all the people dead. Despite the horror of the story, he couldn't keep a tinge of pride from his voice when he told me how Heather, his wife, shot two of the pirates before they got her.

"That's what was running through my mind when you left for the DNA clinic. I...tend to zone out whenever that memory rises up out of the depths of my mind. I can only imagine how that made you feel at the time." Drake looked me in the eyes again. "I'm sorry for that."

It was my turn to wave off an apology. "I can only imagine what you went through seven years ago and go through again every time the memory returns. It must be horrible."

Drake shook his head. "It's heartrending, something I'll never get over. Time dulls the pain, but I'll carry it with me for the rest of my life. Candi—she was my daughter—would be almost ten if she'd..."

Drake broke off and rubbed his face. As he drew several deep, uneven breaths, I said, "You don't have to say anything else. I think I understand—as well as someone who hasn't suffered through what you have *can* understand, anyway."

"No, there's more, and it's important for you to hear it, Jeanine. You see, the real horror came afterwards, when we caught the pirates." Drake sought my gaze again and something feral gleamed in his eyes. "We fought our share of pirates before and this bunch just wasn't the same as those other gangs. This bunch had a nearly new ship, and it was an actual gunship, not some converted freighter like we'd always fought before. There was more about them that just didn't make sense for regular pirates—their discipline, their tactics, stuff like that.

"But they were operating in our backyard and no one knew that asteroid belt better than we did. We tracked them down, came in dark, and only powered up at the last second. The short version is that we got them—blasted their ship, killed most of the officers, and took the rest prisoner. The prisoners kept insisting they were just regular pirates, but we didn't believe them."

Drake looked away from me, no longer willing to meet my gaze. "All of us lost people in that attack. When we didn't like the answers we got, it didn't take much for us to forget about our training. It's appalling just how much torture a man can take before he breaks, but we broke them all. The 'pirates' were house military, part of an undercover mission for House Kahn to drive the settlers away from the asteroid belt so Robert the Butcher could claim the system had been abandoned by our lord's house and take it for himself."

"You were part of House Wilkinson?" I asked.

"Got it in one, Jeanine. But do you want to know what the worst part was? When we reported everything we found, the duke —Arthur's second son, Michael—filed a complaint with the crown. My family was dead at the hands of the Butcher of House Kahn and he *filed a complaint*!" Drake shook his head as if in disbelief. "We all testified, but the Butcher claimed the men had gone rogue. The word of a bunch of commoners wasn't worth a damn against the word of a duke. The court did rule in House Wilkinson's favor, ordering House Kahn to reimburse Wilkinson for its lost assets. That's all our families were in the end—assets for our lord and master."

I slid out of my seat, knelt next to Drake, and wrapped my arms around him. "I'm so sorry. I just wish there was something more I could say or do to ease your pain."

Drake ran his hands through my hair and we just sat there for a little while. Then he said, "Our Lord Michael was kind and generous with the settlement—he told us that, himself—and gave us half of it to split among ourselves. Then he released us from the patrol, claiming we had *sullied* the patrol's reputation."

"That's when you bought the *Rising Star*, isn't it?"

"Yeah. My daughter used to always dance and sing, so I called her my rising star. When I named the ship after Candi, the ship sort of became my family." Drake forced some joviality into his voice. "Anyway, that's my story. Now we need to talk about yours."

"Are you up for it, Drake?" I asked. "It can't be easy telling me all of this. It can wait—"

"No, Jeanine, it can't wait." The man slid out of his chair and sat on the floor in front of me. "Do you remember when Robert the Butcher tried to claim the Duchy of Neert—House Wilkinson's lands—three years ago?"

"I think so. He died in an accident or something like that?"

"It was no accident. Robert requested Recognition as the Lord of Neert from the Star Stone. I don't know all the mystical crap behind it, but as long as all of the direct descendants of Arthur Wilkinson were dead he would have been Recognized. Instead, the Star Stone killed him—it burned him to ashes, in fact."

"So this Butcher guy missed one of the Wilkinson kids?" I asked. "That seems pretty careless of him."

"No, Robert got all of the children Arthur and Evelyn Wilkinson had. But obviously Arthur had another child with another woman—the now-famous Wilkinson Bastard."

"You think it's me," I guessed.

"Yes, I think it's you."

"And you hate the Wilkinson family almost as much as you hate House Kahn," I said.

"Yes, but I don't hate *you*. You have their blood and you were raised by their knight, but you are not one of them." To my surprise, Drake pulled me close and gently kissed me on the lips. "I could never hate you."

Drake held me while I absorbed everything he had told me. It took a while, and even then I hadn't really come to grips with the news. But eventually I pulled away from him and asked, "Assuming I am the Wilkinson Bastard—God, what a title to go through life with—what do you think we should do? Hide on a sparsely populated planet? Leave the kingdom and head to the frontier? Something like that?"

"If that's what you decide you want to do, I'll support you all the way, honey."

I smiled at his endearment. "I sense a 'but' in there. You might as well spill it."

"You could claim your birthright," Drake said. "You could go to the Star Stone and request Recognition as the Duchess of Neert."

Of all the things I thought Drake would say, suggesting we make a run *toward* the hub around which the lives of the nobles revolved was near the bottom of the list. The man suffered horribly because of the nobles' machinations and disregard for the lives of the commoners caught up in them. Yet he wanted to raise me up into that rarified group?

"Drake, I'm just a simple commoner who was raised by a man I thought was my eccentric grandfather. What do I know about the nobles and their responsibilities?" I shook my head, shrugged my shoulders, and gave off every other bit of negative body language I could think of. "Besides, isn't there already a Duchess of Neert?"

"You're already more noble than any of those people who actually hold the titles, Jeanine. You know what it's like living as a commoner, something none of *them* ever learned, or even considered was worth learning." Drake leaned forward, his eyes almost burning with intensity. "And the Duchess of Neert only holds the title by right of marriage. As soon as a true Wilkinson heir is recognized, she loses the title."

"So if I try for Recognition, I'll have two of the great houses after me? It's already cost me far too much having just one of them out to get me." I crossed my arms. I was trying to look defiant, but think I really just looked defensive. "No thank you."

"By all accounts, Lady Evelyn has no love for the title and will gladly step aside for anyone who isn't part of House Kahn." With a visible effort, Drake reigned in his enthusiasm. "Besides, it's obvious that Lord and Lady Wilkinson wanted you to be Recognized at some point. Why else would they send you into hiding with their most trusted defender?"

"Have you ever thought that Sir Jared's job was keeping me *away* from the whole noble scene?" I asked. "Maybe they were afraid that Butcher guy from House Kahn would find a way to use me against them. It wouldn't be the first time one house used another house's bastard that way."

"That's true, but that only happens when the house in question doesn't know the bastard exists. Arthur Wilkinson obviously knew you existed *and* wanted your existence kept secret." Drake's gaze turned inward as he gave this idea deeper thought. "What if Lord Arthur knew—or at least suspected—that the Butcher would come after his family? His legitimate heirs were already in the public eye—tagged and ready for bagging by the Butcher, if you will. Much as he may have wanted to hide them, he couldn't. But if he had a secret bastard hidden away that child would be like an insurance policy for revenge—insuring the Butcher died terribly just at the moment when he thought he had won it all."

I rubbed my temples, trying to ease the tension I felt building inside of me. "That is just too convoluted for words, Drake! My God, how can you even think up something like that, much less believe the nobles are capable of such wheels within wheels within wheels?"

"I've spent the last seven years studying the behavior of the so-called nobles. Trust me, the scenario I just laid out is tame compared to some of the stuff I've read about and seen happen in real life."

"Why would you torture yourself like that?" I leaned forward and carefully brushed Drake's hair away from his eyes, turning the gesture into a soft caress of his cheek. "Why would you subject yourself to a constant reminder of everything the squabbling of nobles has cost you?"

"Know your enemy."

"What are you talking about?" I asked.

Drake caught my hand in both of his and stared hard into my eyes. "Most of the commoners in the kingdom never get crushed like I did, but they go through life keeping their heads down and praying they never earn the attention of their lord and master. There are still millions of people like me in the kingdom—people whose lives casually are destroyed when our 'betters' vie for power and prestige. We've finally grown tired of being pawns in their games, Jeanine, and we're not going to take it anymore."

He brought my hand to his lips and gave it a soft kiss. Then he simply watched me, giving me time to absorb everything he had told me.

"You're planning a revolution?" I finally asked.

"Yes."

"And you want me to join you?"

"Only if you want to. I've put my life in your hands, but I refuse to believe you'd ever betray me." He gently rubbed the back of my hand. "You know I'd never do anything to hurt you. If you want nothing to do with the revolution, I'll help you find a safe place to hide from House Kahn and leave you out of it."

"If I'm out of the revolution, I'm out of your life, too?"

"Until we win, yes," Drake said. "It wouldn't be safe for you, otherwise."

"Do you really think you'll defeat the kingdom?" I couldn't keep the incredulity out of my voice.

"Anyone who starts a revolution expecting to lose, has already lost."

Okay, that made sense to me. Twisted sense, but sense nonetheless. "If you're set on overthrowing the nobility, why do you want me to be Recognized as one of them? Even if I become the Duchess of Neert, it's not like they're going to share all of their defense secrets with me."

"There are a couple of reasons," Drake replied. "First, we can use House Wilkinson's star systems to build our forces and prepare for the revolution. We'd still have to be careful and secretive, but less so than if we did this elsewhere. You'd also lend a certain authority to our cause. No matter how badly the nobles abuse some people, they will more readily believe in our cause if it's led by one of the nobility."

"You want me to *lead* your rebellion?" I pulled my hand back and glared at Drake.

"Not unless you want a position of leadership—and even then you'd have to prove that you're ready to lead." Drake captured my hand again. "But simply having a duchess among our ranks will work in our favor."

Once again, he stopped talking and gave me time to think. One horrible thought rose to the surface.

"How long have you suspected I was the Wilkinson Bastard?"

"It first occurred to me when you told me about Sir Jared," Drake said, obviously surprised at the question.

"You didn't think about it back on Thinda?" I asked.

"No. Why would I think of that? I just assumed you were another poor commoner about to get squashed by an uncaring noble." His eyes suddenly widened as if comprehension was dawning. "Do you think I was pretending to love you just to draw you into the revolution?"

I shrugged. "Wouldn't you do anything to overthrow the nobles?"

"No, I wouldn't. I've done some terrible things in my life and, if we end up fighting for our freedom, probably will again—but I would never use you like that!" Drake's expression was sincere, but he'd been very sincere making love to me, too. After a few seconds of silence between us, his face fell, and he stood. "I'm sorry I can't convince you, Jeanine. Come on, let's find a safe place I can take you to."

I stood up, wrapped my arms around his neck, and kissed Drake. He returned the kiss, but kept it short and didn't really put himself into it. Laying my head on his shoulder, I asked, "Why are you being so distant all of a sudden?"

"I will not use my love for you to draw you into the revolution."

Keeping my arms around his neck, I pulled back enough to see his face clearly. "Are you saying you love me?"

"I never thought it would happen after I lost Heather and Candi, but yes."

"And being distant is a way to make it easier for me to leave you?" When Drake nodded, I continued, "You don't know much about women, do you?"

He flashed a wry smile. "Heather used to say the same thing about me."

"She sounds like a smart woman." I leaned in close, our lips nearly touching. "Now kiss me like you mean it."

Our lips met and this time his response was filled with love and hope and fear and passion and loss and longing and emotions I can't even put words to. I abandoned all restraint for the first time in my life, pouring all of my hopes, my dreams, and my love into the kiss. When our lips finally parted, we were both breathing hard.

I whispered, "After the revolution, I will not be put on a throne. I will not fight to replace one despotic monarchy with another one."

He whispered back, "We want a republic. No kings. No nobles. And definitely no queens."

"Then I'm with you, Drake. Let's plan our Recognition run."

THE SLICER

Drake

"*Are you saying you love me?*" she asked.

"*I never thought it would happen after I lost Heather and Candi, but yes.*"

My universe changed with those words. A single sentence filled with simple words. Simple words with straightforward meanings. But for me, they meant so much more than their definitions.

They meant letting Heather and Candi move on.

They meant releasing the grief that had dominated my emotions.

They meant the end of my old life.

They meant the end of my journey down the path of vengeance.

They meant the beginning of my new life.

They marked my first steps on the path toward justice.

They meant I had finally opened my heart to love another.

Did Jeanine understand just what it cost me to admit my love for her? Did she have any idea what I gave up when I uttered those words?

Of course, she didn't.

Did I have any idea what I gained with those few words? Did I have any idea how those words changed my life?

Of course, I didn't.

But, for the first time in seven years, I actually wanted to live that life.

"Hello in there!" Jeanine sang. "Is anybody home?"

"Hm? Oh, I'm sorry, babe." The endearment—once previously reserved solely for tender moments with Heather—came naturally. It felt right using it with Jeanine. And that changed my life just a little more. "I was...thinking."

Jeanine cocked her head and looked at me. Heather used to do the same thing when she was trying to figure out the true meaning behind my words. "Are you wishing you'd kept quiet?"

"God, no! I don't regret anything I said."

"You had such a pensive expression, I was afraid—"

I pulled her into a tight hug. "Don't be. It's just..." I flailed for the right words and finally just said, "I always feared loving someone else would mean pushing Heather and Candi from my heart—only it doesn't. They're both still in my heart, where they've always been. But now you're in my heart with them and it feels right."

We held each other for a while, neither one of us saying anything. Finally, I pulled back and saw Jeanine's bright blue eyes shining with unshed tears. I kissed her gently and said, "Knowing Heather, if she could say one thing to me right now I think it would be 'It is about damned time, Drake.' Actually, knowing Heather I can't imagine she'd just say one thing. She'd tell you that you're going to have your hands full taking care of me. And she'd remind me that this ship is going to be in hyperspace for at least another couple of hours."

"And what would she suggest you do with those two hours?"

I scooped Jeanine into my arms. "Make passionate love to you."

She laid her head on my shoulder as I carried her to the bedroom. "That sounds like a very good idea."

Much later, Jeanine sat in the co-pilot's chair as I prepared to reenter normal space. I disengaged the hyperdrive, and we watched red stars and blue stars suddenly turn white.

"Do you ever get tired of watching that?" she asked.

"Not so far, and I hope that feeling lasts for the rest of my life."

"I know what you mean," she said, a dazzling smile lighting up her face. "Getting tired of that sight would mean the stars themselves had lost their wonder." Without taking her eyes from the star field, she asked, "Have you decided where to go next?"

"When, exactly, would I have found time to think, much less decide? You're quite the distraction, you know."

"You're not so bad at that, yourself," she responded. "But I also recognize that look on your face. You've already decided where to go, right?"

"Yes, but I want you to hear my reasons before you react."

Jeanine spun her seat to face me. "You want to go back to Bragua."

My eyes widened and my mouth dropped open. "How did you know?"

"You want me to pursue recognition as the next Duchess of Neert, but you also don't want to watch me go up in flames if you guessed wrong about my bloodline. We're going back to get my DNA scan." The woman had the temerity to smirk at me. She had a good smirk, too, managing to look both smug and sexy at the same time. Then the smirk turned into a frown and she said, "I just don't see how we can get the scan from the clinic without running the risk of being caught."

"What do you mean 'we'? *I* will get the scan. *You* will stay safe and sound on the *Star*."

Jeanine's frown turned into a glare. "You can forget that kind of crap right now, buster. I'll take precautions with my appearance, but this is the wrong time to start treating me like I'll break. Fragile people make lousy revolutionaries."

I held up my hands in mock surrender. "You're not fragile—which I never claimed, but consider it duly noted. And there's probably no reason you can't come with me since I'm not going to go to the clinic."

"Where are you going?"

"To visit a slicer who's on our side. He'll be disappointed I'm not asking him to slice into Bragua's defense net, but he'll retrieve your scan faster through the net than we could in person."

We took our time returning to Bragua, making two jumps, so we arrived in the system from a completely different vector than when we left. The time in hyperspace gave me a chance to swap out the *Star's* registration beacon. By the time we arrived in Bragua space, she flew under the name *Arcadia*. We landed on the opposite side of the planet from our previous stop. I fired off a coded message to one of the slicer's many identities and then did a little shopping for Jeanine.

The slicer responded while Jeanine was getting ready to go out in public and we arranged a meeting. Thirty minutes later, I left my ship accompanied by a prim woman who wore her brown hair in a tight bun and clothes that must have been specifically tailored to hide or disguise everything wonderful about women. Even her walk was muted, with little swing to her hips, and she maintained a proper half meter separation from me. No one gave her a second glance and hardly anyone even bothered with a first glance.

As we neared the address provided by the slicer, I felt my pulse quicken and could hear Jeanine taking deep breaths in an attempt to keep calm. When we entered the slicer's apartment building— or, at least, the building he chose for this meeting—and approached the lift chute, her steps faltered just for a second.

"Are you okay?" I asked. "Do you still want to go through with this?"

Jeanine's steps returned to normal. "Absolutely. If powerful people are going to keep trying to capture or kill me, I'm damned well going to make sure I know *why*."

Without another word, we stepped into the lift chute.

We got out of the lift tube on the fifth floor. I took Jeanine's hand and guided her to the last door in the hallway. I rapped on the door in the prearranged pattern. A small compartment opened next to the door, revealing a retinal scanner.

As the scanner light swept across my eye, Jeanine asked, "You've met this guy before?"

"Nope, but several of us know how to contact him if we need his services."

"Then how did he get your retina print? Did your...organization...give him the scans of people who knew how to contact him?"

"No, that's much too risky," I said, looking away from the scanner as the compartment closed. "But this guy wouldn't be very useful to us if he couldn't get that kind of information on his own."

The door slid open, revealing a short hallway three or four meters long. It ended in yet another door. Jeanine looked at me and raised her eyebrows. I shrugged, and we walked through the doorway. As expected, the door slid shut behind us. As unexpected, the door in front of us did not slide open.

"Now what?" Jeanine asked.

"I don't know. He scanned my retina and knows I'm who I say I am."

"I'm scanning you for recording devices and tracking beacons," a disembodied, husky woman's voice said. "It's a low-level scan and takes a minute or so."

Jeanine smiled at me. "It looks like *she* is quite thorough."

"I could be a man using software to disguise my voice and my sex." As the voice spoke, it morphed from the woman's voice into a man's voice and then back again. Then the door slid open and a different, higher pitched woman's voice called, "You're clean. Come on in."

I originally thought we'd find the slicer in some kind of high-tech lair; a room littered with snack containers, electronic equipment I couldn't recognize, and a smarmy, middle-aged guy who would ogle Jeanine while making sexually suggestive comments. After hearing her unfiltered voice, I had mentally replaced 'guy' with 'girl' and thought sexual suggestions were less likely. The rest of my expectation remained the same though.

Instead of my imagined lair, I found a neatly organized,

comfortably decorated room. It did have one wall dedicated to stylish electronic equipment at whose function I could only guess. I got that part right, at least. A young woman with dark blonde hair sat in front of the bank of equipment. She was about Jeanine's age and had a single cable running from the equipment to a data port in the back of her neck.

The woman stood, smiling at the two of us, and said, "It's good to meet you at last, Drake. You can call me Jana. I've heard a lot about you from your compatriots." Her eyes took in our clasped hands. "It seems I can disregard one thing your friends told me about you."

Noting where the slicer was looking, Jeanine asked, "What did they tell you about Drake?"

Jana looked at me as if asking permission to spill some secrets. I said, "I have nothing to hide from Jeanine."

"Your friends warned me that you used sex to hide from the pain you still felt over the loss of your family and, if we met, you'd do your best to get me into bed. They also told me you'd be gone by the morning." Jana's eyes switched back and forth between Jeanine and me. "You don't need to hide anymore, do you?"

"No, I don't," I said. "But Jeanine still does and we need to make sure we understand the reason behind that."

"You gave vague hints about it in your message," Jana said. "Could you elaborate?"

"You're connected to everything on Bragua, right?" When Jana nodded, I continued, "Then you heard about the little drama that played out on the other side of the planet? The one involving House Kahn's Recognized knight and your own lord's Sir Gilbert?"

"Yes, and I know that was you two." Seeing my surprised expression, Jana added, "I sliced into the security cam feeds. I must say the flitter rescue from eighty-something floors above the ground was worthy of an adventure vid."

"Well, that saves a little time," I said. "The office Jeanine leapt from was a DNA clinic."

Jana turned her gaze on Jeanine. "And you went there because...?"

I was trying to figure out the best way to explain our theory when Jeanine said, "We think I'm the Wilkinson Bastard."

Jana's eyes widened and her mouth actually fell open. As looks of surprise go, you couldn't get a better one unless you watched a kids' animated vid.

Jana got control of herself, closed her mouth, and grinned broadly. "Drake, it's about time you guys brought me something really interesting! I'll have her DNA scan results in just a minute."

Jana's eyes unfocused, and it was obvious she was already traveling the net in search of the information. Unsure whether she could hear me or not, I asked, "Don't you need the name of the clinic?"

Her voice distant and her eyes still unfocused, Jana said, "Really, Drake? You've already told me Jeanine was at the clinic when you showed up with the flitter. That was more than enough to find the office. Murray and Mize, right?"

"That's them," Jeanine replied.

"I've got good news for you, Drake," Jana said.

"The scan confirms her identity?" I asked.

"No, the scan is gone," the slicer replied. "Someone completely wiped it from the clinic's system."

"Is this some new definition of 'good news' that I'm not familiar with?" Jeanine asked.

"Sort of," Jana said. "First, it's good news if you want to be the Wilkinson Bastard. No one would bother wiping the scan of someone whose parents were unimportant. Second, it's good news because this means I'll have to slice into the Royal DNA Database."

"I understand the first, but what's so good about the second?" Jeanine asked.

I answered, "Because the Royal DNA Database will be a lot harder to slice, Jana thinks it's a challenge worthy of her skills."

"Exactly!" the slicer said. "This is going to take a lot of concentration, so I won't be saying anything for a long time. If my brain fries or my head explodes or something like that, run like hell and leave Bragua as soon as possible."

"My God," Jeanine exclaimed, "is that really possible?"

"Not really, but it sounds exciting, doesn't it?" Jana replied. "Now, hush while I do my job."

Watching Jana do her thing, I once again found that real life wasn't anything like adventure vids. In the vids, slicers always jerk back and forth in their seats, sweat pours down their faces, and they mutter cryptic phrases that end up making perfect sense later in the vid. Jana just sat in her chair, her entire body relaxed and sweat-free.

For a while, Jeanine and I watched Jana, waiting for her to pop back with the information. Once again the vids steered me wrong. Instead of waiting through one or two tense minutes, we watched the slicer for ten boring minutes. When she was still busy, we settled back on Jana's sofa and took a nap.

"Wake up, love birds!" Jana called. "I'm back and I have answers."

I awoke with a start, shook Jeanine awake, and checked my chrono. "It took you two and a half hours to do the job?"

"I could have pulled a smash and grab in under thirty minutes, but I assumed the idea was to get in and out without getting caught or leaving a trail." Jana disconnected herself from her equipment, stood, and stretched. "Besides, there were some surprising attachments to Jeanine's scan."

Jeanine stood and faced Jana. "What did you find out? Am I the Wilkinson Bastard?"

"Yes."

I stood and wrapped an arm around Jeanine's shoulders. "I... don't know what I should say now."

Jeanine leaned into me. "You don't need to say anything, Drake. I grew up thinking my family was dead, now I know it's true. Thank you, Jana, for finding the answer I sought."

"Hold on, you two," Jana said as we turned toward the door. "That's not all I found."

"Let me guess," I said. "You found evidence that someone working for House Kahn sliced the database and attached a warrant to any scan matching Arthur Wilkinson's DNA."

"Good guess, and reasonable after everything that happened to you two yesterday. I can even give you the slicer's name if you want. I recognize his style. The guy is good. I'm better."

"No need," I said. "If there's nothing else, we'll be going."

"There *is* something else," Jana said.

The slicer's tone of voice caught my attention. Whatever she'd found, Jana thought it was extremely important.

"What is it?" Jeanine asked.

"Shortly after House Kahn attached that warrant to the Wilkinson DNA records, someone else sliced the database and attached something else to it."

"Who did it and what did they attach?" I asked.

"I...don't know who did it." That admission looked physically painful for Jana. She grimaced as if the next bit was even worse. "The file is encrypted and I can't break the encryption."

I sighed in frustration. "If you can't open it, I doubt anyone else in our organization can."

"You're right—I'm the best our side has got." Jana said that so matter-of-factly that you couldn't call it arrogance. She was simply stating a fact. She continued, "I can't open the file, but Jeanine can. The encryption is keyed to her retina print."

I looked at Jeanine. "How would someone get your retina scan if no one knew who you were?"

"Sir Jared knew who I was," Jeanine replied. "He must have given it to whoever sent the message."

It only took Jana a couple of minutes to load the file onto a data pad that wasn't on the net or connected to her system. It's possible she was simply being paranoid, but no slicer worth the name would dare open a file like this one on anything else.

Jeanine sat before the pad and Jana activated the file. The pad scanned Jeanine's retina, and the screen played a vid. A distinguished looking woman on the high end of middle-age appeared on the screen.

"Hello, Jeanine," she said. "You don't know me, but I am Lady Evelyn Wilkinson, Duchess of Neert."

LADY EVELYN'S MESSAGE

Jeanine

Almost of its own volition, my hand snapped out and stopped the vid playback. "Is this some kind of joke, Jana? Did you create this file during the hours when Drake and I thought you were slicing the Royal DNA Database?"

"How dare you accuse me of that! Just because you're *the* Bastard doesn't mean you also have to be *a* bastard," Jana replied. "Even if I was enough of a jerk to try something like that, do you have any idea how long it takes to create a vid that is truly lifelike? It's a lot more than a couple of hours."

"Then you must have created it before we got here." A part of my mind knew I wasn't making sense, but it couldn't silence the larger part of my mind that was panicking. Hell, I didn't even really understand where the panic was coming from, so how could I control it?

"Oh my, Jeanine, you've found out my little secret." Even through my panic, the sarcasm in Jana's voice was obvious. "I used my quantum crystal ball to peer into the future, discovered Drake was bringing the Wilkinson Bastard to see me, and spent the intervening hours crafting a true-to-life animated vid just to play a joke on you. It's all the more astounding because I don't have any talent or training in animation."

The slicer's words made sense, but my brain wasn't interested in sense. "Then how could that woman know who I am? How could she know I'd perform a DNA scan?"

Two calloused hands gently took hold of my head and turned me to face their owner. Drake gave a reassuring smile as he brushed my hair back behind my ears. "You know Jana only did what we asked her to do, and she did it very well. Deep inside, you know that's true. Right, Jeanine?"

Drake's thumb wiped away a tear I didn't even know I had shed. I concentrated on his smile and felt the panic slowly recede. "I'm sorry, Jana. I...I don't know what came over me."

"I do," Drake said. "It's possible that Lady Evelyn has known your name since you were born, but you're afraid of what else she knows. Or, more to the point, you're afraid you'll find out Sir Jared, the man you thought was your grandfather, has been communicating with House Wilkinson throughout your life. And, after everything else you've gone through, that's one betrayal you can't accept."

I closed my eyes and nodded. "I'm sorry, Jana. Every time I think I've adjusted to all of the surprises life has thrown at me lately, something like this comes along and shows me just how raw my emotions still are."

"Yeah, well, I guess it's better to let your emotions out where you can deal with them. That's what I've read, anyway." Jana pointed at the data pad in front of me, "Can we start the vid again? I don't know about you, but I'm dying to find out what that woman has to say."

I tapped the screen, and the vid resumed playing.

"Before I say anything else," Lady Evelyn said, "please accept my condolences over the death of your grandfather, Sir Jared. I know he wasn't your grandfather by blood, but he was in his heart. I'm sure you've wondered if Sir Jared saw you as nothing more than a job for his lord. Rest assured, the man loved you as deeply as if you were his own flesh and blood. He said as much in his last message to me."

I gasped as a knot in my gut relaxed. I stopped the vid a second time as hot tears welled up and poured forth. Drake knelt and rocked me in his arms as I sobbed.

"What is wrong with her?" Jana asked. "That's a good thing, that the guy she thought was her grandfather loved her?"

"Yes," I managed to wail.

"Then what's with the waterfall?"

Gently stroking my hair, Drake said, "When Jeanine thought Sir Jared was her grandfather, she mourned deeply. When she found out he was an assigned guard, she was afraid he never loved her, that his attention was nothing more than a man doing his duty. She'd probably convinced herself that she didn't care that she was an obligation instead of a cherished granddaughter. Lady Evelyn's words told Jeanine that her life may have been a deception, but it wasn't also a lie."

Jana considered Drake's words for a moment. "So, these are just really loud tears of joy?"

"Exactly," Drake said.

"Wow, is life with her always like piloting through an emotional asteroid field at top speed?" Jana asked.

"Pretty much," Drake said, a grin on his face. "But she's had to take the controls and pilot through *my* asteroid field a few times, too."

"It's obvious the two of you were meant for each other." Jana checked her chrono. "Can we get back to the vid? I've got another job to do tonight and need to start prepping for it soon."

I took a few seconds to regain control of myself. "Don't be surprised if I continue this tonight, Drake."

"Whatever you need, babe."

I swiped at my eyes one more time and then tapped the screen again.

"There is much I must tell you, but I won't go into details on a vid—even one as tightly encrypted as this one," Lady Evelyn said.

"Smart woman," Jana murmured.

"You are the result of a short fling between my late husband,

Lord Arthur Wilkinson, and a lovely young woman who was one of my ladies-in-waiting. I won't name her just in case this vid ends up in the hands of House Kahn.

"Your mother thought she was in love with Arthur—he was quite a charming man when he wished, not to mention devilishly handsome. After the inevitable happened and Arthur finally coaxed her into his bed, your mother tearfully confessed the whole thing to me. There was never much love between Arthur and me and it was long gone before your mother joined my staff. I told her she wasn't his first dalliance, wouldn't be his last, and gave her my relieved blessing to continue the affair if she wished.

"Your mother had a proper birth control implant, but any doctor will tell you that no implant is effective one hundred percent of the time. You were conceived against extremely long odds. Before Arthur learned of the pregnancy, Robert the Butcher of House Kahn killed my eldest child. She was only fifteen and... and..."

Lady Evelyn's image in the vid jumped, leading Jana to say, "She stopped recording or had her emotional outburst edited out."

"Please excuse me," Lady Evelyn said. "Twenty-five years dulls the pain, but it never goes away. Everyone was sure Robert killed my Bianca, but no one could prove it. Arthur was always very good at extrapolating future events from current ones. Instead of seeing you as a threat to the family line, Arthur saw you as a possible last line of defense against House Kahn. He kept your mother's pregnancy secret and, after you were born, sent you off under the protection of House Wilkinson's Recognized knight. If the Butcher ever succeeded in killing Arthur and all of our children, Arthur knew you would be his secret weapon for revenge—a role you filled admirably, I might add.

"After burying six children and a husband, I took great pleasure watching the Butcher burn for his sins against me. But of course that same event revealed the existence of the Wilkinson Bastard to the galaxy. Since that day, Lady Olivia of House Kahn has dedicated herself to finding and destroying you. I hoped you'd reach your twenty-fifth birthday before she found you. Then we could have simply slipped you into court and gotten you Recognized as the new Duchess of Neert before anyone even knew who you were. Now, Olivia will do everything in her power to kill you before you can appear before His Majesty and petition the Star Stone for Recognition."

"Tell us something we don't know," Drake said.

"I can provide little aid to you, Jeanine, and wouldn't blame you if you simply ran for the frontier and a safely anonymous life." Lady Evelyn cocked her head and gave a rueful smile. "From what Sir Jared has told me of you, I doubt you'll do that. In that case, I strongly recommend you find allies and come up with a way to get into the chamber with the Star Stone. Olivia is smarter than her brother was, but she's not as cunning nor as bloodthirsty. If you can achieve Recognition, she'll have a much harder time killing you. Good luck, Jeanine."

I stared at the blank screen for a moment, trying to sort out my feelings. Finally, I muttered, "It looks like you were right, Drake."

Drake placed his hands on my shoulders and kneaded them gently. I'm sure they were hard as rocks because I damned sure didn't feel relaxed. He asked, "Right about what, Jeanine?"

"Right about me being part of some ridiculously convoluted failsafe revenge plot Arthur Wilkinson cooked up." I tried my best to keep calm and speak in a level tone, but my voice broke midway through the sentence. I closed my eyes and sniffed back the tears I knew were coming. Dropping my head, I whispered, "Dammit."

"I'm sorry, honey," Drake said.

"I'm obviously missing something," Jana said. "You've just had a *duchess* give her blessing to take her place as the head of one of the most powerful families in the kingdom. Wealth, power, luxury, and a huge staff ready to fulfill your every whim and desire. What is there to cry about?"

I almost snapped at the slicer, but just didn't have the energy.

Instead, I asked, "When was the last time you saw your father, Jana?"

"Huh?"

I caught Drake's hands and pulled them down and around me. "I'm sorry, is your father still living? I don't want to dredge up painful memories."

"No, Dad's alive. I had lunch with him last week. He asked about my work, potential boyfriends—you know, the usual stuff fathers ask daughters." The slicer drew a sudden breath. "I'm sorry, Jeanine. You *don't* know, do you?"

"No, but that's what I always imagined it would be like. The thing is, you're a real person to your father, someone he loves and wants to be happy in life."

"Well, yeah."

"My father didn't see me that way. I was nothing more than a valuable tool to him, his chance to strike from the grave against House Kahn."

"You don't know that!" Jana exclaimed.

"The very first thing Lady Evelyn did was reassure me that Sir Jared truly loved me like the granddaughter he never had. The only thing she said about my father was that he saw me as the last line of defense against his enemies." I raised my head and looked Jana in the eyes. "Don't you think she'd have given me similar assurances about my father if he had any deep feelings for me?"

"Oh." The woman looked away as if she was embarrassed for having missed that. "I'm sorry—I should have thought it through better than I did."

"My situation is hardly a typical one, Jana." I stood and shook hands with the slicer. "I appreciate everything you've done for us. Can we take the data stick with the encrypted message from Lady Evelyn?"

"Sure, that's why I put it on the stick in the first place. Do you want to take the data pad, too? It's an old junker I keep around for just this sort of thing."

Drake scooped up the pad, ejected the stick, and put it in his pocket. "Thanks. We'll do that. I don't need to tell you how dangerous it would be to keep a copy of the message, do I?"

In response, Jana crossed her arms and glared at him.

Neither of us spoke on the trip back to the *Rising Star*, now sporting a beacon identifying it as the *Arcadia*. On the ship, we kept our conversation to the minimum necessary to prep and launch the ship. Only when we were clear of Bragua's atmosphere, did I bring up the future.

"Where are you taking me, now?"

Drake kept his eyes on the pilot's console, but I doubt he really saw any of the readouts. "Did anything you learned today make you change your mind about joining the revolt and getting Recognized?"

"No," I said. "Did any of it change *your* mind? I might still get Recognized if I'm on my own, but I won't find your revolution without a guide."

"No, though I hate the idea of putting you in danger just because I'm part of the revolt."

"It's dangerous enough just being me these days." I gave a mirthless laugh. "I doubt your revolution will be much worse."

"Right now, you've got one of the great houses out to get you," Drake said, his tone earnest. "Once the revolution starts, *all* of the great houses will want you dead."

"Not all of them." I smiled faintly, "If I'm still alive by then, I'll almost certainly be the Duchess of Neert. I think I can convince myself to come down on the side of our revolution."

"I'm serious, Jeanine."

"So am I, Drake. Yes, the revolution is dangerous. Yes, one or both of us could get captured and executed or killed in battle. But I'm not going to run and hide from it all. And even if I did that, you know you couldn't turn your back on the revolution and come with me. You said as much when you first told me about the revolution."

"I've given that a lot of thought over the last few hours," Drake said. "I think I could do it if that's what you wanted, Jeanine."

"Maybe, but you'd hate yourself for abandoning your compatriots and, eventually, you'd hate me for taking you away from your chosen path."

"It's *my* path, Jeanine. I don't want you to feel compelled to take it with me."

"I'm *choosing* to join you on that path, you dolt! Dammit, Drake, why are you arguing so hard against my choice?"

Refusing to meet my eyes, Drake said, "I've already lost everything once and one reason I threw in with the revolution was because I didn't have anything to lose. Now, all of a sudden, I've got everything to lose."

I took Drake's hand in mine and pressed it against my cheek. "Then let's make damned sure we win."

A ROYAL PLAN

Olivia

Accepting the queen's offer to marry her son was only the beginning of our relationship. We talked long into the night that first time and many nights thereafter. Once we had the political details hammered out, we finally got down to planning my romance with Prince William.

"My dear, this courtship is going to be devilishly difficult to orchestrate," Queen Charlotte said. "I'm afraid you must put aside your pursuit of the Wilkinson Bastard for a few months and concentrate on your coming marriage."

"But that woman will come of Recognition age in a few weeks, Charlotte," I said. "It's vital that I bend all of my attention to finding her."

The queen's eyes turned steely, showing the true strength beneath the queen's benevolent face. "Olivia, I am offering you a kingdom and a throne upon which your children will sit. Do not throw that away for a mere duchy."

"I... You're right, of course, Charlotte," I said, hanging my head slightly. "I've dedicated so much time and effort into finding the bastard, I hate putting her aside when she's almost within my grasp."

"You don't have to give up trying to capture this girl, Olivia."

The steel in Charlotte's eyes faded a bit, and she gave me a maternal smile. "But you do have to trust your own people to handle the details. Surely, your man Colin can handle this in your absence?"

"My absence? Where am I going?"

"You're coming to Xapreathea, dear. How else will William rescue you?"

I frowned. "Rescue me from what? A life of too much paperwork?"

Charlotte laughed, her eyes merry once again. "Amusing as that is, it won't play well in the news cycle. No, William must rescue you from mortal danger so you can swoon in his arms—all of it recorded for replay throughout the kingdom, of course. The two young lovebirds will have a whirlwind romance, during which the handsome prince will surprise his beautiful lady love with a heart-felt proposal. As the kingdom rejoices, the young lovers will beg for a fast wedding. The doting king and queen will accede to their wishes by throwing the grandest wedding in centuries."

"Won't the people see through such a fairytale story?"

"Oh, some will," Charlotte agreed, "but if we plan this just right, the vast majority of your future subjects—including the nobles and the so-called intelligentsia—will be too swept up in the story to give it much thought."

"How are we going to stage mortal danger in a manner convincing to everyone?"

"This is the truly difficult part, Olivia. The danger must be real and people must die as a result of it. We'll minimize your risks as much as possible, but if something goes wrong with the plan, you may be injured."

"Or killed?"

"That will be a remote possibility, yes." Charlotte leaned forward to the cam on her subspace transmitter. "Are you willing to take that risk, Olivia?"

I gave the matter careful thought. "Do you think we can stage this event in space, preferably above Xapreathea?"

Charlotte arched her perfect eyebrows in surprise. "I suppose so."

"And William—he's quite the sportsman, but does he have much training or experience operating a space suit in a vacuum?"

"All members of the royal family have such training. William is actually quite good at it and makes a point of suiting up and going outside every time he takes his sports ship into space. What do you have in mind, Olivia?"

The queen listened carefully to my explanation. When I finished, a smile of true pleasure spread across Charlotte's face.

"Olivia, my dear, you and I are going to get along very well."

Jeanine

During the trip to the rebel base—or whatever the revolution calls their headquarters—I questioned Drake a lot about the goals of his revolution, the people in charge of it, and how they planned on overthrowing the kingdom. He gave me answers with enough detail to satisfy me but without giving me enough information that I could betray the organization to Royal Intelligence. I could tell Drake was afraid I'd be hurt or offended by his evasive responses, but Grandfather—I reinstated that name for Sir Jared after hearing what Lady Evelyn had to say —included training in operational security along with all the martial arts training he gave me.

In truth, making sure Drake understood that I approved of his precautions also made me examine why Grandfather never told me of my true heritage. Stripped of emotion, his decision was textbook security protocol. He kept me in the dark because knowing the truth wouldn't help me any and could get me in real trouble. Had he not been killed, I'm pretty sure he'd have told me everything when I turned twenty-five and could pursue Recognition if I chose to do so. Examined from that point of view, I liked my decision to go back to calling him Grandfather all the more.

By the time we reached the home system for the rebellion, I

was satisfied with their cause and their methods. I didn't recognize the system, but it had a couple of sparsely settled planets and a very large asteroid belt. Drake piloted into the asteroid field and I lost all sense of direction after that. He flew for another couple of hours before a huge, somewhat cylindrical asteroid loomed up before us. Drake thumbed on a transponder and keyed the comm.

"Ares Control, this is the *Rising Star* requesting permission to land," he said.

"Acknowledged, *Rising Star*. We have you on our scopes. Be advised several of our weapons systems have a target lock on you. If you break course or fail to follow the approach course we give you, you will be destroyed."

"Noted. You know you'd never actually hit me, Barney."

"You're quick, Drake, but not that quick!" Barney responded. "Now give me your pass phrase so neither of us has to find out which one of us is right."

"Heather would kick my ass if I gave that out over an open channel."

I expected something more cryptic for the pass phrase, but Drake's choice could be worked into a conversation without a problem.

"Got it, *Star*. Use approach beacon eight. I'll tell the brass that you're back."

"Thanks, Ares Control. After you alert the brass, can you comm Kelly and ask her to meet me at the docking bay? I've got a guest with me and I'd like Kelly to take care of her while I'm being debriefed."

"*Her*? God above, Drake, please tell me you didn't bring one of your one-night-stands home with you."

"I'm not discussing it over the comm, Barney. Just call Kelly for me, okay?"

"Will do. Ares Control out."

I waited a few seconds to make sure Drake wasn't going to comm someone else, then said, "You've had a lot of one-night stands, have you?"

"You heard the warning my compatriots gave to Jana, and you guessed at a lot of it during our first morning together onboard the *Star*," Drake growled. "This can't come as a surprise to you."

"No, I just wanted to see how much you'd squirm after your new girlfriend called you on it. You didn't squirm once, which is no fun at all."

"I'm sorry you're so disappointed, Jeanine."

"Don't be. Your matter-of-fact response is pretty reassuring from the new-girlfriend point of view."

Drake gave me a puzzled look. "Wait, you're saying it's reassuring that I admit I had a lot of one-night stands?"

"Sure. A guy with a guilty conscience—one who might keep pursuing overnight flings—would downplay the number or even try claiming his reputation far exceeded his deeds."

"Because I admit I've screwed around a lot before, you're saying you can trust me to stay faithful to you in the future?"

"Yes."

"That makes no sense at all."

I gave Drake the last word, falling quiet so he could concentrate on landing the *Star*. As he brought the ship into the docking bay, I took a look around at the other ships in there. From what I saw, I was pretty sure the phrase 'ragtag fleet' was directly inspired by the collection of ships in the docking bay. A handful of mechanics guided tool carts between ships while others worked on ships ranging in size from two-man scouts to freight haulers converted for combat.

I spotted some actual warships though they were few in number and not exactly what you'd call new ships. On the other hand, the *Rising Star* was an old ship, and she was easily as good as any ship I'd ever seen. I found myself wondering how big House Wilkinson's fleet was and the quality of its ships. If the rebels managed to get me to the Star Stone, perhaps I could give their fleet a significant upgrade.

Several men and women wearing military-looking uniforms met us as we exited the ship. Not being in uniform himself, Drake didn't salute the officers. He briefly introduced me, without going into any further details. I assumed he was saving that for a more private and secure location. Then he motioned to a uniformed woman who looked a few years older than me.

"Kelly, this is Jeanine," Drake said. "Can you take care of her while I'm off being debriefed? Maybe take her to grab a bite to eat, wash clothes, take a shower, whatever."

"Of course, sir," Kelly responded, giving me the once over.

"Kelly was part of my crew when we were in the Space Patrol. She'll take good care of you," Drake said before walking away with the officers.

I watched him leave until Kelly said, "Why don't we get your bags off the ship, ma'am."

I led the way onto the *Rising Star.* "It's just Jeanine. And I only have the one bag."

Without a second thought, I went to the bedroom I shared with Drake to get the bag. When I turned around again, Kelly was right in front of me, an intense expression in her eyes as she looked up into mine.

"You're sleeping with Drake, aren't you?"

I saw no reason to keep that a secret. "Yes."

"You know he's never...stayed with the same woman for more than a night or two since..." Kelly said. "And he's never brought one with him on the *Star.*"

"He told me."

"He told you what?"

I tried side-stepping around Kelly, tired of being trapped against the closet door. Kelly side-stepped, too.

"He told me everything, Kelly. He told me about Heather and Candi and the false pirates." I tried side-stepping yet again. "Would you please back off a bit? I don't like being crowded like this."

"I don't care what you like and don't like," Kelly sneered, side-stepping to block me again. "But I care a lot about Drake. All of us who served under him do. It looks like he's decided you're something special. Maybe you are, maybe you're not. Just know that I'll cut your throat if you break his heart."

"Seriously? We've known each other for one minute and you're threatening me?"

Kelly poked me in the chest. "Yeah. You got a problem with that, Red?"

This wasn't exactly how I'd imagined my first few minutes as a revolutionary, but I wasn't the one who chose the script. "Yes, I do have a problem with that."

Kelly grinned and poked me again. This time, I caught her hand and jerked it up and to my right. Surprised, Kelly shuffled her feet to keep her balance. I twisted her arm and swept a foot under her. Kelly lost her balance, and I drove her down onto the deck. Keeping hold of her arm, I dropped on top of the prone woman, trapping her twisted arm between us. Kelly yelped in both pain and surprise.

"Listen up, Cutthroat Kelly," I hissed, "you can try to kill me if you want, but I recommend you use a blaster. Hand-to-hand combat is all about strength, speed, size, and training. I've got you beat on all four of those."

I released the woman and stood up. Then I offered Kelly a hand up. "And I would never intentionally do anything to hurt Drake."

The woman accepted my hand, giving me a lopsided grin without a hint of embarrassment. "Well, now that we've got that out of the way, welcome to the revolution, Jeanine!"

SUSPICIONS

Drake

I was surprised anyone from the senior staff met me in the docking bay, much less Intelligence Chief Colonel Stephen Gregg, ground forces commander General Richard Harrison, and their aides. Not wanting to make Jeanine nervous, I didn't tell her which positions they held when I made introductions. Still, their presence set off all sorts of mental alarms. What happened during the months I was out gathering information that made these men meet me at the docking bay?

We walked in silence for a couple of minutes, but I broke it when we passed the corridor to the Intelligence offices. "In the past, I've always been debriefed by Intel. Why isn't that the case today?"

"This time, you brought us a new recruit," Colonel Gregg said.

"Begging your pardon, sir, but so what?" I replied. "I've brought in quite a few recruits over the years."

"This one is different, Captain Haral," Gregg said. "We'll discuss just how different once we're behind closed doors."

Gregg's response actually reassured me. Someone made a subspace call to headquarters with information about Jeanine's DNA scan. That someone was almost certainly Jana, the only other revolutionary besides me who knew Jeanine's true identity.

That the high command was taking the report seriously gave me hope that our planned Recognition run would have their full support.

A couple of minutes later, we entered a large conference room filled with senior officers and staff. I recognized a couple of them—Admiral Juliette Pierson and Revolutionary President Diana Sutcliffe—but the rest were unknown to me. Of course, I spent most of my time away from the base and rarely met with anyone outside of Intel when I was here. Colonel Gregg motioned to a chair and, trying to contain the excitement building inside of me, I took a seat.

President Sutcliffe said, "Captain Haral, please tell us everything leading up to your meeting with the woman known as Jeanine Langston. Tell us everything that has transpired since you met her. Leave nothing out."

"Including personal information that will be of no military value, ma'am?" I asked.

"*Especially* personal information, Captain."

That set off even more mental alarms, but I was certain everyone would settle down once they had all the information. Keeping that thought firmly in mind, I launched into a full description of everything that happened to me over the previous several weeks. My audience listened carefully, interrupting only to request more details about one thing or another. I did my best to contain my temper when they delved into the exact nature of my physical relationship with Jeanine. At least, they stopped short of asking what positions we preferred.

When I wrapped up the story, including my suggestion we help Jeanine achieve Recognition, Colonel Gregg was the first to speak. "Captain Haral, is it correct that the base personnel hold you in awe due to your reputation as a lady's man?"

"Why does that have anything to do with Jeanine?" I demanded.

Gregg ignored my question and pushed on. "In fact, don't they call you 'Driller Drake' when referring to your prowess with women? Aren't you known for having a different woman on your arm and in your bed each night you're in a port?"

"That has never stopped me from doing my duty, as you well know, Colonel," I snapped.

"I'm not questioning your dedication to duty, Captain. I'm simply verifying the standard by which you have lived since joining us all those years ago. Are my statements correct?"

"Yes."

"But since meeting Jeanine Langston, that has all changed."

It wasn't a question, but a response was expected. "Yes."

"And since that meeting, you have not had physical relations with another woman."

With a sinking feeling, I saw where this was going. "No, I have not, but there's nothing sinister about it. I've simply found a woman I care about at a time when I was emotionally ready for a relationship committed to one woman."

"Do you truly believe that, Captain?" Gregg asked. "No, don't answer that. It's obvious you love this woman and do, indeed, believe exactly what you just said."

General Harrison said, "Have you taken the time to consider all of these events dispassionately? To expose your story to the light of reason? A strange man attaches himself to you in a market—"

"I attached myself to him by giving him money and offering to buy him lunch," I said.

"Yes, but you're quite well-known for your generosity to those in unfortunate circumstances. The Langston woman told you the man did this sort of thing on a regular basis," Harrison replied. "There's no question the man conned you into believing you initiated contact. There are many questions concerning the reason he did so."

"I've already been over that," I said, feeling my temper slipping out of control. "He either knew danger was near or suspected it. He simply wanted his granddaughter—"

Harrison said, "Who wasn't actually his granddaughter."

"Fine. He simply wanted Jeanine to have a way off of Thinda if his suspicions were correct—which they were."

"Did you witness this attack?" Harrison asked.

"I've already told you I didn't, but Jeanine was very nervous and distracted when she met me. At the time, I just assumed she was nervous about our date and what it would lead to. Instead, she was already mourning the death of her grandfather." I caught myself before one of the officers could correct me. "Make that, mourning the death of the man she grew up believing was her grandfather. And note that I certainly *did* witness a Recognized knight ordering a customs team to trash my ship, the *Rising Star*."

"And yet they didn't find the woman who was, quite literally, hiding right under their feet," Harrison said.

"That's because my smuggling holds are extremely hard to find and shielded against scanners. They're one of the reasons you recruited me into the revolution in the first place."

Harrison flicked a wrist, waving that point off. "Then, after all of this excitement, the woman—"

It was my turn to interrupt. "Stop calling her 'the woman.' She has a name."

"Very well, Captain. On the very evening Miss Langston claimed her grandfather was killed, and she learned a Recognized Knight of the Realm was after her, she invited you to share her bed." Harrison looked at me, his stare boring into me. "Is that correct, Drake?"

That's when I finally lost my temper. "Yes, it is correct, Richard. May I call you Richard? Or would you prefer Dick since you're acting like such a big one right now."

Harrison's face turned red, and he opened his mouth for what I expected would be a verbal thrashing. That's when President Sutcliffe spoke for the first time. She never raised her voice, but it cut across both of us like a whiplash.

"That is enough. Both of you will now be quiet." She glared at Harrison until he sat back and then turned her glare on me. "You are a man trained in intelligence, Captain Haral, but you're letting your emotions cloud your judgment. Try looking at your story from our point of view. Can you not see why we're suspicious of it?"

"But what of Sir Jared's and Sir Phillip's public records? What of the DNA scan results and the message from Lady Evelyn?"

"I have no doubt the records of the two knights are accurate and that you met Sir Phillip. It's possible you met the real Sir Jared, but it's just as likely you met someone who was surgically altered to look like him. As for the DNA scan, who better to falsify royal records than Royal Intelligence?" President Sutcliffe's gaze was more gentle than Harrison's but no less penetrating.

"But why go to all of this trouble, ma'am?" I asked. "I'm nobody important to the revolution."

"Isn't it obvious, Captain?" she asked. "Royal Intelligence wants someone on the inside of our revolution. Someone we wouldn't expect and who came with an enticing reason to send back into the wider galaxy once she learned the location of our base."

"Jeanine would never do that, ma'am."

"How do you know that?"

Because I've looked into her eyes when she was at her most vulnerable and seen the truth behind her pain and fear. Because people who have lost something near and dear to them can recognize the same thing when they see it in others. But I didn't say any of that because it was obvious they'd already made up their minds.

Taking my silence as an acknowledgment of her point, President Sutcliffe said, "We cannot risk letting Miss Langston leave the base. Furthermore, we must assume your cover is blown until we discover otherwise. Both of you are confined to this base until further notice."

I sat still for a moment, stunned at the pronouncement. Finally finding my voice, I said, "You can't be serious!"

"For once, I agree with Captain Haral." To my surprise, this came from General Harrison. Then he continued, "We cannot allow this woman to wander free around the base. I suggest we take her into custody and put her under lock and key."

"*What?*" I shouted. "Are you out of your f—"

"Stop right there, Captain," President Sutcliffe's voice cracked through the murmur of the others in the room. "General Harrison's suggestion has merit—"

I opened my mouth to protest, stopping only when the president turned her famous glare on me and continued, "*But* I will not follow through with it if you keep Miss Langston with you at all times. While Miss Langston is here, she is not allowed anywhere except the base's common areas and your personal quarters."

"I don't have quarters," I said. I kept my voice low, but it carried to every corner of the packed conference room. "I stay on the *Rising Star* when I'm visiting the base. Jeanine and I will be quite comfortable there."

"I'll have quarters assigned to you, Captain Haral," Sutcliffe said. "Miss Langston will not be allowed in the docking bay. Furthermore, the revolution has need of your ship."

That brought me up short. "Excuse me?"

"We cannot afford to let such a valuable asset sit idle while we...assess...the situation with Miss Langston," Admiral Pierson said, speaking for the first time. "We'll assign another crew to the ship. They will use it for normal intelligence operations until you are cleared for active duty."

"The *Rising Star* is my personal ship, and *she* is not part of your command. Only I fly the *Star*," I said. "I made that very clear when I joined the revolution and all of you agreed to that."

"Times change, Captain, as do the needs of the revolution," Pierson snapped. "You will provide all of the codes necessary to unlock the ship and train the new crew on its—excuse me, *her*—operation."

"Of course, my Lady. It shall be as you command, my Lady." I stood, glared at the three leaders of the revolution, and bowed deeply. "If it pleases my Ladies and my Lords, your subject humbly begs your permission to take leave of your august selves and go about his menial duties."

"How dare you imply we are anything like the nobles we are

working to overthrow?" President Sutcliffe's tone was controlled but her face was red with anger.

I met her glare with one of my own. "After you leave, I suggest you read the transcript of this meeting. Replace your names with, say, Lady Olivia or Queen Charlotte and then ask yourself if your words aren't a perfect fit for either of those nobles. Now, if you'll excuse me, I have to go tell the woman who could have become our single greatest ally that the daring leaders of this rebellion are too cautious to trust her."

Ignoring the voices raised in protest, I strode from the room. My only regret was my inability to slam the automatic door to the conference room.

It took me a few minutes to make my way back to the common area and several more to find Kelly and Jeanine. To my surprise when I found them I also found the other eight members of my old Space Patrol crew. They were listening with rapt attention as Jeanine, perched on the edge of Kelly's bunk, recounted our adventure escaping from the DNA clinic.

I thought Jeanine was the only one who noticed my arrival at the back of the room until Sam said, "Damn girl, you jumped out of an eighty-second-floor window trusting the Skipper to hold the flitter in one place? I don't know if you're the bravest person I've ever met or the most foolish."

"Ha, ha," I said.

Everyone in the room spun about in mock surprise and, his voice a monotone, Sam said, "I did not know you were there, Skipper."

Everyone except Jeanine laughed. I tried playing along, but I just couldn't make myself do much more than flash a quick, wan smile. Frowning, Jeanine rose and came to me.

"What's wrong?" she asked.

At Jeanine's question, the laughter came to a sudden end and everyone studied my expression. Kelly was the first one to speak.

"Damn, one glance at the Skipper and Jeanine knew something was wrong." Kelly shook her head and continued, "Whatever else is going on, I gotta say you fell for the right woman, Skipper. Heather is the only other woman I knew who could read you that quick."

Everyone else added their agreement, which helped ease my soul just a bit. Obviously, my old crew saw the same things in Jeanine that I see every time I look at her. More than ever, I didn't want to deliver the message I had to deliver.

Seeing me struggling to find the right words, Jeanine said, "Just say it, Drake."

I looked at the floor, unable to meet her eyes. "The senior staff are suspicious of you and your story. They think you could be a member of Royal Intelligence sent to infiltrate our organization."

My old crew gave cries of outrage, every last one of them firmly in Jeanine's corner. Jeanine raised her hands, obviously asking everyone to leave off. To my surprise, they fell silent immediately. That's more than they usually did when they served under me.

"There's more, isn't there?" she asked. "They're sending me away, right?"

"I could take you myself if that was the case. This is worse." I forced myself to meet Jeanine's gaze so she would have no doubt as to my feelings. "They won't let you leave at all. You're restricted to the base's common areas and must be accompanied by me at all times. And I'm restricted to the base because they assume my cover is blown."

"Oh."

That's all Jeanine said, but that single word all but ripped my heart out. I could hear the anguish and uncertainty hiding behind the word, but had no idea what to say to comfort her.

"So, do I get to take a long shower before we go back to the *Rising Star*?" she asked.

"We're not going back to the *Star*," I replied. "The docking bay is off limits for you. And the *Star*...um, the *Star* is..."

My voice finally broke under the strain and I just hung my head. Jeanine immediately wrapped her arms around me and held me close. In a gentle voice, she asked, "What about the *Star*? What are they doing to her?"

"They want to assign a new crew to her." My old team gasped and Jeanine hugged me more tightly. I dropped my forehead onto her shoulder and said, "I'm supposed to train the new crew to fly her and give them all of her access codes."

"The hell you say!" Hemlata spoke in a whisper, but everyone heard her just fine.

That's when Kelly pushed her way through the crowd, pulled Jeanine and me completely into her quarters, and shut the door. Guiding us back to her bunk, Kelly said, "Jeanine's told us the highlights of your adventure together but also told us there were some things we had to hear from you. So sit down and tell us everything."

Sitting on the bunk, with my arm wrapped around Jeanine, I looked each of my former shipmates in the eye. They all had the same determined look I saw in their eyes seven years ago when we went after the pirates.

"I'm positive the senior staff doesn't want you to know what I'm about to tell you. Hearing it could get you restricted to the base, too. I know how important this cause is to each of you, so if anyone wants to back out and insure they can keep going out on missions, no one will be offended." I waited for a few seconds, giving each of them a chance to think through the consequences of sticking around.

Before I was ready to go on, Kelly said, "None of us are leaving, Skipper. Now spill it."

"Okay," I said, pleased they all chose to stay. "The short version is that Jeanine is the Wilkinson Bastard."

I don't know what they theought I was going to say, but it definitely wasn't that. Mouths dropped open. Eyes bugged out. Heads shook as if trying to make sense of my simple pronouncement.

Predicting the questions to come, I said, "Yes, we're sure. Jana even hacked the Royal DNA Database to verify the test results. Not only did she verify the results, she found evidence that House

Kahn planted a false warrant on any scan results with at least a fifty percent Wilkinson match. She also found a vid from Lady Evelyn of House Wilkinson. The lady called Jeanine by name and acknowledged her as the bastard child of Arthur Wilkinson."

Zach was the first one to find his voice. "You better start at the beginning and tell us everything, Skipper."

For the next thirty minutes, Jeanine and I did just that. My old crew bristled when I described how Sir Phillip had the *Rising Star* trashed and got downright outraged when I wrapped up with the debriefing by the senior staff.

Everyone was quiet for a few seconds after I stopped speaking. Then Kelly said, "Well, it's a damned good thing that knight trashed the *Star*."

"You've lost me, Kelly," I said.

"You have to fix up the *Star* before that new crew can fly her, right?" When I nodded, Kelly continued, "And who better to help you do that than us, the people who helped you fix her up when you first bought her."

I shrugged. "That makes sense, but I'm still lost."

"It's simple, Skipper. We get started fixing the *Rising Star* and, once everyone is used to us coming and going from her, we smuggle Jeanine onboard." Kelly grinned broadly. "Then you fly us the hell out of this rock and we make that Recognition run you told us about."

After Kelly finished speaking, it took me a moment before I could find my voice. Jeanine beat me to it.

"You'd do that for me?" she asked. "You'd risk court martial and God only knows what else for someone you just met?"

"Sorta," Kelly replied. Her expression turned serious, and she caught Jeanine's eyes. "I think I speak for everyone here when I say we like you, Jeanine. You seem like a nice girl caught up in some really nasty infighting among noble houses. That really sucks, but we've only known you for a few minutes."

"So, you're doing it for Drake." Jeanine made it a statement rather than a question.

Kelly nodded. Her gaze swung to me even though she was still speaking to Jeanine. "Drake kept us together when our world fell apart. He gave us a purpose, a place to focus our hurt and anger. After we got those fake pirates, he fought tooth and nail to get House Wilkinson to pay attention to our claims. If it wasn't for him, our so-called Lord Wilkinson would have pocketed the whole settlement from House Kahn. And when Drake joined the revolution, so did we. He might not be in our chain of command anymore, but by God, he'll always be my commanding officer."

Jeanine gave my old crew a genuine smile of pleasure. "Good."

Kelly's eyes swiveled back to Jeanine. "It doesn't bother you that we're doing this for him and not for you?"

"I love Drake. How could your loyalty to him ever upset me?" A bit of mischief crept into Jeanine's smile. "Besides, you'll try all the harder because you won't want to let him down. What kind of future noble would I be if I didn't exploit that?"

The crew all got a laugh from that. Then Kelly sat down next to Jeanine and said, "Remember, we're also sorta doing this for you. Ever since we joined this revolution, we've all spent a lot of time worrying about Drake. It was like once he got our lives back on track, *his* life went off the rails. He's been head-down gathering intel and recruits for the revolution, only looking up long enough to screw some girl."

"Hey, I wasn't *that* bad!" I protested.

Everyone but Jeanine shouted me down, with Kelly telling Jeanine, "Don't listen to him. We were all afraid he'd find some way to die heroically once the actual fighting started. He put our lives back together again but never figured out how to rebuild his own. We couldn't figure it out, either, but it looks like you're a natural at it. For the first time in years, I see a glimmer of the Skipper I knew all those years ago. So, I guess you could say we're helping you because you can help Drake."

Jeanine wrapped Kelly in a sisterly hug. "I'll do my best."

My vision blurred. With a start, I realized tears were filling my eyes. I looked down, hoping to hide the motion as my hands swiped at my eyes. After all of these years and all the time I spent worrying about my old crew, I never realized they were even more worried about me. I thought I was hiding my emptiness behind the grinning mask of a womanizing spy. Apparently I did just the opposite—at least among those who know me best.

"I've never seen the Skipper cry—no matter how much he needed to—in all the years I've known him," Hemlata said. "Now I *know* we're doing the right thing."

That's the kind of comment that was supposed to make my tears dry up in a flash while I told the team I sure had them fooled. That's how this would have played out just a few weeks ago, before I met Jeanine. Back when I only cared about people in passing, like when I bought lunch for her grandfather. Back when caring was done at arm's length in an unconscious effort to keep me from getting involved beyond a quick helping hand. If I'd ignored Jared the same as everyone else at the market or if I'd met him later after I'd found company for the evening, where would I be now? Worse, where would Jeanine be right now?

"What are you thinking about, Skipper?" Kelly asked.

I thought about making a joke and evading the question. But that's what the old, lonely Drake would have done. Pushing that man aside, I tried out the new version of myself. "I was wondering what would have happened to me if I hadn't met Jared when I did. Then I realized I was actually worrying over what would have happened to Jeanine. I imagined her all alone, on the run, and cornered by Sir Phillip and his team of mercenaries. I've even dreamed about it. In my dreams, Heather's ghost appears next to Jeanine and calls for me to come help. But I can't help because I'm not there and don't even know who Jeanine is, or that she needs help. And—"

Without warning, grief rose up from my gut and overwhelmed me. My tears turned into the wracking sobs I'd held within for all these years. Tears flowed down my cheeks like miniature rivers.

Tears of love.

Tears of loss.

Tears of rage.

Tears of horror.

Tears of betrayal.

Tears of fear.

Tears of discovery.

And, finally, tears of joy.

Eventually, I cried myself out. I don't know how long it took. All I know is I finally purged all of those pent up emotions and became aware of my surroundings again. I was curled up on the floor of Kelly's quarters with a pair of arms wrapped around me. Warm breath blew across my neck from the person curled up against my back. I didn't have to see her to know it was Jeanine. I turned around to face her and wasn't surprised to find we had the room to ourselves.

Jeanine kissed me lightly on the forehead and asked, "Better?"

Rather than toss out a reassuring answer, I took careful stock of myself. How did I feel? Lighter. That's the first word that came to mind. I felt as if I'd cast off a heavy burden that had been weighing me down for years. And brighter. That's the next word that occurred to me, as if I was seeing the world clearly for the first time since my patrol ship returned home all those years ago. Jeanine's eyes shone like blue stars, clearer and more lovely than ever before. Her hair, her smile, everything about her looked as if someone had stripped away a film that kept me from seeing just how lovely she truly was.

"Yes," I said. "I'm lighter, the universe is brighter, and I'm damned happy to be alive and with you."

Kissing me lightly on the lips, Jeanine said, "I know this should be just like when you told me you loved me, where we are consumed by passion and make frantic love right here on the floor. Only, this is Kelly's room and your old crew is waiting just outside the door." Jeanine raised her voice, "And those walls look pretty thin to me."

Muffled laughter came from the hallway as Jeanine and I got

up. I took one more swipe at my eyes and then opened the door. "You can have your room back, Kelly."

Entering, Kelly hugged me tightly. "Welcome back, Skipper. We've missed you."

Then she hugged Jeanine just as tightly. "Welcome to the team, Jeanine."

To my considerable surprise, each member of my old crew did the same thing. Thank God I was cried out, otherwise I'd probably have lost it again.

Once everyone was back inside, Kelly closed the door. "Now that we've got all that mushy stuff out of the way, let's work out the details of the escape plan."

By the time we broke for supper, we had covered every contingency we could think of. As usual, life had different plans for us.

PRINCE WILLIAM TO THE RESCUE

Olivia

One week after the planning session with Queen Charlotte, my heart hammered in my chest as my personal yacht came out of hyperspace and began its approach to Xapreathea. I told the crew that I didn't feel well and retreated to the privacy of my suite. I had never done that before, always staying on the bridge during the ship's approach and landing. It's a small detail, but one vital to our plan. The coming explosion would be centered on the bridge, where I had always been during the last leg of my spaceflights, rather than on my suite.

Once inside my suite, I dismissed my maids—poor, doomed souls that they were—and quickly pulled out the only airtight trunk I owned. It's a family heirloom and I always travel with it. That fact was also vital to the plan since I didn't have to change any of my packing habits to survive the vacuum of space. Tossing the clothes from the trunk, I climbed inside, pulled the lid shut, and braced myself.

Despite my preparations, the explosion jarred me violently. The trunk tumbled and bounced all about my suite, but it stayed in one piece and protected me from flying debris. Then gravity vanished. My stomach lurched and heaved out the little bit of food I'd eaten for lunch.

When debris stopped banging off of the trunk, I strained to hear if air was leaking from the chest. I prayed to a God I didn't believe in to protect me from a disaster I had created. Terrible as the explosion and its aftermath was and as terrifying as the sound of air hissing out of the trunk would have been, the absolute silence was far worse.

Had the trunk been blown too far from the wreckage to show up on any scanners? Or was it floating in the midst of large pieces of my ship that blocked scans? Had anyone even noticed the explosion? With no sense of time and no idea what was happening outside of my trunk, I found the waiting was far worse than everything that came before.

I was barely holding back fearful sobs when I heard something bang against the outside of the trunk. Praying it was a person and terrified they wouldn't realize I was in the trunk, I screamed, "Help me! Oh, God, someone please get me out of here!"

My eyes filled with tears when I heard William's voice. "Olivia? Is that you? Can you hold out while I get this trunk into my ship?"

"Yes! Just, please, help me!"

A minute later and after a bit of gentle banging, the lid opened and light streamed in. Arms reached into the trunk and gently pulled me out. William's handsome, concerned face swam into focus before me.

"I've got you, Olivia. Everything is going to be okay. Are you hurt?"

I shook my head, wrapped my arms around the prince, buried my face in his neck, and sobbed.

Now that I was safely inside William's little sport ship, he cleaned me up and comforted me while I cried out my terror. He stroked my hair, held me tightly, and whispered comforting words to me until I finally quieted.

William tried to give me a friendly kiss on the cheek but I turned my head and caught it on my mouth. My lips parted and returned his chaste kiss with a passion I never expected to feel toward any man. The prince was surprised but responded with equal fervor. Neither of us spoke for several minutes.

When I began pulling off William's clothes, he said, "Olivia, are you sure you—"

I place a finger over his lips. "I have never been more certain of anything in my life."

I knew William was more experienced than me at this sort of thing, but my close brush with death—even if it was a close brush I'd orchestrated for myself—fueled an enthusiasm that more than made up for my inexperience.

At last, our passion spent, I held the prince tightly and whispered, "I love you, William."

To my surprise, I realized I meant it.

YOU'RE BEING OVERLY DRAMATIC

Jeanine

Drake and his old crew worked on their plan well into the night. Since there really wasn't much I could do to help with that, I just listened. I didn't get the details—too many of those required knowledge of the base and its supplies—but I got the basics. When it was time to plan the route out of the asteroid field and into open space, I had an easier time following the discussion because Drake brought up a map.

Stripped of all the details, the plan boiled down to fixing the *Rising Star*, smuggling me aboard in a big, floating toolbox, and then running like hell for open space while also avoiding the revolution's external sensors and picket ships. Simple, straightforward, and with very few moving parts.

Sometime during all the planning, Drake got a message assigning us quarters. We'd hoped for a room close to Drake's crew, but someone in the revolutionary council put us on the far side of the base near the quarters used by the senior staff. That put the docking bay between the crew and us. Since the docking bay was off limits to me and senior staff quarters are mostly off limits to enlisted personnel that meant a long walk for Drake and me if we wanted to visit with the crew.

Drake grimaced as he read the message to us. When he was

finished, he said, "This might be the first step toward isolating Jeanine and me from everyone else. After a few days, base personnel will get used to us not being around very often. It's a short step from there to restricting us to our quarters, effectively cutting us off from everyone we know."

"But why go to all that trouble when they can just go ahead and restrict you to quarters immediately?" Kelly asked.

"Probably because isolating your own people is something nobles do and very much *not* something the plucky revolutionaries do," Drake replied. "If we gradually fade from sight, hardly anyone will notice, much less say anything. They get the same effect while making it seem as if it's our choice."

"That's pretty devious," Zach said.

"A bit, yeah," Drake said, "but remember that neither the senior staff nor us are looking at this situation dispassionately. We'll hope they'll come to their senses soon, but we won't wait around for that to happen."

I had a feeling the senior staff was done thinking about me for the time being, but there wasn't any point in discussing it. Once the plan was as complete as possible, the gathering broke up. It took Drake and me another thirty minutes to walk around to our quarters, which were barely larger than Kelly's single room. At least it had a double bed. Exhausted, we got undressed and climbed into bed. I was barely aware of Drake's arm draping over me before the universe faded away.

The next morning, Drake was whisked away to meet the new crew Admiral Pierson was assigning to the *Rising Star*. I got to tag along because Drake was supposed to be with me at all times. The admiral got a sour expression when Drake pointed that out to her, but she didn't say anything else about it. Then Drake got a sour expression when they introduced his replacements.

A lithe man with close-cropped hair gave Drake's hand a firm, no-nonsense shake. "Captain Ron Landry, pilot. Pleased to meet you, sir. And this is Lieutenant Brody Shaw, my navigator."

Shaw, a compact man who almost vibrated with energy,

pumped Drake's hand once. "We've examined your record, sir. It's most impressive."

Drake's eyes slid to Admiral Pierson. "I'm happy to hear my record carries weight in some places."

Pierson's cheeks reddened slightly, but when she didn't rise to the bait, Drake said, "I have no doubt that these gentlemen are very good at their jobs, but they'll never be able to replace me."

Pierson's lips compressed into a thin line while Landry and Shaw exchanged a puzzled look. Landry asked, "Could you explain your rationale, sir?"

"Have you ever done recruiting, Captain? Or you, Lieutenant?"

"We both have. That's why Admiral Pierson chose us," Landry replied. "We both closed out our service in the Royal Navy in a busy recruiting center."

"Don't worry about our loyalty to the revolution, sir," Shaw said. "What we saw and were ordered to do during our service is why we joined."

Drake shook his head. "I don't question your dedication to the revolution. Out of curiosity, how did you end up joining?"

"A woman we served with recruited us, sir," Shaw replied. "She knew how we felt about the situation in the kingdom and recruited us personally."

"I see. Do you have any idea how she was recruited?"

"Same as us, sir," Landry said. "I believe the person who recruited her was brought by a..." He frowned, "Smuggler."

"Why does that bother you, Captain Landry?" Drake asked.

"Smugglers are criminals, sir!"

Drake leaned toward Landry and, in a stage whisper, said, "So are revolutionaries."

Landry's frown deepened. "But we are only criminals because the nobles forced us down this path. *We* are fighting for a better galaxy."

"How do you know most smugglers weren't also forced into their line of work by the government? Royal import taxes are quite high, Captain." Drake vented a sigh of exasperation. "Do you even have any idea what the punishment is for smuggling?"

Landry drew himself up to his full height and glared at Drake. "No, nor do I see any need to know."

"Admiral, these men are fine recruits who will, no doubt, prove excellent serving in any flight-related position. If they make any attempt at recruiting, they will be caught and interrogated—during which they will almost certainly give up this base's location and the names of everyone they know in the revolution. Then they will be executed."

"You're being overly dramatic, Captain Haral," Pierson said.

"If anything, I'm underplaying it, Admiral." He waved a hand at the two men, both standing almost ramrod straight. "Look at them. They'll stand out like a couple of sore thumbs. I will not be complicit in a mission to get these men killed.

"Gentlemen, you have my utmost respect for your abilities and your dedication, but some people just aren't suited for some jobs. I hope you understand." Heading for the door, Drake said to Pierson, "I've got to start working on my ship so she'll be ready when you find people who can handle the kind of recruiting I do."

He ushered me out of the door and away from the sputtering admiral. Step one of our plan—reject the crew—was complete.

PLANNING ANOTHER ESCAPE

Drake

We hadn't gotten more than ten meters down the corridor before Admiral Pierson's assistant came hurrying after us. "Wait one moment, Captain!"

Jeanine and I obligingly stopped and waited for the aide. I let the irritation I currently felt with the entire revolution show through on my face as the man quick-marched up to us. "I have quite a lot of work to do on the *Rising Star*, so please make this quick."

The commander's face reddened at my brusque tone. Representing an admiral, I'm sure he was usually treated with more respect than was due his rank. Since I outranked him and had shown an ample lack of respect for the admiral, I don't think he really had any idea how to deal with me. He could complain to Pierson, but flag officers rarely take kindly to officers who whine about such things. The senior staff had already taken away my ship—my own, personal ship, no less—and restricted me to the base, too. What else could they do to me? In the end, the commander settled for frowning deeply at me. It was a comical sight, but I kept my laughter in check.

"Admiral Pierson orders you to return to her office."

The man's tone was so supercilious, I decided a little pettiness was called for on my part. I simply stared at the man and waited for him to remember proper military protocol. The Space Patrol was fairly lax about that sort of thing, especially in a casual setting like this, but I know the Royal Navy—where many of our revolutionary officers came from—is big on it.

The commander withstood my glare for five full seconds, before adding a grudging, "Sir."

I gave the man my best patronizing smile. "Of course, Commander. Lead on."

Landry and Shaw left the office as we approached. They rather pointedly ignored us, which didn't bother me in the slightest. Then we were through the door and standing before a glowering Admiral Pierson.

"I suppose you think you're very clever, Captain?" she spat.

"At the risk of bragging, ma'am, I most definitely do." I kept my tone level and precise, giving the admiral no chance to 'read' anything into my reply beyond the actual words used.

"Yes, I'm sure. Don't think I'm not aware of your big plan, Captain."

I felt a spike of panic but quelled it quickly. There was no way anyone outside of our little group knew about our true plans. The admiral was either fishing for information or, more likely, had the completely wrong idea.

"I was unaware I had a big plan, ma'am." Keeping my face as expressionless as possible, I asked, "Perhaps you could explain it to me?"

"You think if you reject every qualified replacement crew, the senior staff will simply cave in and allow you to go back to your normal duties."

"Do you truly think that pair was qualified to replace me?" This time, I let irritation creep into my voice. It was either that or call into question the admiral's intelligence. "I gave you my absolutely best judgment of those two officers. Based on our brief conversation, I would happily select them to lead a military mission. My mission is not military. It is, in essence, an undercover operation and those two men aren't cut out for that."

"Very well, Captain. Since it appears I must defer to your expertise in this matter, I'm putting the search for your replacements squarely in your hands." Pierson's smile was too predatory for this quick acquiescence to bode well for me.

"I think that's best, ma'am," I said, again striving for a level tone. "Is there a catch?"

"I suppose you could call it a catch, Captain. You have twenty-four hours to find a suitable replacement crew."

"And if I can't find one, ma'am?"

"Then we'll just have to send Landry and Shaw. You *will* begin training your replacements at oh nine hundred tomorrow morning —whoever they happen to be. Is that clear, Captain?"

"Crystal clear, ma'am."

"Commander Adams, here, will see that you are given access to the proper information so you may perform your search. He'll arrange for interviews with any personnel you deem worthy of such." The admiral flicked on her data pad. "Dismissed."

Jeanine asked, "And what about me, Admiral Pierson? I can't imagine you want me looking through your personnel records."

"You are restricted to your quarters while Captain Haral is busy, Miss Langston."

An idea occurred to me. "I know Jeanine is restricted from the docking bay, but if someone escorts her on and off of the *Rising Star*, she could help my old crew with the repairs on the inside of the ship. There is a lot she can do that doesn't require working with the engines or any of the ship systems. Besides, she's already fully familiar with the *Star* and her capabilities."

Admiral Pierson took a moment to consider my suggestion, then gave a quick nod. "Very well. Take her to your ship. Your former crew is responsible for her until further notice."

Pierson waved us away, her attention already shifting to the data pad. Adams followed us out of the admiral's office.

"Come with me, Captain Haral," Adams said, "I'll get you started and then take Miss Langston to your ship."

"I'm sure you'll have to assign office space to me, grant me access to the personnel records, and that sort of thing. Why don't I take Jeanine to the *Star* while you get that taken care of?" I tried a friendly smile on the Commander. "I'm sure it'll go more smoothly if I'm not under foot."

Adams just nodded, pointed to an office, and said, "I'll be in my office making the arrangements, sir. Please join me once your... friend...is on the ship."

When Jeanine and I had the corridor to ourselves, Jeanine murmured, "That was clever, getting me assigned to work on the *Star*. I really wasn't looking forward to squeezing into a tool chest or something like that just so Kelly could smuggle me aboard."

"I wasn't even thinking about that," I said. "I just imagined how bored you'd be stuck in our single room all day and night."

"Whatever the reason, I appreciate it. Now I'll have time to get to know your crew better—and get them to tell me all of their stories about you."

"Even if those stories involve Heather and Candice?"

"*Especially* if those stories involve your family." Jeanine took my hand. "They're part of you, Drake, so learning about them is learning about you. And you are a most fascinating subject to study."

"I bet you say that to all the dashing revolutionaries you go planet-hopping with."

"Why, yes, I *have* said that to every single one of them," Jeanine said, a smile tugging at the corners of her mouth.

When we reached the *Rising Star*, I quickly explained the situation to the crew. As expected, they were happy to have an extra pair of hands for the work. Zach voiced the one concern caused by this change in the plan.

"It's great that we've already got Jeanine on the *Star*," he said, "but will you be able to get away from your new duties and join us?"

"I think so," I replied. "If necessary, I can always select a new crew and bring them to the ship for training."

"That means we've got to figure out a way to get the new crew off the ship before we can make a run for it," Kelly said.

"You just concern yourself with putting the *Star* back in ship-shape. We'll worry about the other problems when and if they arise."

I saluted my crew, kissed Jeanine, and then headed back to Adams' office. Despite the crew's worries, I liked our situation and was confident we were much better off than when we woke up that morning.

Jeanine

To my surprise, Drake's old crew brought all of their repair questions to me. I found myself making decisions about colors and materials and cushions and offering opinions about shelf space and—with much ribald ribbing—whether the bed in the captain's cabin should be larger. Despite my situation and the senior staff's distrust of me, I had fun.

Grandfather and I spent so much time on the move and keeping a low profile that I never had many friends. He only enrolled me in local schools when absolutely necessary and I never played any kind of sports. Sometimes, Grandfather let me enter martial arts tournaments, but even then he never let me show my full range of skills and had me lose before I advanced far enough to attract attention.

I was working with Hemlata in one of the storerooms when I realized I was humming while I worked. In books, I'd read about people who did that sort of thing but never understood it—and, for the first time in my life, I found myself doing that same inexplicable thing. For God's sake, why? I stopped what I was doing and tried to figure it out.

"Is there something wrong, Jeanine?" Hemlata asked.

"No..." I said. "It's just—I was humming and didn't even realize it."

"Yeah, I find myself doing that when I'm in a good mood," Hemlata replied without looking up.

That's when it hit me. I finally felt as if I was part of a team, people whose presence made me happy and gave me a sense of belonging. I finally had...friends. I knew I could tell Hemlata all about this new feeling—or anything else—and she'd listen, offer advice, give hugs, or just hold my hand while I cried. Before Drake and his friends, the only person who ever did that for me was Grandfather. Knowing that, I felt no need to explain it. My smile widened and, very consciously, I resumed humming.

We worked hard throughout the day, bringing lunch back to the *Star* so we could take stock and decide what to do next while we ate. By dinnertime, the *Star's* interior looked much better. We still had a lot of work to do—damn those customs inspectors back on Thinda and their thoroughness—but the end was in sight.

"Okay, people, we've been onboard the *Star* since breakfast. I think we all need a change of scenery," Kelly said. "We're eating dinner in the mess hall."

As everyone filed toward the hatch, I stood in the middle of the common area taking in all the work we'd done. "Can you bring something back for me? I'm not really hungry right now. Besides, I need to figure out the answers to the next set of repair and design questions you're going to hit me with."

"Are you sure?" Kelly asked. At my nod, she said, "Okay. We'll be back in an hour or so."

"That's fine. Oh, if they have any kind of chocolate for dessert..."

Kelly grinned, "We'll bring you two."

I wandered around the *Star*, making a mental checklist of the most pressing repairs remaining. We really had made a lot of progress during the day, so my list was complete within fifteen minutes. I thought about getting back to work but decided I deserved a little rest and relaxation, too. Settling into the copilot's seat, I leaned back and closed my eyes. As much as I enjoyed working with my new friends, I'm still not used to being around other people that much. Make that, I'm not used to being around other people who know me and want me around. Whatever the reason, I reveled in a few minutes of quiet and solitude.

It lasted less than ten minutes.

The sound of voices entering the *Rising Star's* airlock was the first indication I had visitors coming aboard. I immediately recognized Drake's voice, but it took me a few seconds to place the other two. Just before I walked into the ship's common area, I realized the other two voices belonged to Captain Landry and Lieutenant Shaw. Drake gave me a tired smile followed by a quick kiss. Landry and Shaw gave me curt nods.

Raising an eyebrow, I asked, "Did you decide these two were the best team available, after all?"

Drake sighed dramatically. "Not exactly, though I haven't found anyone better suited than them so far. They caught me as I was heading to dinner and asked to see the *Star.* You know how much I enjoy showing off my pride and joy, so I couldn't say no."

In fact, I knew the exact opposite. Drake was never comfortable with strangers onboard the *Star.* That's why he never spent more than one night with the same woman—until he met me, that is. That told me he wasn't comfortable having Landry and Shaw onboard, but couldn't think of a good reason to refuse their request.

The two men looked around the common area briefly and then headed for the cockpit. Without asking, they settled into the two seats and studied the control panels. Drake and I wore matching expressions of irritation, but I let him take the lead in response to their poor manners.

"Please, make yourselves at home, gentlemen," he growled. "Don't let the fact that you're on *my* ship get in the way of your enjoyment."

"You heard the admiral, Haral," Landry said, his tone even. "This ship is part of the revolutionary fleet, now. It will be used as needed and by those deemed best suited to use it."

"All right, that's it!" Drake snapped. "Get off of my ship right now."

"I don't think so," Shaw said.

He spun his chair around to face us. He held a blaster pistol and had it pointed at my chest.

"What the hell do you mean, no?" Drake demanded. When he caught sight of Shaw's blaster, his hot anger turned ice cold. "Huh."

The controlled response confused Shaw. "What do you mean by that?"

"Call it professional respect," Drake said. "I'd never have guessed you two were Royal Intelligence agents."

I couldn't match Drake's level tone when I added, "It can't be a coincidence they're risking their undercover position to get us. I think that means they're probably agents for House Kahn."

Anger flooded into Shaw's face. "Shut up! You don't know anything about us."

The man's emotional reaction surprised me a bit and made the subject worth pursuing. "I don't know, Drake, maybe you're right and they really are Royal Intelligence. But if that's the case, why would Shaw get so upset over the idea of them working for House Kahn?"

"Maybe they have an under-the-table arrangement with Lady Olivia," Drake suggested. "Feed information to the duchess in exchange for money or favors or whatever."

"Oh, I get it," I said. "They're traitors just like us."

"I'm *not* a traitor!"

The Lieutenant's finger tightened on the trigger before he caught himself. I'd hit a nerve with the treason bit, though I couldn't really imagine why. Had Shaw really convinced himself he was a royal patriot even as he sold information to the most ambitious house in the kingdom? Whatever the reason, he didn't have the same emotional control Captain Landry had. I'd have to work the treason angle a little harder and see how far I could push Shaw. If I could get the man concentrating hard on *not* shooting me, it might give us one second when we might act. When you're fighting up close, one second can be a very big advantage.

"Shaw." Landry didn't raise his voice and his inflection was flat, but the single word affected the Lieutenant as if his Captain had hit him. "Take the woman out of here and close the airlock. Shoot her if she tries anything." Landry tapped a control on the communications board. "I've turned on the ship's intercom system. Shoot her if you hear any sound over the intercom you can't identify. And shoot her if the intercom goes off."

Landry finally spun around and faced us. "Captain Haral, you heard my orders to Landry. If you do anything I don't like, Landry will shoot Miss Langston. Is that clear?"

Drake nodded. "And if I hear a blaster shot, I will kill both of you. Is that clear?"

"You'd be welcome to try," Landry replied. "Once Shaw and Miss Langston are out of the cockpit, sit down in the copilot seat and unlock the controls. Just to make sure we're all on the same page, Shaw will shoot Miss Langston if you don't unlock the controls."

"I figured that out all by myself," Drake growled.

Shaw was very cautious getting out of the copilot seat, never taking his gun or his eyes off me. A few seconds later, the two of us were out in the common area, with Shaw ordering me to seal the airlock.

I decided to explore around that nerve I'd struck earlier. "As a royal agent, I'm sure you know I'm not wanted by the crown. House Wilkinson will pay you twice what House Kahn is offering for me."

Shaw gave a humorless laugh. "The Wilkinsons are finished as a major house. Why would I throw away a connection with the rising power just for a little money?"

As the airlock hatches sealed, I said, "I can't match any offers of patronage you've got from Lady Olivia, but why drag Drake into this? If you release him before we leave, you have my word that I will cooperate with you."

This time, Shaw's laugh held contempt. "Lady, you are so far off track with this it's ridiculous."

"Then why not put me on track." I gave Shaw a mocking smile. "Unless you'll commit even more treason doing that."

Shaw glared at me and said, "Why not. It'll do you good to learn the galaxy doesn't revolve around you. Our mission was to find the guy who coordinates recruiting for this band of traitors. Imagine our surprise when it turned out to be Haral. Everyone in the RIA thought he was a small-time shipper and smuggler for the revolution. Instead, he uses his well-earned reputation as a woman-izer—you knew about that bit, didn't you, honey? Anyway, he uses that reputation to receive and send messages to his recruiters. And he does such a good job at it that no one would have figured it out. But he screwed up and fell for you."

I already knew the rest of the story. "So this is all about Drake. And I'm just along to make him behave?"

"Nah, we can handle Haral. You're just an added bonus because Lady Olivia really wants you. She'll clear the path for us to advance and probably give us a nice, fat bonus, too." Shaw grinned. "So you could say it's about the money, after all."

Over the intercom, I heard Drake say, "Docking bay control, this is the *Rising Star*. We've made some adjustments to the engines and need to fire them up for a test burn. Do we have clearance?"

"*Rising Star*, we copy. All personnel are clear of your position. You are go for a test burn."

"Roger that, control. Firing up now."

With a muted roar, the engines fired up. After a few seconds, the sound increased.

"*Rising Star*, what are you doing?" Control's voice was still level, but there was definite tension in it.

"Just testing the repulsers, Control," Drake replied. "We'll bring her back down in a minute."

"Land the ship *now*, *Rising Star*," Control barked. "You have no authorization for such a maneuver."

Without another word, Drake gunned the engines and the *Rising Star* blasted out of the docking bay and into space.

PRISONERS

Drake

Despite Jeanine's ability to needle Shaw, she couldn't push him into making a mistake. At least, she hadn't yet. To my disgust, Landry kept his emotions in check far better than Shaw did. As soon as I unlocked the control panel, he calmly bound my hands behind my back and fastened the manacles to the back of the copilot seat.

"You know, threatening Jeanine isn't exactly a smart move on your part," I said as the engines warmed up. "After all, she's your prize capture."

Landry didn't even glance up from the controls. "What makes you think Miss Langston was our target? I will admit she's a nice bonus, but that's all she is." Landry paused long enough to give me a flat stare. "House Kahn wants her alive, but they'll accept her corpse. Bear that in mind during this flight."

Landry's fingers danced lightly over the controls, displaying obvious experience piloting starships. Control squawked when Landry engaged the repulsers—which he made me 'explain'—and continued calling to us as he flew the ship out of the docking bay and into the asteroid field.

People have the idea that asteroid fields are tightly packed with small, large, and gigantic tumbling rocks. Fed by games and adventure vid images, they assume only a daredevil pilot with hyper-fast reactions can even hope to pilot through one with any chance of survival. There are some places in any large field where that is true, but no one ever takes a ship into those areas. Beyond that, any competent pilot can fly through an asteroid field. A highly skilled pilot can do it at high speed. Landry didn't fly as fast as I could have, but he was as fast as anyone else I've ever met.

The comm was quiet for several minutes after Control gave up on us. Then it was Admiral Pierson's turn to yell at me. I learned all sorts of stuff about myself from her rant, ranging from her distrust of 'irregular space forces'—I can only assume she meant the Space Patrol, not the revolutionary force she led—to her certainty that I was just another man acting stupid around the first hot babe who smiled at me. She ended with dire threats and, belatedly, entreaties to my loyalty.

When Pierson cut off the comm, Landry said, "My superiors will be pleased when I tell them Pierson is in command of your navy. She doesn't have a particularly stellar reputation among her peers in the Royal Navy."

I didn't respond because, from a certain point of view, the Royal Navy was right about Pierson. Her interpersonal skills are sorely lacking for someone of her rank. I have no doubt her subordinates disliked working for her and her superiors disliked having her work for them. Whatever else I'll say about Pierson, she is a logistical mastermind and very good at strategy and tactics. During peacetime, those skills aren't highly valued or rewarded. When the revolution finally expands beyond the small skirmishes we fight throughout the kingdom, the Royal Navy will quickly re-evaluate Admiral Pierson's abilities.

Our final contact with the rebel base came a few minutes later. It nearly ripped my heart out when Kelly came on the comm. "Hey, Drake. Are you out there?"

Landry cocked an eyebrow—the most expressive his face got during our flight from the base—and turned the volume up so the sound carried clearly over the internal comm.

"What's the deal, buddy? Why did you cut and run? Didn't you trust the senior staff to figure out Jeanine was on the up and up?" She paused for a few seconds, waiting for a response. "I know Jeanine has you all hot and bothered, Drake, but how many times have I told you to think with the brain above your shoulders instead of the one between your legs?" Kelly's tone hardened as if she was losing her temper. "Hell, I even skipped eating *my* dessert tonight so I could bring it back for you. I love chocolate but I know you love it even more."

Clever, Kelly! All of my old crew know I can't stand chocolate. On our patrol ship, whoever had kitchen duty made it a point to only make chocolate desserts so there would be that much more for everyone else. Since I brought my own sweets, it was all in fun. And now it was Kelly's way of telling me she figured something was very wrong about this situation.

I felt the tension in my gut loosen just a bit. Unlike Landry and Shaw, Kelly knew the *Rising Star* extremely well—better than anybody except me, in fact. She performed the engine mods. She helped me install the electronics. And she knew the frequency of the *Star's* emergency subspace tracking beacon. The very same beacon I turned on when I unlocked the ship's control panel for Landry.

They would never get their hands on a ship as fast as the *Rising Star*, but Kelly and the crew would get their hands on some ship and they would come after us. I could only pray they would catch us before Landry turned Jeanine over to House Kahn.

THE PROPOSAL

Olivia

Every news service on the planet was there when William's ship landed. They all recorded William carrying me from the ship, me with my arms wrapped around his neck and my head resting on his shoulder. He took me to a waiting ambulance and rode with me to the hospital. William was as sweet as he could be, never leaving my side as the doctors ran their tests and then kept me overnight for observation. By the time we left the hospital the next morning, he was mine.

The prince and I were *the* news story for the next two weeks. Cams followed our every public move and an adoring public followed the story with rabid interest. Vids of us adorned every newscast. Fashion mavens deconstructed every outfit I wore and explained to the public what each article of my clothing said about our romance. I was quite amazed at the accuracy of their predictions, all the more so because I wasn't consciously choosing my outfits to send any messages.

The queen offered me a suite at the palace during my 'recovery' from the explosion. It played well in the vids, allowing Charlotte and Bernard to play the part of doting parents and caring monarchs.

During a public appearance the day I moved into the palace

suite, Charlotte joked, "I feel as if I must keep poor Olivia under my wing. It's for the girl's own protection. Who knows what those two lovebirds might do unchaperoned at Olivia's estate? I can promise you there won't be any shenanigans going on in *my* palace!"

Her comments drew delighted laughs from the crowd. It also drove speculation that Their Majesties were keeping a tight rein on their womanizing son, ensuring he didn't do anything to ruin our storybook romance. In truth, William and I engaged in 'shenanigans' every night—every bit of it enthusiastically encouraged by Charlotte.

Two weeks to the day after William rescued me, he took me to a lovely public park. Crowds of commoners and newsie cams followed us as we held hands and ate ice cream. Then William led me to a wishing fountain. Digging into his pocket, he pulled out a few coins.

"Are you familiar with the legend associated with this fountain, my dear?" William asked.

"No," I said, my tone playful. "Are you going to tell me?"

"Of course, I am," he said. "When you toss your coins into the fountain, throw them as high as you can. If you can make your wish while the coins are in the air, and if all of the coins land in the fountain, your wish will come true."

"That sounds simple enough," I said. "But what should I wish for?"

"Only you can choose your wish, darling," William replied before giving me a quick kiss on the lips. "It's terribly ungentlemanly of me to go first, but I *do* know what I'm going to wish for. Do you mind?"

"Not at all!" I said as my heart beat quickened. "Perhaps your wish will inspire me."

"I do hope so, Olivia."

William took several coins and threw them high into the air and then immediately dropped to one knee before me. He pulled a beautiful engagement ring from another pocket, looked up at me, and said, "I wish, more than anything in the universe, that you will marry me!"

I caught my breath and found tears forming in my eyes. Blinking rapidly, the tears cleared just in time for me to see the splashes as all of William's coins landed in the fountain.

"You spoke your wish while the coins were in the air and they all landed in the fountain. That means your wish is going to come true," I said, my voice suddenly tight with emotion. "Yes, William, I will marry you! There is nothing I wish more in the universe, either."

The prince slid the ring onto my finger, swept me into his arms, and kissed me quite soundly as the crowd around us cheered. I laid my head on his shoulder, recognizing I truly wanted to marry William for himself and not just for the throne that came with him.

As we smiled and waved at the crowd, I understood just how good my life was. I had a man I loved and a public that, to my surprise, adored me. Once I got my hands on the Wilkinson Bastard, my life would truly be perfect.

AN EARLY WEDDING PRESENT

Jeanine

The flight to Gaunner was just as bad as you might imagine. I got to needle Shaw, who almost always rose to the bait in some way or another. Unfortunately, Landry kept a tight rein on him, so he never quite got so upset he resorted to violence. Since my goal was to get him to do just that, it was frustrating. All the martial arts training in the galaxy is wasted if you can't get the guy with the blaster to come close enough for you to disarm him.

I guess the pair didn't really consider me much of a threat since they rarely bound me, but they also didn't exactly give me free run of the ship. All the doors were locked open, and they watched me at all times—even in the bathroom. Landry was dispassionate about it, merely watching me shower or do my business. Shaw, looking for a little revenge from my taunts, openly leered at me every time I was in there. Early on, I struck provocative poses to lure Shaw closer, but gave up when they didn't work.

The most difficult part was not being able to talk privately with Drake. They let us spend time together—sometimes bound to each other if both men were busy with something—but we weren't allowed to whisper. It can be hard to give voice to your deepest emotions when a couple of royal spies are listening to every word you say, but we got over it long before the trip ended.

Drake was worried about everything except himself. He worried most about me, afraid Lady Olivia would have me killed outright or would 'loan' me to Royal Intelligence to threaten while they interrogated Drake. He worried how his supposed defection would affect his former crew's standing in the revolution. He worried Landry would tell the Royal Navy where the hidden base was and the navy would attack before the revolution could move. At least subspace comm units were so hideously expensive the *Rising Star* didn't have one. He even worried about the *Star* more than he worried about himself.

"You don't have to worry about me, Drake," I said, trying to reassure him. "The only reason Lady Olivia wants me dead is because of my claim to the Duchy of Neert. If I officially renounce my claim, perhaps we can put this whole thing behind us."

Shaw laughed when I said that. "If you believe that, you're stupider than I thought. Her butcher brother died because of you. If you're really lucky, she'll just kill you outright. I'm betting she wants to burn you alive, just like what happened to her brother."

Hard though I tried to remain impassive, I shuddered at the thought of such a death.

"And there's another problem with your plan, girl. You've got to be touching the Star Stone when you renounce your claim, otherwise, anyone else requesting Recognition gets smoked, just like the Butcher did." A wistful look crossed Shaw's face as if he regretted missing such a sight. "The thing is, the words for both requests are almost identical. At the last second, you could change 'reject Recognition' to 'request Recognition' and snatch the title away from Lady Olivia."

"You're remarkably well informed about the Recognition ceremony," Drake said.

"It's all part of RIA training," Shaw replied. "You'd be amazed how often that knowledge is vital to a mission."

Landry maintained comm silence as much as was practical

when we reached Gaunner, responding only to Gaunner Control. He did have Shaw scan for Royal Navy ships, no doubt with the plan of giving them the location of the rebel base. To our relief, there were no naval units around the planet. That only delayed the inevitable, since Landry would have no trouble making a subspace call from Lady Olivia's palace, but even a few extra hours is better than nothing.

On the ground, Landry escorted me to the palace. "I don't want to attract attention on the streets, so I'm leaving your hands free. Just remember that Shaw is back here with Captain Haral. Do I need to tell you what will happen if you don't cooperate fully with me?"

I shook my head. "Can I at least give Drake one last kiss?"

"As long as you keep your hands behind your back, you may."

With my hands clasped behind my back, I leaned down and kissed Drake. I tried to put everything I felt for the man into that final kiss and could tell Drake was doing the same. Eventually, Landry called a halt to it.

As I pulled away from Drake, I said, "I love you."

His expression fierce, Drake said, "I'll come for you."

"I'll be waiting."

Shaw laughed, shaking his head at our foolishness, as Landry led me to the airlock. I got one last look at Drake before the steel door slid shut behind us.

The trip to the palace passed in a blur as I followed Landry's instructions mechanically. We took a cab to the palace, riding in silence. Deposited at the tourist entrance to the palace, Landry led me around to the business entrance. He flashed his credentials to the guards on duty and waited patiently while their commanding officer called inside for clearance.

Happy for even this small distraction from their normal boring routine, one of the guards said, "It's pretty amazing news about Lady Olivia and Prince William, huh?"

"What news is that?" Landry asked.

"You haven't heard? The prince rescued Lady Olivia when

those damned rebels sabotaged her ship. I guess it made both of them look at each other in a different light because they fell hard for each other. Yesterday, the prince popped the question right out in the open in a public park on Xapreathea. My wife said it was the most romantic thing she's ever seen."

"Lady Olivia isn't on the planet?" Landry asked.

"Gee, that's too bad," I said. "Just think, you could have gone straight to the capital."

The guard commander exited his office and motioned for us to get up. "Come with me. The duchess's assistant has cleared his schedule and will see you now."

I got the idea Landry would prefer returning to the *Star* and making haste for Xapreathea, but he also wanted to make that subspace call to RIA headquarters. Besides, irritating the assistant of the future princess of the realm is probably not a good way to ingratiate yourself with her.

The guard commander led us deep into the business wing of the palace, finally dropping us off in a large, ornately decorated outer office. Before alerting her boss, the assistant to the assistant asked, "What may I tell Mr. Colin this is about?"

For the first time since I met him, Landry actually cracked a smile. "Tell Mr. Colin I've brought a wedding gift for Lady Olivia."

The woman heaved a sigh. "Really, sir, that's insufficient reason to interrupt Mr. Colin's schedule. I'll call a guard to escort you to my lady's social director."

"You don't want to do that," Landry said. "My gift isn't really appropriate for a social director."

The assistant scowled at Landry. "Fine, I'll bite. What is your gift?"

Landry caught my arm and pulled me forward. "I've brought Lady Olivia the Wilkinson Bastard."

WE'VE GOT THAT COVERED

Drake

Jeanine's little psychological warfare campaign against Shaw, waged across four star systems and through three hyperspace jumps, was more successful than she realized. Landry and Jeanine hadn't been out of the ship for more than fifteen seconds when Shaw casually backhanded me.

"That's for all the lip that bitch of yours gave me throughout the trip. If I had *my* way, I'd have taught her a few lessons about proper respect. Damn Landry and his insistence on delivering the goods in pristine condition." He leered and grabbed his crotch. "Who knows, maybe she'd have enjoyed some of those lessons."

Without conscious thought, my leg shot out at Shaw and his cupped hand. I almost got him, but he jumped back at the last second. He flashed an unpleasant grin, walked widely around my seat, and cracked something hard against the back of my head.

"As long as you're still in good enough condition to answer the interrogator's questions, he's not as particular about you. Maybe that's because Royal Intelligence is going to keep hurting you and healing you and hurting you again. Somehow, I don't think Lady Olivia is going to be quite so generous to the bastard." Shaw walked around to face me, carefully staying out of kicking range. "What do you think the duchess is going to do to the woman who made her dear brother go up in flames? Can't you just imagine her pretty red head surrounded by crackling red flames?"

Shaw kept his eyes on mine, enjoying himself immensely. I took advantage of his distraction to pull the heel of my right foot out of my shoe. Once again, I kicked at Shaw. He just opened his mouth to laugh when the shoe smashed into his nose. I wish I could tell you it knocked him out and gave me a chance to escape. In truth, the shoe bloodied his nose a bit and really pissed him off. For the next little while, Shaw danced around behind me and to both sides, pummeling me all about my head and shoulders and hurling taunts and threats the whole time.

Eventually, he got tired of the sport—or maybe he just got tired of thinking up new and supposedly inventive jibes to go with his jabs. Whatever the reason, Shaw stopped and dropped into one of the chairs in the *Star's* living area. He ignored me and I returned the favor.

For the next hour, I welcomed the aches and pains Shaw gave me. They gave me something to concentrate on besides the internal ache I felt for Jeanine. It took agony to distract me, so I flexed my shoulders and shook my head and did everything imaginable to increase the pain. Even when I succeeded, the distraction only lasted a minute or two.

The ship's comm sounded, surprising Shaw and me. Assuming the call had to be from Landry, Shaw answered, "Yeah?"

A few seconds later, he said, "No, the captain's not on board right now...I don't know when he'll be back...Yes, I'm his new crewman...The cute redhead? She left the ship...Yeah, well, too bad...No, I don't know if he already has a cargo...Look, I don't really give a damn how much business you've done with him. He's not here and I don't know the answers to any of your questions... Yeah, you do that."

Shaw cut the comm connection and tossed it on a chair next to him and scowled at me. "Somebody you worked with before is going to ask you to talk to me about my attitude."

"Who?"

"How the hell should I know? Do you think I paid any attention to that?" Shaw said. "What difference does it make, anyway? You're never going to carry another cargo."

"Come on, Shaw, don't you know they haven't built a prison that can hold me?"

To my right, barely within my peripheral vision, the airlock warning light blinked red. Someone had just opened the *Star's* outer hatch. I willed Shaw to keep his eyes on me for just a few more seconds, hoping it wasn't simply Landry coming back. With a soft pop, the inner airlock hatch opened.

Shaw turned idly and said, "That didn't take as long I thought it would. Have—"

Kelly and Zach stepped through the hatch, both holding blasters trained on Shaw. Kelly opened her mouth but, before she could say anything, Shaw grabbed for his own blaster. Zach's hand twitched as he adjusted his aim slightly and squeezed the trigger. The sharp crack of his blaster filled the room.

In shock, Shaw watched his right hand spin across the room. He found his voice and his screams echoed off the walls. Then Kelly smashed the butt of her blaster against the side of his head. It took another two blows, but Shaw finally slumped unconscious in his chair.

"That guy has a good set of lungs and a really hard head," she said, already checking his pockets for the keys to the manacles binding me. "That shot was pretty amazing, Zach, even for you."

"It was only five meters," Zach replied, his tone dismissive. "My normal practice range is twenty."

As the rest of the crew piled in through the airlock, she freed me and asked, "Has Landry already taken Jeanine to the palace?"

Rubbing my wrists, I said, "Yeah. For all I know, the duchess has already killed her."

Kelly shook her head. "Nope. Dear Lady Olivia is off planning her wedding to Prince William. We've got time to rescue her."

"How?" I asked. "I want to, of course, but we don't know the layout of the palace or the placement of guards or—"

Kelly covered my mouth with her hand. "We've got that covered, Skipper."

"You do?"

"Of course! We put in a subspace call to Jana before we left the base and asked her to get everything she could find on the palace. Everything we wanted was waiting for us when we landed."

"The senior staff let you use the subspace comm? And they must have let you take a fast ship or—"

"Yeah, about that..." Kelly gave me a look of mock contrition. "We, uh, might have drugged the comm operator and made an unauthorized subspace call."

"And the senior staff didn't give us jack—but they did increase security around the faster ships in the navy." Sam said. "Kind of stupid to do that *after* their best ship was taken, but you know how it is with officers."

"So you stole a ship?" When Sam nodded, I asked, "What did you steal?"

"There was an RS300 freighter nobody was paying much attention to," he responded.

"That old tub? You guys should still have at least one more hyperspace jump left! How did you-" Comprehension dawned on me. "You took a riskier course, didn't you?"

"Of course," Hemlata said. "We knew we'd be too late if we didn't. And you know Grant is one of the best astrogators in the business."

"How many jumps?" I asked Grant.

"I was real careful, Skipper!" Grant said. "Ran the numbers half a dozen times and—"

"How. Many."

Grant met my eyes. "One."

"Holy hell, Grant! You know the whole idea of hyperspace routes is to *avoid* gravity wells—not plow right through half a dozen of them!"

"I'm an astrogator. Of course, I know that, Skipper. We skirted eight gravity wells, but the odds were with us."

"And what, pray tell, were the odds?"

"We had a sixty-three percent chance of surviving the trip."

My eyes widened in horror. "And you didn't think that was too dangerous? What kind of fool are you?"

"He's your kind of fool, Drake," Kelly said. "We faced longer odds than that against those fake pirates from House Kahn and I didn't see you backing away."

"This is different," I protested.

"No, it's not. We take care of our own," Kelly said, "and today that means we're rescuing Jeanine."

Starting with Kelly, I looked into the eyes of each of my former crewmen. From each pair of eyes, defiance and determination looked back at me.

"I want all of you to think about what you're agreeing to," I said. "You'll be risking your life for my woman, not—"

"God, Drake, will you just shut up already?" Kelly said. "We'll be risking our lives for our friend."

"And I appreciate that, Kelly, but Jeanine—"

"Is the friend we're laying our lives on the line for," Kelly interrupted again. "That you love her is just a bonus, as far as we're concerned."

"Oh," I said. "In that case, what's your plan?"

Grant pulled out a data stick. "Where's your data pad?"

While I got the pad, a couple of the crew dragged the unconscious Shaw off to a storeroom. For grisly effect, they tossed his hand—minus the blaster still clutched in it—in with the intelligence agent. By the time they got back, Grant was opening file after file of data gathered by Jana.

Staring at the collection of maps, building plans, duty rosters, and God only knows what else, I was astounded. "Why did Jana have all of this stuff on hand? Has she got something against House Kahn, too?"

"She didn't have it on hand, Skipper," Grant replied.

"Then how did she get it? Bragua is in a different duchy. They wouldn't have this stuff in any of their databases."

"That agent must have hit your head harder than we thought," Kelly said. "Jana used a subspace connection to hack the systems here on Gaunner and then routed the information to a drop box for us."

My eyes widened at the thought of the exorbitant cost of just one minute of subspace time. "How long did she keep the connection open?"

"Let me check. She left a note for you," Grant replied. He opened one of the files, scanned it, and whistled. "It took her four hours and twenty-six minutes to finish the job."

I winced. "If I sell the *Rising Star*, I think I can reimburse her for the connection."

"Jana has other ideas. Here's what she wrote." Grant began reading from the file. "Drake, you owe me big time, but don't worry about that right now. Concentrate on getting Jeanine out of the clutches of House Kahn and then meet me on Xapreathea. I'll be working on a plan for Jeanine's Recognition. How does the title Jana Ward, Data Mistress to Her Grace the Duchess of Neert sound to you?"

I couldn't help laughing and then wincing as my head ached again. "Could someone get the med kit? I'm going to need some good drugs if I'm going to lead this rescue."

Kelly shook her head. "Oh hell no, Drake! You are in no condition to even go with us, much less lead."

"But—"

"We need someone to fly the *Star* to the palace at just the right moment," Kelly said. "That's your job, so you have to stay here."

"I can't—"

"You can and you will. You know the drill, Drake. The best person for the job gets the job," Kelly said. "You're the pilot so you stay here to fly the ship. Grant stays here to calculate our hyperspace jump out of here and run Jana's intrusion programs. The rest of us slip into the palace and get Jeanine."

Much as I hated to admit it, Kelly was right on two counts. I wasn't in condition for the physical demands of leading the rescue and I was far and away the best pilot among us—even more so when it came to flying the *Rising Star*. I met Kelly's glare and said, "Aye aye, Admiral Powers."

The corners of Kelly's lips turned up slightly. "Good. Now, here's our plan. We like it, but feedback is welcome."

We had the details all worked out and were waiting patiently when Landry finally returned to the ship. He took one look at the blasters trained on him and raised his hands.

"Shaw?" he asked.

"Alive and locked in a storeroom," I said. "We can show him to you if you insist. Then we're locking you in a different storeroom."

Landry didn't insist. Once he was locked away, Kelly led the rescue team out of the ship. Frustrated to be on the sidelines for most of the action, I calmed my nerves as best I could and waited for Kelly's signal.

BREAK OUT

Jeanine

I was somewhat surprised when Lady Olivia's guards took me to a comfortably furnished, windowless room. Call me silly, but I expected a dank dungeon, a stone floor, a thick wooden door bound with iron, and rats. I guess I read too many fantasy tales growing up and never realized dungeons were out of fashion. The two men used restraints on my hands, otherwise, they treated me as a family guest.

As the guards ushered me into the room, I said, "It's illegal to lock me up like this. I haven't done anything wrong and haven't been charged with a crime."

One of them smiled at me though his eyes looked sad. "That's not for us to say, miss. I'm sure everything will work out fine after Lady Olivia reviews your case."

"Not bloody likely," I muttered. "Look, if you can get me out of here I'll make it more than worth your while."

The guard sighed. "You're a very attractive young woman, miss, but—"

"I didn't mean sex!" God in heaven, why do men automatically assume the only thing a woman can offer them is naked gymnastics? I glared at the guard and said, "I meant money. Safe, free passage to my duchy for you and your family. Land, a house, and a job when you get there."

"I beg your pardon, my lady." The man's tone was insufferably patronizing. "I was unaware you were a duchess. Which duchy is yours?"

"Once the Recognition ceremony is complete, I'll be the Duchess of Neert."

The other guard spoke for the first time. "So, you're the Wilkinson Bastard?"

"I am."

The first guard looked at his companion. "Is she the fourth or fifth bastard this month?"

The second guard tapped his fingers, counting. "Fourth."

"Did you include the old man from last week? The one who was older than his 'father,' the late Lord Arthur?" asked the first guard.

"Oops, I forgot him." The second guard smiled at me. "Don't you worry, miss, the medical staff will do a quick DNA scan and then you can be on your way."

The first guard gave me a quizzical look. "One thing I never understood is why so many of you come here to make the claim. Why didn't you just go to Neert?"

"I was brought here under duress," I replied. "Believe me, I would quite literally rather be anywhere else in the galaxy right now."

"As you say, miss," said the first guard, releasing my hands from their restraints. "We'll knock when the medical crew gets here. Would you care for something to eat while you wait?"

I shook my head, and the guard shut the door. The light next to the door turned from green to red, indicating the door was locked. With a sigh of frustration, I waited and weighed escape plans. After an hour or so, a medic came, took a DNA sample, and left. I stopped pacing and settled onto the surprisingly comfortable sofa. The tension of the last two days caught up with me and I found myself fighting to stay awake. Then I remembered something Grandfather told me long ago

"If you don't know what else to do, take a nap."

The last time I followed Grandfather's advice—getting 'properly laid' by Drake—worked out incredibly well. With Drake uppermost in my mind, I stretched out on the sofa, imagined his arms wrapped around me, and drifted into sleep.

I woke up when the lights went out. My eyes snapped open, but the room was absolutely dark. I closed my eyes again, essentially telling my brain it could ignore sight, and concentrated on listening. I heard muffled voices from the direction of the door; probably my two guards. Wanting to be in position to take advantage of even the slightest opportunity, I rose, stretched my arms out before me, and carefully shuffled toward the sound.

Half a minute later, I found the door seam and the control panel. I positioned myself next to the door and waited, hoping there was a way to open it while the power was out. If the guards decided to check on their 'guest' while it was still dark, I just might have a chance to take them down before they knew what was happening.

Waiting in absolute darkness messes with your sense of time. I felt as if I stood next to the door for years before I heard several thumps and more muffled voices. I heard the door slide open. I tensed, ready to make a hit-and-run attack on the guards as soon as they entered the room.

Then a woman whispered, "Jeanine, it's me—Kelly. Here, put this on."

Kelly put a pair of goggles into my hands. As soon as I put them on, I recognized them as low-light and infrared vision goggles. Kelly and five more of Drake's former crew came into eerie focus. I felt dread coil around my heart when I realized Drake wasn't with them.

"Did you find the *Rising Star*? Shaw is holding Drake prisoner."

Kelly smiled, pulling me down the dark corridor. "Don't worry, honey, Drake is safe and waiting for us to give him a call. He'll come get us in the *Star* when we're ready to go."

I stepped over my two guards, who were sprawled on the floor outside. "I hope you didn't have to kill them. They were as kind as their position allowed."

"Nope, we just knocked them out," Kelly said. "Now let's get a move on. We left Zach and Sam guarding our route out of here and don't want to give the guards time to regroup and overwhelm them."

As we set off at a run, I asked, "Is Grant with Drake?"

"Yes," Kelly said as she started panting.

"What about the city's air defenses? Won't they shoot down the *Star*?"

"Don't you...ever run...out of...breath?" Kelly asked, her breath coming in gasps.

"Grandfather made me train for long distance running."

"Hate you...right now...Jana wrote...program...scrambles... tracking."

"Jana is with you?"

"No...and now...shut...up!"

I stopped asking questions and trusted in my friends. We ran through dark corridors, past other guards lying on the floor, making so many turns I quickly lost my sense of direction. After a couple of minutes, Kelly signaled a stop. Ahead was a large room. Lights burned off to the right, out of our line of sight. Our goggles automatically compensated, keeping the light from blinding us.

Kelly took a few seconds to catch her breath, then said, "Crap, the lights are a new development." She pulled out a comm and thumbed it on. "Zach? We're close but the guards have portable lights set up in the ballroom."

"Roger that," Zach responded. "I'll be there in thirty seconds. Make a run for it when I take my first shot."

"Will do. Sam? Call Drake and have him standing by," Kelly said. "Tell him to take off as soon as Zach starts shooting."

"Got it," Sam said.

As we waited for Zach to get into position, the six of us crept slowly toward the ballroom. Dozens of voices sounded in the room as guard officers gave commands and directed their men. From the fragments we picked out, none of them was quite sure what was happening. But with both the power and emergency power out, they were treating it as an attack.

"It sounds like they're waiting for someone to bring low-light goggles," Tanner whispered. "We're going to be in deep—"

We heard the flat crack of a blaster followed closely by the sound of a portable light blowing apart. The light in the ballroom dimmed appreciably and voices rose in alarm.

"Let's go," Kelly said. "And stay in the shadows."

Praying the guards wouldn't see us, we sprinted into the ballroom.

As Drake's former crew and I ran through the deep shadows in the ballroom, Zach steadily blasted apart the portable lights set up on the far side of the room. Four shots, four lights. Five shots, five lights. Did the man ever miss? The guards returned fire, but they were literally firing blind. In those brief few seconds, I thought Zach held their attention so thoroughly the rest of us were going to make it through the ballroom unnoticed.

Then a voice shouted, "Captain, there are people against the far wall!"

"Pick up the speed, crew!" Kelly urged.

"How the hell did that guy even see us?" Hemlata wondered.

"Squads two and three, direct fire at the back wall," a commanding voice called. "Squad one, the shooter is providing cover for them. Keep firing at him."

"Everyone, we're too easy to hit bunched up like this," I said. "Spread out. Run side-by-side in pairs."

No one asked why I was issuing orders, they just did as I said. Those in front kept up their sprint while the rest of us slowed down for a few seconds. By the time we were strung out in a ragged line of three pairs, blaster bolts were flying all around us. Ahead of us, more blaster bolts splashed all around the corridor where Zach was firing from, but he just crouched lower and kept picking off lights.

"All squads, advance," the security commander ordered. "Once you're out of the light, turn on your low-light goggles."

"Dammit!" Kelly panted. "Jeanine...run...faster."

"I'm not leaving you guys behind!" I snarled.

"Not...request...order."

Next to me, Tanner pushed me gently in the back. "Go...You're why...we're here...Revolt...needs...duchess...Skipper...needs...you."

Reluctantly, I kicked into high gear and surged past my friends. Kelly flipped me off as I passed her, a fierce grin making the signal more of a compliment than an insult. At least one or two guards saw me make my break and their fire tracked after me. They were still forty or fifty meters away, though, and their shots weren't accurate. A couple of shots came within a meter of me, but that was all. And then I reached the corridor and dropped down next to Zach.

Reaching for his holster, I said, "I'm taking your pistol. Nice shooting, by the way."

Zach's last shot blew out the only remaining light in the room, so he smoothly turned his aim on the security guards. He sighted, exhaled, and fired. A guard cried out and dropped to the ground holding his side. I pointed the pistol toward the guards streaming our way and began shooting. I had about as much chance of hitting the guards as they did me, so I didn't really try. I just wanted to lay down covering fire for the team.

I ran through half of the pistol's charge in a matter of seconds. Then Kelly joined me, huffing and puffing, and began firing even more wildly than I was.

When Hemlata got there, she grabbed my arm and pulled me up, gasping, "Come on...Got to...go."

Once again, I reluctantly ran while my friends stayed behind. We hadn't gone ten meters when a man cried out behind us. He was much too close to be a guard, so I tried to stop and go back. Hemlata kept a firm hold on my arm and dragged me on.

"We've got to go back," I said. "One of the team is hurt!"

"Tanner," Hemlata gasped. "But we...keep going...Whole crew... agreed."

"But—"

Hemlata roughly jerked me down the corridor, away from the rest of the crew. "Run...or all...wasted."

I blinked back tears, something I *really* couldn't afford while wearing the goggles. I could break free of Hemlata if I wanted to, but I recognized the truth in what Tanner told me when he shoved me forward. If I stayed behind to fight, I jeopardized everything the crew was trying to do. Yes, they wanted to rescue me for Drake's sake, but they also saw the much bigger picture. They dedicated their lives to the revolution and having a duchess on their side could make a real difference—and that was something they believed was well worth dying for.

My eyes cleared, and I stopped fighting against Hemlata. "I understand."

Behind us, Kelly issued quick commands in a low and urgent voice—too low for me to interpret. Then even that faded into the background as Hemlata and I ran on through darkness so deep only our goggles made it possible for us to run. We took a left turn into a corridor with meager light from a distant window or door. We turned right after another sixty or seventy meters and Hemlata pulled up at the corner.

"Just head...straight down...this hall," she said around gasped breath. "I'll...wait for...others."

Again, I wanted to argue. I wanted to tell all of these people I wasn't worth the sacrifices they were making. Instead, I gave a curt nod. "You're still coming, right? Because you know Drake won't leave without you."

Hemlata gave me a thumbs up and then turned her attention back in the direction we'd come from. I saw Sam waiting at the end of the hallway and, without another word, ran toward him. Seconds later, I stopped next to Sam and pulled off the goggles.

Light came through a door that opened onto a large and peaceful courtyard.

Before I could ask Sam for an update, a loud roar shook the whole wing of the palace. The *Rising Star*, looking more beautiful than she'd ever looked before, came in low over the palace and settled into the courtyard.

Yelling to be heard over the landing spaceship, I asked, "How did they get past the air defense batteries?"

"Ask Jana when you see her," Sam yelled back. "She gave us a lot of programs to temporarily take out stuff like that."

Watching the *Star* crush a lovely collection of flowers, I asked, "Any word from the others?"

"Hemlata has them in sight. Tanner's body is slowing them down, but they're close."

Body? Damn, damn, damn! I barely knew the man, but he was friendly, outgoing, the kind of guy you always liked having around. Drake told me Tanner lost his parents, sister, and the girl he planned to marry in that long-ago raid. And now he was with them again.

Damn my father!

Damn Robert the Butcher!

Damn the Duchess of Neert!

And especially damn the Duchess of Gaunner and her stupid vendetta against me!

"You'd better watch your back, Olivia," I muttered, "because now I've got a score to settle with you."

The sound of blaster fire came from down the hall. Sam turned that way and lifted his goggles into place. "They're coming. You'd better get to the *Star* now."

"It's just a short dash to the ship. I'll stay and help lay down covering fire."

Never taking his eyes off the hallway, Sam pushed me toward the door and said, "No, you won't. Go!"

For the fourth time in the last five minutes, I turned and ran from a friend in desperate need of help. As soon as I came through the door, the *Star's* airlock cycled open. Grant leapt through it, a blaster rifle clutched in his hands. He gave me a lopsided grin and lifted the gun in half-salute as we passed each other.

I charged through the airlock and into the *Star*. Drake caught me in his arms. "Are you okay?"

"I'm fine, Drake." Eying the blaster rifle he had propped against the inner wall of the airlock, I asked, "Have you got another gun?"

He pointed to the other airlock wall. A second rifle was propped up there. I grabbed it and the two of us took up positions on either side of the airlock.

"What's your situation?" Drake asked.

I almost answered before I noticed he was wearing a headset. Drake listened for a few seconds and his already grim face turned grimmer. "Sam, you and Grant were supposed to stay at the door."

He listened to Sam's reply and then said, "Kelly, keep falling back toward the courtyard. Jeanine and I will take Sam's old position and give you covering fire."

Kelly must have yelled because the voice from the headset was loud enough for me to hear. "Goddammit, Drake, you will stay on the *Star*! Is that—"

Blaster fire rained from the doorway I ran through less than a minute before. A couple of shots came in through the open hatch though most splattered harmlessly on the *Star's* exterior.

"You've got guards between you and the courtyard!" Drake yelled into the comm.

Kelly shouted something that made Drake shake his head violently. "No! There's got to be another way!"

After another shout from Kelly, Drake hung his head and slapped the airlock control. The hatch slid quietly shut, muting the sound as it closed. His face set, Drake walked toward the pilot's compartment.

"What about the others?" I asked.

"They're not coming, babe," Drake said, his voice husky with emotion. "Come on, Jeanine. Let's go finish this."

Drake was quiet as we boosted straight up toward space, leaving behind a charred garden. He ignored multiple warnings to stop or be destroyed. All of those threats came from ground-based defenses compromised by Jana's many intrusion programs. But her software couldn't affect Gaunner's orbiting defenses nor the duchy's space fleet.

As we roared through the planet's atmosphere, I watched the fleet converge on our course. "Do you know how we'll get past all those ships?"

Drake's fingers flew across the pilot's controls. "Grant took care of that. Tell me when we reach an altitude of one hundred kilometers."

"We're passing forty-three now. What happens at one hundred?"

"We jump into hyperspace."

I couldn't keep the incredulity out of my voice. "We do *what*?"

"Grant calculated the course, and he really knows his stuff." Drake took a second to look me in the eyes. "I won't use his calculations if you don't want me to."

"Use them." I smiled at Drake. "If we don't make it, well, we've both got people waiting for us on the other side."

We both turned back to our consoles. I checked our altitude. "I'll count the kilometers to one hundred... Ninety-seven... Ninety-eight... Ninety-nine... One hundred!"

Drake's finger stabbed at the hyperspace controls. "Will you marry me, Jeanine?"

I held my breath. Released it when we didn't explode. "Nothing would make me happier, Drake."

A bittersweet smile spread across his face. "Not even having Olivia turning on a spit over an open flame?"

"Not even. But I'll make sure that's included in my wedding gift registry."

"Kelly left a message for you and asked me to give it you if she didn't come back from your rescue." Drake leaned back in his seat and took both of my hands in his. "Do you want to watch it now or wait?"

I blinked rapidly to clear the tears threatening to flow. "Sure, let's watch it now."

Drake tapped a few buttons and a small vid screen rose between the two control panels. Kelly's smiling face materialized on the screen, but she wasn't alone. The rest of the old crew were arrayed behind her.

"Hi, Jeanine. If you're watching this, you're safe on the *Star* and at least one of us didn't get away after the rescue. Maybe none of us did. However many of us died or were captured, we don't want you to feel guilty. We're all adults and we chose to rescue you."

Behind Kelly, the rest of the team nodded in agreement, some of them adding a muttered "Yeah" or "Kelly's right."

Kelly continued, "By now, one of us must have told you how important a duchess will be to the revolution. We've all agreed that's what we're going to tell you if we need you to leave us behind. And we won't be lying, either, but that's not the main reason we're coming to get you. Drake will never admit it, but he is the only reason any of us survived the attack on our old mining settlement. Without his firm guidance, I'd have opened my suit right in the middle of our town square and joined my family in death."

Again the crew nodded and voiced their agreement again. Kelly let them wind down. "Drake kept us together—as a crew and as people. We told you it hurt watching him self-destruct over the last few years. Just between you and me, I was giving him another year at most before he managed to get himself killed.

"After we got to know you and saw how Drake reacted to you— let's just say we added you to the very short list of people we were willing to die for. That's why we don't want you feeling guilty over any of us. You make Drake whole again—and *that* is something worth dying for!" Kelly stopped and swiped a hand across her eyes. "When you crazy kids get around to starting a family, feel free to name a daughter after me."

One by one, the rest of the crew offered a personal message along the same lines as Kelly's. Kelly closed out the vid with one last comment.

"If Drake isn't already watching this, pause it and go get him. The last bit is for him." Kelly pretended nonchalance for a few seconds and then returned her attention to the cam. "Drake, old friend, take care of Jeanine. She's part of our family now, so stop wasting time and ask her to marry you."

The vid winked out. This time, when my tears flowed I didn't blink them back.

TOUGH DECISIONS

Drake

Our reckless hyperspace jump was short—just long enough for a quick emotional purging before our next big decision. Sixteen minutes and a fifth of a light year later, the *Rising Star* popped back into normal space.

I gave Jeanine one last squeeze and sat back in the pilot's seat. "I know it's tough to put our friends out of mind, but we've got some decisions to make."

Jeanine nodded, wiping her eyes. "Like what to do with Landry and Shaw?"

I shook my head. "I'll turn them over to the revolution if I can and space them if I can't. No, we've got to warn the revolution that Royal Intelligence knows the location of the base."

Jeanine knocked her fist against her forehead. "Right. Landry would have made that subspace call right after leaving me at the palace. There's nothing to decide, then. Is there a way to send a subspace call to the base?"

"Yes, but you can be sure Lady Olivia's security team has every planet in the region on the lookout for us. They'll search every Helldiver class starship that comes along, so we need to go straight back to the base."

"Can we get there in time to evacuate the base?"

I ran a hand through my hair. "Maybe. Grant left a course that takes us straight from here to the base. It'll get us there in twenty-six hours, but it's dangerous. Make that *really* dangerous."

"How bad, Drake?"

"Grant gave us a forty-one percent chance of making it. The odds suck, but I don't see any other way."

Jeanine suddenly perked up and leaned over the navigation console. She brought up charts and tapped a few buttons. A few seconds later, a course flashed up on her console. "What about a safe, fifteen-hour jump to a subspace relay?"

Maybe the emotional burden was affecting Jeanine's memory. "No one around here is going to let us land, much less make a subspace call. Warnings from House Kahn, remember?"

"Of course, I remember, honey. But I'll bet I know someone who will ignore the warning." Jeanine turned a tired smile my way. "Don't you think it's about time I met my stepmother?"

"Holy hell! I never even thought of that."

I keyed in Jeanine's course and the *Star* leapt into hyperspace again. Then we checked in on our two prisoners.

Landry was awake and patiently waiting for whatever came next. He didn't say anything, merely nodded when I tossed a couple of ration bars and a bottle of water to him. Shaw was more entertaining, letting his pain and anger overwhelm him. He flung vile curses at us and, when those had no effect, threw his hand at Jeanine. She caught it without flinching.

"You know, Shaw doesn't really have the temperament for a spy." She idly examined the hand. "The RIA must really be hard up for good agents."

"I don't know, Landry is pretty good. From casual brutality to calm indifference, it's all part of the job to him."

Jeanine nodded as she tossed the ration bars and water bottle to Shaw. "Yeah, Landry is...professional."

We turned away, but turned back when Shaw made a frustrated sound. We found him struggling to break the seals on the food with only one hand.

Jeanine met his white hot glare with a smirk. "Are you having trouble opening those, Shaw? If you need help, all you have to do is ask."

"Go to hell!" Shaw snarled.

"Temper, temper, Shaw. Fortunately for you, I'm a generous woman. Despite your insults, I'm going to give you a hand." Jeanine tossed Shaw's hand back to him and closed the door.

"You can be cruel, babe." I slid an arm around her waist. "What should I do to stay on your good side?"

She looked up at me with irresistible eyes. "Fix dinner while I grab a shower?"

"It shall be as you command, my love." I patted her backside as she headed for the bathroom. "Remember, we've only got the shipboard water tank."

The simple routine of cooking let my mind wander, replaying bittersweet memories of my missing friends. Some made me smile or even laugh. Others brought sharp pain. As they were all I had left of my old crew, I treasured every emotion.

Jeanine, wearing one of my shirts and making it look much better than I ever could, joined me and I shared the stories. Like me, she laughed and cried and shared in my celebration of the people who had meant so much to me. To us. And, unworthy as I felt, I bowed my head when Jeanine prayed that my crew had been captured rather than killed.

After dinner, we comforted each other as men and women have done for thousands of years. Finally, emotionally and physically spent, we fell asleep in each other's arms.

Hours later, we arrived at Neert, where House Wilkinson's security fleet was on high alert. "This is the Shield class gunship *NS Rapier* to Helldiver class transport *Rising* Star. You are ordered to reduce speed and prepare to be boarded."

Jeanine gave me a quick look. "You didn't change the transponder?"

"I didn't see the point. It's not like we're going to get in to see Lady Evelyn without making a lot of noise." I keyed the comm and responded to the hail. "This is Drake Haral, captain of the *Rising Star*. We will comply with your command if necessary, but we'd really rather skip all of this and go straight to our audience with Lady Evelyn."

"We have the report from your visit to House Kahn's palace. Rest assured we will blast you into a million pieces if you don't follow my orders to the letter."

"That won't be necessary, *Rapier*, but we are in a bit of a hurry. If you would, please send word to Lady Evelyn that Jeanine is here to see her."

"Her ladyship is a busy woman, *Rising Star*. We do not bother her on the whims of starship captains."

"Trust me, *Rapier*, she'll want to be bothered this time."

"Give me one good reason, otherwise prepare for boarding."

I offered the comm to Jeanine. "Do you want to do the honors?"

She took it. "*Rapier*, my name is Jeanine Langston, but you probably know me better as the Wilkinson Bastard."

Less than a minute later, Neert Control provided landing coordinates on the palace grounds.

MARRY HIM TODAY

Jeanine

I sat in the copilot's seat as Drake shut down the *Rising Star*. He stood and waited for me to join him. To my surprise, I found myself frozen in place. I couldn't even make myself look at Drake.

He held a hand out to me. "I think we're supposed to leave the ship now, babe."

"I know, but..." I waved a hand vaguely. "I don't know."

"If you'd rather not do this, Jeanine, just say the word. I'll fire up the *Star* and we'll leave."

I shook my head. "No, you still have to make that subspace call. I can't let my nerves take away our chance to warn the revolution."

"Then let's get this over with." Drake looked out a starboard viewport. "We shouldn't keep all those uniformed men and women waiting out there. Trust me, standing at attention gets uncomfortable very quickly."

Curiosity thawed my muscles. I stood and took a look at the precision ranks formed up next to the ship. "Do you think they're here to take us into custody before throwing us into the palace oubliette?"

"They look more like an honor guard than prison guards, but

you never know with nobles." Drake shrugged and took my hand. "There's only one way to find out which they are."

I let him lead me to the airlock. Somehow, the airlock cycled far too slowly and much too quickly at the same time. Finally, and before I was ready, Drake and I stepped out of the *Rising Star*.

Every one of the guards snapped to attention as we descended the ramp. Their commander marched up to us and saluted.

"My lady Jeanine, on behalf of Duchess Evelyn and the people of Neert, allow me to welcome you home at last."

Home? How could this place be home to me? I was born on the planet, but Grandfather took me away the very next day. I never came within twenty-five light years of Neert until today. And now this man offered me welcome and called it my home? I opened my mouth to correct him and then closed it again.

Instead, I drew a deep breath and said, "Thank you, commander...?"

"Captain James Pennington, commander of your personal guard, my lady."

I inclined my head in the way I imagined a noblewoman would. "Thank you, Captain Pennington. Please tell these men and women they may relax."

The captain broke his salute and, without a word from him, the rest of the guards settled into...what do they call it in the military vids? Parade rest? Sure, let's go with that.

"Captain Pennington, are all of these men and women my bodyguards?" At the captain's nod, I continued, "This is Captain Drake Haral, formerly of House Wilkinson's Space Patrol. Protect him as you would me."

"Yes, my lady." Captain Pennington motioned toward a waiting ground car. "If you and Captain Haral would come this way? Lady Evelyn awaits you in the palace."

After a very short ride, we followed Captain Pennington down a long hallway to a huge set of double doors. Guards, or maybe uniformed servants, opened the doors as we approached. The captain stopped just within the room.

He snapped to attention once more. "My lady, I am pleased to present Lady Jeanine and Captain Haral."

A tall, regal-looking woman of perhaps sixty years turned my way. Dark eyes regarded me from under equally dark hair though the hair showed occasional streaks of silver. The woman smiled at me and, to my complete surprise, her eyes were as warm as her lips.

"Thank you, Captain Pennington." She nodded to the man. "That will be all for now."

The captain bowed to Lady Evelyn and then to me before backing out of the room. The uniformed men outside closed the doors, leaving us alone with my stepmother.

While I tried to figure out what to do next, Drake gave a proper bow to Lady Evelyn. "My lady, thank you for granting us permission to land."

"It is I who should thank you for bringing my stepdaughter safely to me." To Drake's obvious surprise, Lady Evelyn stepped forward and took his hands in hers. "I know it is far too little and far too late, but please accept my deepest condolences for the loss of your wife and daughter."

His voice stiffly polite, Drake said, "You're too kind, my lady."

"No, I'm not. Had I been kind, I would have said this to you and your crew seven years ago."

Drake's tone softened. "You were still mourning the death of one of your own sons at the time, my lady. He was but two months gone at the time. As a parent, albeit for only a few years, I understand all too well the depth of your loss."

Lady Evelyn shook her head. "That gives me even less excuse, for I also understood what you were going through. Can you find it in your heart to forgive my lapse?"

A genuine smile spread across Drake's face. "I can and I do."

The duchess held his hands for a second longer before dropping them and taking mine. "I shall not wait seven years to offer my condolences over Sir Jared's death. He was a good and honorable man who loved you more than life itself."

"Thank you, my lady."

"Tut, dear, let's drop all of the formal titles. Please call me Evelyn. The same goes for you, Captain Haral."

"Then you must call us by our given names," I said. "But before we do anything else, could Drake use your subspace relay to make a call?"

Evelyn's eyebrows rose in surprise. "Of course. I can have a servant take him there."

"Can you also ensure my call is private and not recorded?" Drake asked.

Evelyn grinned. "Why? Is it likely to get me executed?"

Drake did not respond to her grin. "Only if Royal Intelligence learns of it."

"I see." The grin vanished as soon as it appeared. "Considering how you've been treated by the crown, I suppose I shouldn't be surprised. And considering how the crown stood by and let that butcher from House Kahn slaughter my family, I most sincerely hope your revolution succeeds."

Seconds later, a servant led Drake away, leaving me alone with my stepmother. Once the door was closed again, we sat and faced each other. An awkward silence stretched for several seconds before Evelyn broke it.

"From what I can tell, Drake is a good man. He's a bit of a womanizer, but I suppose you already know that."

"He's not a womanizer anymore," I responded.

"You're in love with him."

"And he's in love with me." I smiled wistfully. "He asked me to marry him."

"I assume you said yes?" At my nod, Evelyn leaned back in her seat. "May I offer you a bit of advice along those lines, Jeanine?"

"You can if you want to," I said, "but it won't do any good. You can't stop me from marrying Drake."

"My dear, I wasn't thinking of stopping you! Quite the opposite." Evelyn leaned forward, her gaze intent. "Marry the man *before* you get Recognized as duchess. Marriage is much more difficult and fraught with complications for nobility, so make sure you're already married before you're elevated. Hell, girl, marry him *today*. I can summon a priest right now if you like."

I felt a thrill of excitement run up my spine. Before I even considered how to answer her, I heard myself say, "Yes, please do!"

Half an hour later, Drake returned from making his call, his step lighter and his face less strained. I met him with a quick kiss and whispered, "You got through and the warning was in time?"

"I did. It took some persuading, but Admiral Pierson is organizing the evacuation now." He looked around at the small gathering of people on the far side of the room. "Um, who are those people with Evelyn?"

"Witnesses. And a priest."

"Have you got to swear an oath or something before you can be recognized?"

"No, honey. They're here for us. You and me."

Drake's eyes widened in sudden comprehension. "Oh. We're getting married."

"Evelyn thinks it's a good idea to marry before I'm duchess, because nobles have all sorts of pressure to marry for political reasons. Since I want to marry for love that means I want to marry you. But only if you want to. I mean—"

Drake placed a hand over my mouth, cutting off my babbling. "Did I ever mention how much I dislike long engagements?"

And so, with a duchess and the captain of my personal guard as witnesses, and without pomp, Drake and I were married.

THIS IS NOT REASSURING

Olivia

"**N**ow, darling, calm down and tell me what's wrong!"

I had a lot I wanted to say. Like *I'll calm down when I damned well choose!* Also, *Don't tell me what to do!* Then there was *Don't take that patronizing tone with me!* And, as much as I wanted to deny it was there, *Be man enough to come over here and make me calm down!*

It all got jumbled up and emerged as another scream of rage as I threw yet another wedding gift at Prince William. He ducked—the man has extremely quick reflexes, I'll give him that—and the crystal whatever-it-was hit the far wall with an extremely satisfying crash. I reveled in the tinkling echo of expensive crystal bouncing across the floor and looked for something else fragile on the tables laden with gifts.

"Olivia, stop that immediately!" The sharp tone cut through every other sound and burrowed past my rage to my reason. When I dropped my arms to my sides and hung my head, Queen Charlotte nodded. "That's more like it."

Her gaze swept the room, taking in the servants scurrying around cleaning up in the wake of my destructive rage and her son only now emerging from his crouch. "All of you—out. Now."

The servants hastened to obey, no doubt thrilled to get away from this scene. William hesitated, looking back and forth between his mother and me. I waited for him to assert himself and demand the right to stay and calm his future bride himself. After a few seconds, the prince averted his gaze from the two women in his life and slunk from the room.

Charlotte interpreted my expression correctly. "You knew what William was like when you agreed to this marriage, Olivia. He has many fine traits, but a backbone is not one of them. At least, not where you and I are concerned."

I knew the queen was right, but I still wasn't quite ready to let go of the last vestiges of my rage. With no other target in sight, I took aim at my future mother-in-law and hurled my barb. "He can be remarkably assertive in bed."

Charlotte smiled, as if giving me a little credit for trying, and said, "Like father, like son. I strongly recommend you take advantage of William's true area of expertise. You're a passionate woman. Oh, your intellect is more than capable of reining in that passion in public, but that makes it all the more necessary for you to let it run wild in private. Trust me, I know this from…intimate… experience."

I conceded defeat, realizing yet again that nothing I said would ever shock the queen. So I settled for striving to meet her extremely high expectations. I released my anger and forced myself to calm down. "Thank you, Charlotte. I'll try to remember that."

The queen regarded me for a moment as if searching my soul and then nodded. "Now, dear, what's all of this about? I assume that subspace call from Gaunner is behind it?"

"Yes. Two members of Royal Intelligence delivered the Wilkinson Bastard to my palace. Quite the wedding gift, you'd think. Only things did not go as planned."

"She escaped?"

"With considerable help. A commando team infiltrated the palace, shut down all of its defenses, and broke her out. My guards captured the commando team, but the Bastard got away in a spaceship someone landed in a palace courtyard." I grimaced at the images Colin showed me of the garden. When my mother was alive, it was her favorite place to relax. "The ship jumped into hyperspace a mere one hundred kilometers above the planet."

"Well, that was quite daring of the pilot. Too bad he doesn't work for us." Charlotte considered the situation and then asked, "Do you think the ship was destroyed making that jump?"

"I doubt it. The Bastard has always been lucky like that, ever since we tracked her down."

Charlotte gave me a stern look. "Consistent luck is called skill, dear. Never get into the habit of attributing to luck anything that can also be the result of skill. It is far better to overestimate an opponent than to underestimate her. At worst, you'll be properly prepared for her. At best, you'll crush her utterly."

I considered Charlotte's words carefully before nodding. "I understand, Charlotte, and you make quite a lot of sense."

"Good, I'm glad you think so. You're not going to like what I'm about to say, but you must keep a tight rein on your temper and consider this carefully." The queen watched me until she was certain she had my full attention. "When I asked you to marry William, I did not fully comprehend the depths of your obsession with the Wilkinson Bastard. If I had, we'd have held this conversation before I offered you the throne."

That got my attention. Was the queen tossing me aside because of this thrice-damned Bastard? If I lost the prince because of the Bastard, I'd dedicate my life to destroying her and House Wilkinson.

"In most ways, Olivia, you are exactly what I hoped you would be—thoughtful, relentless, cunning, observant, and appropriately manipulative enough to handle my son and, through him, the nobles. You're almost the perfect daughter-in-law."

My chin rose in challenge. "Almost?"

"Yes, dear, almost." Charlotte met my challenging gaze with one of her own. "You are too provincial in your thinking. You are about to have the entire kingdom laid at your feet, yours to rule, yet you remain obsessed with this Wilkinson child." The queen's gaze softened just a bit. "I know you blame her for your brother's death and wish to crush her under your heel. That's fine—provided it doesn't distract you from ruling the kingdom."

"It won't, Charlotte. Especially once the Bastard is dead."

The queen sighed. "Listen to yourself, child. In one sentence you assure me your attention is on the prize before you. In the next, you demonstrate just how obsessed you are with this woman. This is not reassuring, Olivia."

I struggled to keep my expression impassive while my mind raced to find the right words to reassure the queen. I found them quickly enough, but also realized just how difficult they would be to utter. I did not let that stop me.

"When I take my wedding vows, I will also renounce my claim to the Duchy of Neert. Here and now, I give you my word that I will abandon my pursuit of the Wilkinson Bastard at the same time."

Charlotte smiled and her eyes lit with pleasure. "Well done, Olivia. Though you need not renounce your claim to Neert. That will happen automatically when you complete your vows."

I felt my eyes widen in surprise. "I...did not know that, Charlotte."

"Very few do, dear. Between now and the wedding, you and I will select an appropriate minor noble in Neert for promotion. We can offer it as a surprise ending to the wedding ceremony." Charlotte gave me a slight smile. "And you may maintain your vendetta against the Bastard, just treat it as more of a hobby than your reason for living. But should the opportunity present itself, by all means crush the young woman. Just make sure it can't be traced back to us."

"I wouldn't have it any other way, Charlotte."

The queen took my arm and led me toward the door. "Let's clear out of here so the servants can clean up and find replacements for the gifts you broke."

"Must they? That crystal thing was hideous!"

"Yes, they must. I'm afraid that hideous thing was a gift from Bernard's mother." Charlotte patted my arm. "Now, let's go find that son of mine. You can teach him that rage and passion are intertwined and the greater the rage, the greater the passion afterward."

Along the way, my future mother-in-law offered several very detailed techniques she claimed would enthrall any man. She was right, too.

A BRILLIANT PLAN

Drake

I woke up next to Jeanine, just as I had for the last several weeks. This morning felt different. Our surroundings were luxurious in the extreme, but that wasn't it. Despite the vast bed, we lay so close I felt her warmth. I gazed on the same lovely face, relaxed and surrounded by tousled locks of flame. I heard the same deep, even breathing as she slept. Her same scent, sweet and promising of passion, tickled my nose. I longed to reach out and caress her soft skin, but touch was the one sense I didn't allow myself. Not yet. Not while my sleeping wife played this sensuous symphony of the senses for me.

My wife. *That* was what was truly different. Not that I had a wife, but that 'wife' no longer meant anger and anguish. Now, 'wife' was restored to its true, glorious meaning. Now, wife meant love and longing. Love for the woman before me. Longing for the life we would build together. Now, 'wife' meant Jeanine.

She stirred, her hand moving beneath the covers. I gasped as she touched me. A sultry smile spread across her face. Heavy-lidded eyes opened, revealing bright blue eyes.

"I see you're already up." Her voice was soft. Her warm breath played across my face. "I'd hate to waste that."

She flowed into my arms. The symphony of senses, now

directed by Jeanine, moved from adagio to allegro. But still sensuous—deeply, lovingly sensuous.

Eventually, hunger of a more pedestrian kind drove us from our honeymoon room. A patiently waiting servant led us to Lady Evelyn and a lavish breakfast. The dowager duchess welcomed us warmly. She led the conversation while we concentrated on eating. By the time our appetites were sated, Lady Evelyn had our story from the time we met until we landed in her backyard. We glossed over our involvement with the rebels, simply referring to it as a secretive organization. Our hostess wasn't fooled, but it gave her some plausible deniability.

When we pushed our plates away, Evelyn turned a smile on Jeanine. "I have a visitor who would very much like to meet you, Jeanine."

My wife's hands flew to her mouth as her eyes widened. "My... mother?"

"Yes, dear. Are you up to meeting her?"

Jeanine nodded, her eyes blinking rapidly. She stood and reached a hand to me.

I gently kissed the hand. "Unless you need me, I think this should be a private reunion, babe."

She paused for a thoughtful second, smiled, and followed Evelyn from the room.

Several minutes later, Evelyn returned and took a seat across from me. She answered my unasked question. "All things considered, the reunion is going well. I sent for Peggy—that's Jeanine's mother—last night and explained the situation. Arthur told Peggy her baby was stillborn, and I never told her otherwise. The poor woman hates me right now—as well she should—but she is happy to finally meet her daughter."

"How is Jeanine handling it?"

"She was stone-faced and under rigid control until Peggy held out her arms to her." A wistful smile stole across Evelyn's face. "Despite the twenty-five years she's lost with her daughter, I envy

Peggy the time to come. What I wouldn't give for more time with even one of my children..."

Before I could offer any comfort to her, Lady Evelyn followed Jeanine's example and reigned in her emotions. "I'm afraid I don't have time to be maudlin. We have to decide what you and your lovely wife are going to do next."

"Jeanine and I have given that careful thought. We have a plan, but we'll need your help."

One of Evelyn's eyebrows rose gracefully. "As I told Jeanine in the vid message attached to her DNA scan results, there is little I can do to help. I hold my position only until the Star Stone Recognizes a legitimate heir. My political position is weak, so I have no allies among the nobles in Court. Beyond granting you access to my communications array, I can't think of any other aid I can give to you."

"I can. Or, in truth, Jeanine could. This is all her idea." I considered how best to proceed and decided on a gradual approach. "Am I safe in assuming you won't be attending Olivia's wedding in two weeks?"

"And provide a handy target for the barbed tongues of nobles? No, thank you."

"Jeanine and I want you to reconsider." Evelyn opened her mouth, but I silenced her with a raised hand. "And we want you to bring Jeanine and me to the ceremony as part of your retinue."

Evelyn considered this. "Go on."

"The ceremony culminates with Olivia and Prince William requesting Recognition of their union and elevation of Lady Olivia to Princess Olivia, right?" Evelyn nodded, and I continued. "I assume every eye will follow the newly married couple from the Star Stone to present themselves to King Bernard."

"Of course. A handsome prince. His beautiful princess. The heady allure of power. Yes, they'll attract gazes like a magnet attracts iron filings." Evelyn shrugged. "What of it?"

As I explained our plan, a sharp smile slowly spread across Lady Evelyn's face.

When I finished, she said, "That is brilliant! And deliciously cruel. I wouldn't miss it!"

Before Evelyn and I could discuss Jeanine's plan further, my wife burst into the room. I couldn't tell if Jeanine was hugging or towing the woman next to her. A mere glance showed the women were related. Both redheads. Both slender, though the older woman's weight had settled a bit with age. Both with blue eyes still bright with tears. Their expressions differed though.

Excited anticipation was written on Jeanine's face. Peggy wore nervous trepidation.

Jeanine spoke as she came toward me. "Drake? This is my mother. Her name is Peggy. Don't you think we look like each other? I mean, you don't even need a DNA test or anything, right?"

I put a finger on Jeanine's lips. "You're babbling, babe."

"I know, honey, but I'm just so excited!" She gave me a quick kiss. "A few weeks ago I was all alone. But now I've got a husband and a *mother*." Jeanine suddenly wrapped her arms around Peggy. "I always wanted a mother."

And the two women dissolved into tears again. I simply smiled and watched, remembering another mother hugging her daughter. My eyes misted, but pain brought by the memory was tempered with the contentment brought by the scene before me.

A slight sound drew my attention away from the joyful mother and daughter. Lady Evelyn slipped from the room. Her shoulders heaved. A hand covered her mouth, muting the sobs she couldn't stifle. It gave me a glimpse of the woman hidden by the title. A glimpse of a woman who buried six children. A glimpse of pain six times worse than my own. A glimpse of a woman without hope for the happiness Jeanine rekindled in me.

Then Jeanine pulled me into the hug with her mother. "Drake, aren't you going to say something to your mother-in-law?"

"Only if you let me." Jeanine punched me in the arm. I grinned at Peggy. "Do you see what I have to put up with, ma'am?"

Peggy pretended offense at my words. "Don't you ma'am me,

Drake. Even if we don't really know each other yet, we're family. You got that?"

"Yes, ma'am!" I held my hands up, ready to fend off more arm punches. "I mean, yes, Peggy. And thank you."

Peggy's brows drew down. "For what? Treating my son-in-law like family?"

"A little of that, but mostly for Jeanine."

"Much as I regret saying it, I didn't do anything to make Jeanine what she is today."

"Of course you did." I took Peggy's hands and looked into her eyes. "*You* created her. *You* carried her. *You* gave birth to her. *You* did all that because you loved her. And you kept loving her, even when you thought she was stillborn. I believe love has power, Peggy. I believe your love crossed light years. I believe it guided and protected Jeanine throughout her life. So, yes, thank you."

The next thing I knew, two redheads enveloped me in another hug and the tears flowed again.

Through her tears, Peggy said, "I can see why you love him, Jeanine."

"Yeah," my wife said, sniffling, "he is pretty damned wonderful."

It went like that for a long time. Smiles, memories, tight hugs, sudden tears. Dry your eyes. Repeat. Eventually, Jeanine and Peggy ran out of tears and questions and rambling stories—at least for the moment—and we managed to fit in some lunch. After I told Peggy of Evelyn's tearful departure, my mother-in-law was even willing to have Evelyn join us for lunch. While conversation lagged, and we all leapt at any conversational gambit, it was a start. By the end, Peggy was at least cordial with the duchess.

After lunch, I settled in with the palace's subspace relay and a list of message drops Jana included in the data packet she sent to my crew. Jana already knew what happened on Gaunner since the news was playing up the 'terrorist attack' on the princess-to-be's home. Royal Intelligence laid the blame squarely on revolutionary forces, the same ones who, according to Lady Olivia, blew up her ship on its approach to the capital.

Of more interest was the news that wasn't reported to the public. The Royal Navy found our rebel base, but not before the evacuation I fought for. I felt my gut relax at that news and wondered where the fallback base was.

I filled Jana in on our plan, asking her to find out as much as she could about the Recognition ceremony. We made arrangements to reconnect when Jeanine and I landed on Xapreathea. Then we wiped all of our messages and abandoned the IDs and message drops we used.

Next, I paid a visit to Lady Evelyn's makeshift prison, ensuring Landry and Shaw were well contained. Satisfied with those arrangements, I returned to my new family. The next day, we held a quiet celebration for Jeanine's twenty-fifth birthday as she came of Recognition age.

The following morning, Jeanine and I joined Lady Evelyn's advance retinue, those sent ahead of the duchess to prepare for her arrival. We boarded one of the duchy's starships and began the last leg of our Recognition run.

The trip from Neert to Xapreathea felt...odd. The starship was too crowded. Our room was too big. Our bed was too big. The food was too good. There was too little for us to do. You can only do so much advance planning before you repeat yourself for the third or fourth time. By the end of the second day, Drake and I had done what we could. Plans were set. Messages were sent. Arrangements were out of our hands. We were at loose ends.

Did I mention the big bed? I think I did. I should mention it again. And again. And again. And...well, you get the idea.

During one of our entwined moments-after, I summoned the courage to ask Drake a question. "When this is all over, do you want children?"

His eyes cracked open. "Hm?"

Great, Drake was taking an after-sex nap. I almost backed off from the question. Then my resolve strengthened. "Children. You know, miniature humans?"

"I know what children are, babe." A sleepy smile stretched his lips. "And I know where they come from—as I hope I proved to your satisfaction."

"Multiple times." I propped myself up on one elbow and

captured Drake's eyes with mine. "Please, I'm serious. Do you want children? And don't dodge the question by asking what I want."

Drake nodded, looking thoughtful. He was quiet for so long I feared he was trying to find a way to let me down gently. When he finally spoke, he didn't meet my eyes.

"Nothing in the universe brought Heather and me more joy than Candi. Everything was brighter and better because she lived. And everything was darker and worse because she died."

I looked away from Drake, blinking away tears. His reaction was what I'd feared. I did my best to take a light tone of voice when I said, "I understand. I just had—"

"I'm not finished, Jeanine." He took my head in his hands and turned my gaze toward him. "I want that brightness back in my life. I want to rock our babies to sleep. I want to tell bedtime stories. I want to dance with our daughters while you dance with our sons. I want to share that boundless joy with you." He pulled me close and kissed me lovingly. "Yes, Jeanine, I want children. With you, just in case you weren't sure of that."

Then words were no longer necessary. We practiced making babies well into the night.

Six days later, we landed on Xapreathea, directly on the grounds of the Duchy of Neert's capital-world palace. Armed with the best false identities the duchy could provide, Drake and I were ready for anything. Needlessly so. Already overwhelmed by pre-wedding traffic, we were brusquely put in a landing queue and landed without a visit from customs. A single low-level bureaucrat met us at the landing field. She checked us off from a list, barely glancing at the proffered identity cards.

An hour later, we met with Mr. Dogan, Lady Evelyn's local head of security. The duchess assured us he was absolutely trustworthy, noting he had been her eldest daughter's bodyguard. He confirmed our instructions were followed to the letter and relayed everything he'd gotten from Jana.

"The young woman requests a call from Lady Jeanine at m'lady's earliest convenience," he wrapped up.

"I'm not lady anything, yet, Mr. Dogan. Everyone called me that on Neert, and it never felt right," I told him. "Just call me Jeanine. If you truly insist, you can add 'Lady' to that after I'm Recognized."

"That wouldn't be proper, Miss Lang-." The man stopped himself and paused in thought for a few seconds. "Now that you're married, 'Miss' isn't proper, either. Might I call you Mrs. Haral?"

My eyes widened in surprise at the name he chose. I'd never even given thought to what others would call me. All my life, I was simply Jeanine. I gave my husband a sidelong glance, wondering how he would react.

He met my gaze and smiled, unbothered by the old fashioned form of address. With Drake's tacit agreement, I said, "That would be fine, Mr. Dogan. And quite proper."

"Thank you, Mrs. Haral." The security man smiled at me. "I'll pop off and call Miss Ward while you and your husband settle in."

"That's very kind of you, Mr. Dogan."

"Not at all, ma'am." The older man stopped at the door, looking back at me. "I've waited nearly half of my lifetime for you to come along, Mrs. Haral. I've never forgiven myself for surviving when those bastards—no offense intended, ma'am—killed Miss Bianca. I enjoyed watching the Butcher burn three years ago. And I'll enjoy watching you ruin that Kahn woman's wedding just as much."

"I know what it's like to lose someone, Mr. Dogan, as does Drake. We won't let you down." An idea came to me and I voiced it immediately. "I do hope you'll stay on with us after I'm Recognized as the Duchess of Neert. When Drake and I have children, we'll want an experienced man in charge of their security detail."

The man stared at me for so long I wondered if I'd struck him dumb. His mouth opened and closed twice before he finally found his voice. "That's very kind of you, Mrs. Haral. But I couldn't protect Miss Bianca. You don't want a failure watching over your children."

"You're right, I don't want a failure. But I do want you."

"Why, Mrs. Haral?"

"Because you won't let yourself fail again. I can see that in your eyes." I walked to the man and stared hard into his eyes. "I won't take no for an answer."

"Bless you, ma'am. I- I'd be honored."

"Good." I returned to Drake's side. "Please bring Jana to us when she arrives."

After the door closed behind Mr. Dogan, Drake lifted me up and gave me a big kiss. "Your people are going to love you."

"Because I gave a loyal man a job? I think you—"

"Not because you gave him a job. He *has* one of those." Drake put me down but held my eyes with his. "God above, woman, don't you realize what you did? You gave Mr. Dogan absolution."

"I think you're overstating the case, honey, but I won't argue with you. Especially since we still have a lot to do before Jana arrives."

Drake was off making some arrangements with the palace staff when Mr. Dogan brought Jana to our room. She gave me a congratulatory hug, adding, "I'm not mad at you for not inviting me to the wedding, but I'll be very displeased if you don't invite me to the formal wedding."

"Um, what formal wedding?"

"Jeanine, duchesses do not get married in tiny weddings with just a priest and two witnesses."

"But I'm not a duchess yet. I'm just Jeanine."

Jana rolled her eyes dramatically. "But you're going to be a duchess. You've seen how excited everyone is for the royal wedding. Don't you think the people in the Duchy of Neert deserve a little excitement, too?"

"Okay... Why don't we wait until all of this is over? Then we'll see about a fancy wedding." We sat down in facing chairs. "Have you got anything new for us?"

"I think so. While doing the research into the Recognition ceremony, I stumbled across something very interesting." Jana looked around the suite. "Is Drake here?"

"No, but he'll be back soon."

Jana shrugged. "Maybe it's just as well. He might not like what I've got for you."

Jana launched into a succinct explanation of her find and the uncertainties behind it. But she was wrong about Drake—he wouldn't merely dislike what she was telling me. He would absolutely hate it.

"I wouldn't blame you if you didn't do it," Jana wrapped up, "but I thought you'd want to know."

I nodded slowly. "You were right."

"Do you think you're going to do it?"

Before I could answer, the door opened and Drake asked, "Do what?"

"Hold a fancy wedding after I'm recognized as duchess," I replied, giving Jana a significant look. "Jana thinks the people of Neert would really go for it."

Drake didn't even give this any thought. "We'll do whatever you want, babe."

I smiled at Drake, all the while wondering if I had the courage to act on Jana's information. The wedding was four days away. Surely, that was plenty of time to make a life or death decision.

TRANSFORMATIONS

Drake

Jeanine and I were run ragged in the days following our arrival. After we got our bearings, we spent a lot of time with a variety of specialists Jana found for us.

We toured the grounds with a woman who truly deserved the title 'lady thief.' That's not just because she had impeccable manners and dressed in the latest fashion. She also had enough noble blood to actually *be* Lady something-or-other. No, she didn't give us her real name. Nor do I blame her. She pointed out seven different blind spots in the palace's vid coverage where an assassin or thief could enter the grounds. She provided a comprehensive list of problems with the alarm system. When examining the locks, she actually said, "Tut tut. These will never do."

Leaving the security issues in Mr. Dogan's hands, Jeanine and I next met with a surveillance expert. We presented him with the section of the estate that would be open during Lady Evelyn's pre-wedding party.

If you're like me, you're thinking, "Why would Lady Evelyn throw a party for the prince and soon-to-be princess?" The answer, apparently, is that's how things are done among the great houses. Of course, parties aren't merely celebrations among the nobility.

Every single decision—from silverware patterns to food selections to decorations to the seating chart—conveys a message to those in the know. Though Lady Evelyn's party was announced late and, as a result, was an afternoon soirée with a late lunch rather than an evening dinner gala, Lady Evelyn's social secretary assured me everyone who was anyone would attend.

"They will flock to the palace in hopes of salacious gossip and to see how elegantly Lady Evelyn presents her slights and insults to Lady Olivia," she told me. "My lady is a master of the art."

I couldn't wrap my brain around this approach to partying. "I guess calling Olivia a conniving bitch is right out?"

The secretary's eyes widened in dismay. "Goodness, gracious no! Lady Evelyn would never do something so...comm- um, *uncouth*...as that."

"Okay. Can you give me an example of something Lady Evelyn *would* do?"

"All of the stemware is made from fire crystals." The secretary beamed at me, obviously pleased with her lady's selection.

At a complete loss, I shrugged. "So?"

The woman rolled her eyes. "It's an obvious reference to Lord Robert's fiery death three years ago. The true insult occurs when Lady Evelyn toasts the happy couple and Lady Olivia has no choice but to drink from the fire crystal stemware. People will speak of it for years to come!"

I simply nodded, pretending I understood and then escaped back to our surveillance expert. His team installed hidden cams and directional audio receivers all over the ballroom and surrounding rooms. We left when they began training Mr. Dogan's security personnel in the operation of the new equipment.

I don't know where Jana found the team of make-up artists we visited next, but they were amazing. The process of selecting a new look for a person is far more detailed than I ever imagined. And far more tedious for the person receiving the new look.

They examined us in minute detail. Skin tones were noted. Then they made lewd suggestions until we blushed. That skin tone was noted. Hair color was carefully examined. As was eye color. The shape of our ears. The height of our cheekbones. The curve of our necks. Our posture—sitting, standing, bending, kneeling, squatting. Our walk. Our run. The shape of our backsides.

After having my groin carefully evaluated—to laughter from Jeanine, no doubt remembering my amusement when the attention was on her breasts—I finally said, "This is ridiculous. Just change our hair color and give us some make-up to change our faces and let us get on with our lives."

The woman in charge of the crew confronted me. "Do I tell you how to do your job? Whatever your job is."

"I'm a starship pilot," I growled.

"And what would you say to a passenger who asked why you wasted time calculating a course when you could just point the ship in the right direction and go?"

"I'd say they should stick to something they knew."

"Precisely. We are not merely changing your appearance slightly. We are changing who you are." She returned to her notes. "When we are finished, your own wife won't recognize you."

The woman was right. Her teams transformed us to the point I didn't recognize Jeanine until she spoke. The teams worked with us far into the night, altering our walk, our posture, everything about us, until I felt there was nothing left of the original Drake.

After they returned us to ourselves, the woman in charge said, "We shall return each day to work on your transformation. It's a pity we don't have time for a speech coach, but perhaps you can simply remain silent until it is time to reveal yourselves."

"Wait, you know what we're doing and why we need the…transformation?" Jeanine asked.

"Not at all—nor do I wish to know," the woman replied. "But most of those who engage my services want a public revelation in the end."

When Lady Evelyn arrived at the estate, Jeanine and I attended fully transformed. The duchess didn't so much as look at us during the procession to the palace. She greeted members of her staff—

from the highest to the lowest positions—by name. Then she asked her seneschal for introductions to the new members of the staff.

Lady Evelyn turned to us and smiled. "You may start with these two."

Without batting an eye, the seneschal said, "My lady, I am pleased to present Lady Jeanine Langston and her husband, Captain Drake Haral."

The duchess's eyes widened just a bit, the only visible indication of surprise she gave. "Well, I think those disguises will do."

Bowing slightly, I said, "Transformations, Lady Evelyn. According to she who recreated us, mere disguises are for actors and costume parties."

"Indeed," she nodded, then her mouth widened into a smile. "I come bearing good news, Drake. My spies report that all but one of your crew survived. They are being held captive by House Kahn. I swear, we will find a way to get them back."

"Thank you, my lady!" My vision blurred for a few seconds, "I... cannot say how much that news means to me."

Lady Evelyn patted my arm and smiled in understanding before leading us into the house.

The next afternoon, three days before the wedding, Lady Evelyn threw the palace open and welcomed everyone who was anyone. Jeanine and I attended, fully transformed and identified as Lady Evelyn's third cousins, visiting Xapreathea for the first time.

It started out quite well. Being little more than the galactic equivalent of country bumpkins, no one expected Jeanine or me to provide scintillating conversation nor possess knowledge even remotely interesting to the guests. Beyond simple pleasantries, no one spoke to us. According to the social secretary, even those pleasantries were veiled slights, jabs to see if we were cultured enough to take offense. We weren't, saving us the trouble of pretending we didn't understand. Quickly ignored by the guests, Jeanine and I were free to roam and listen in on any conversation we wished. We didn't learn anything of interest, but it was good practice.

A fashionable hour past lunchtime, a fanfare announced the arrival of His Highness Prince William and his intended, Lady Olivia. Jeanine and I took our positions behind Lady Evelyn and awaited an introduction to the couple. After everything we'd been through—the tears, the fighting, and the anger—we were finally coming face-to-face with the woman behind our misery.

Watching Lady Olivia approach, I felt as if she looked too... normal. Her blonde hair, blue eyes, and pale skin were offset by an elegant black gown that showed exactly the proper amount of cleavage and leg. I was so busy trying to see the evil manipulator inside the lovely woman coming our way that I didn't notice anything else until Jeanine gasped. I followed her gaze, which went past Lady Olivia to the man behind her.

It was the man who killed Jeanine's protector. It was Sir Phillip, Recognized knight of House Kahn.

LADY EVELYN'S BALL

Olivia

William and I entered Lady Evelyn's ballroom as the royal fanfare sounded throughout the vast room. Played by our usual royal musicians, the music was uplifting and alive with a pomp and majesty I never heard before. The musicians had not improved overnight, so something else affected their playing. It was easy to figure out what—the ballroom itself.

Superior design—in the architecture and in the decorating—provided superior acoustics. The fanfare reached every corner of the room but did not echo back to the listener. I wished the royal palace was this well designed. Damn the ballroom for impressing me. Damn the Wilkinsons for building it. And damn me for wanting it!

Evelyn directed a warm and inviting smile toward us. Unless you looked deeply into the woman's eyes you'd never notice her hatred. I looked. I saw. And my false smile turned genuine.

Lady Evelyn dropped into a deep, graceful curtsy. Just behind her, a woman I didn't know gave a clumsy imitation of her hostess. The bow from the man at the woman's side was more successful, but bowing takes little practice. All around the ballroom, the other guests followed their hostess's lead.

"Thank you for your kind welcome. Please, do rise," William called. Taking Lady Evelyn's hand, my intended kissed it lightly. "You have been too long away from the capital, my lady. It gladdened my heart when you accepted our invitation to the ceremony."

William sounded completely sincere. That's because he was. Like most men, William was ridiculously direct. If he dislikes a man, he cannot hide it. Nor does he even make the attempt. What must it be like to engage in social interactions void of subtle slights and veiled insults? How relaxing it must be to laugh simply because a jest is funny. How refreshing it must be to say whatever comes to mind without considering the consequences from a dozen different angles. How lovely it must be to meet biting insults with the slap of a glove and the point of a blade. But that freedom is only for men.

It falls to women to tally the social scores. It falls to women to interpret the civil hierarchy. It falls to women to navigate safely around the sharp shoals of society without sinking their family and their fortune. It falls to women to continue the family line. Women civilize their sons. Women educate their daughters. Women guide their men through dangers men cannot perceive.

Exhausting as a woman's life can be, I do not know any woman who would trade their life for that of their man. And so I sharpened my verbal daggers and prepared for the battles to come.

William concluded his pleasantries with our hostess and stepped aside.

"You look as beautiful as ever, Olivia. You wore black three years ago when last I saw you." Lady Evelyn took my one of hands and her smile widened. "As always, you wear it *so* well. In truth, I believe black is a most appropriate color for *all* members of House Kahn."

Leave it to the bitch to throw my brother's fate in my face right from the start. Well, two could play *that* game.

"Nonsense, my lady. You've worn black many times over the years and always looked devastated." My free hand flew to my mouth. "Oh dear, I meant devastat*ing*. Please accept my humble apology!"

Evelyn's eyes narrowed ever so slightly. I let actual humor creep into my eyes. Yes, you conniving harpy, I *did* just use your children against you.

"No apology is necessary," Evelyn replied. "With the patter of tiny feet in your future, I find myself wondering if your children will inherit your facility with black? Or will it fall to you to wear the color for them?"

The bare susurration from gasps reached my ears as the women around us reacted to this exchange. Damn, but the woman was good! Unable to find an appropriate counterattack, I withdrew from the field.

Turning to the out-of-place pair behind Evelyn, I asked, "And who have we here? I don't believe I know them."

I felt movement behind me. Sir Phillip appeared at my elbow, his attention riveted on the pair. I jostled him with my elbow. When he looked my way, I glared him back several steps.

Ignoring this byplay, Evelyn motioned to the man. "This is Marcus Cherral, my third cousin, and his wife Alice. They're visiting Xapreathea for the first time, drawn from their distant colony to be as close as possible to your royal wedding."

The man bowed stiffly over my hand and spoke. In a truly atrocious attempt at a capital accent, he said, "Honored am I to bask in the radiance of your light, Your Highness."

His wife attempted another graceless curtsy. Her capital accent was less pathetic than her husband's, but only marginally. "As am I, Your Radiance."

Evelyn almost hid her dismay at the antics of her bumpkin relatives. I caught the slight flattening of her smile though. True delight lit the smile I bestowed on the pair before me.

"How very sweet of the two of you!" I turned my smile on William. "Can you imagine, traveling this far just to be *near* our wedding, darling?"

William, already bored with the exchange, didn't even try to say anything original. "Yes, quite...um...sweet."

I beamed at the fools, their expressions all agog. "But why settle for being near when you could *attend* the ceremony with Lady Evelyn. Please tell me you will!"

The bumpkins' eyes widened in amazement and their heads bobbed up and down. In a comical parody of her embarrassing relatives, Lady Evelyn's narrowed in dismay and her head shook back and forth.

I clapped my hands together in delight. "Perfect! Now, Evelyn, I expect to see these two with you at the ceremony. Don't disappoint me."

Having unexpectedly regained the societal upper hand from our hostess, I let William lead me away. My prince spoke to one of his friends, giving me a chance to confront Sir Phillip.

"Why did you crowd me back there?" The knight took a step back from my anger. "You could have distracted me at the wrong moment."

He gave me a perplexed expression. Yet another man totally blind to the combat waged right before his eyes. The knight sketched a slight bow. "Your pardon, my lady. Something about that pair just didn't feel right."

I resisted the urge to roll my eyes. "Of course, they didn't feel right. They're completely out of their depth and are too stupid to realize it."

"Not that, my lady," Sir Phillip said, his expression thoughtful. "They seemed familiar somehow."

"Perhaps you spend too much time on the fringes of the kingdom and among *their* kind. You've forgotten how civilized people act."

I meant that as an insult, but the knight nodded slowly. "You may be right, my lady. Thank you."

I dismissed the thanks with a wave of my hand and resumed my place on William's arm. Basking in my victory over Evelyn, I found the party far more entertaining than I'd anticipated. I didn't even bat an eye when the servants passed out the fire crystal goblets and Lady Evelyn toasted the fires of passion consuming William and me.

A MOST IRREGULAR DISPLAY

Jeanine

As the last of Lady Evelyn's guests left the grounds, I relaxed for the first time in hours.

I leaned against Drake. "God, that was exhausting. Grandfather trained me to play roles, but only for a short time—pretending to be someone else to get through checkpoints or away from various officials."

Drake kissed the top of my head. "I know what you mean, babe. You did great though. Especially all those times Lady Olivia circled back around to us."

I lifted my face to him and stole a quick kiss on the lips. "Do you think Sir Phillip saw through our transformations?"

"How would the knight see through your transformations?" Lady Evelyn asked. "I've spent days with you and they fooled me. According to your story, he only spent a couple of hours with you, Drake, and that was weeks ago. He's never even met Jeanine."

"Would you have recognized us if you heard us speak, my lady?" Drake released me and began loosening the adhesive holding my wig in place. "Sir Phillip spoke with both of us. You can bet he would have recognized us if we used our normal voices."

"That's why you both used those horrible capital accents?"

"It was Drake's idea," I replied. "We didn't have time to discuss it. I just copied him when it was my turn to speak."

"That was a stroke of unintentional genius, Drake. Olivia was floundering in our conversation until you put on your bumpkin show."

"Is it always like that between you and Olivia?" At Evelyn's nod, I continued, "The two of you were so cutting, I'm surprised there wasn't actual blood flowing."

Drake looked back and forth between Evelyn and me. "What *are* you talking about?"

"I'll explain it after I transform back into myself." Drake pulled off my wig, freeing me to work on his. "That includes taking a nice, long, hot shower."

"The important thing is Olivia thinks she insulted and embarrassed me by inviting you," Evelyn said. "If you really were a couple of bumpkin relations, she'd be right. Without that accent, though, it would have taken a lot more work for me to convince Olivia to issue the invitation. Well done, Drake."

"It was sheer luck on my part, so please stop complimenting me." Drake pulled off his wig, sighing with relief as he did. He took my hand and led me toward our suite. "Would you like help scrubbing your back, babe?"

"Take your time and enjoy yourselves," Evelyn said. "I'll visit Dogan. Perhaps we recorded something interesting from Olivia, William, and Phillip during the party."

A couple of hours later, refreshed from our shower and a nap, Drake and I joined Evelyn for a light dinner. The duchess filled us in on her findings while we ate.

"Your lady thief's analysis proved useful. Dogan's men stopped an intruder armed with the latest surveillance tech. They relieved the man of his equipment and—taking a cue from your handling of Landry and Shaw—have him locked up in the basement." Evelyn flashed a conspiratorial smile at us. "I suggest you release him once Jeanine is Recognized as the Duchess of Neert. It never hurts to have such a man in your debt."

I grew up thinking my grandfather was a criminal genius, so forging a tie with an actual master criminal appealed to me. Nodding in agreement, I asked, "Did we get anything from the cams or audio receivers?"

"Yes. I'm afraid Drake was right to worry about Sir Phillip. He felt there was something familiar about the pair of you." Evelyn made calming motions with her hands at our startled expressions. "He never once used your names, so don't get too worked up about it. Olivia was still reveling in her 'victory' over me and summarily dismissed his concerns. I think you're safe, though I don't want you leaving the house until it's time for the wedding."

Drake glanced my way. "I completely agree with your step-mother. We're much too close to our goal to take foolish risks now."

"Okay." Despite my assurance, Drake kept watching me. Finally, I dropped my fork and glared back. "What do you think I'm going to do, honey? Walk down the street wearing nothing but a sign that says Wilkinson Bastard?"

"No, of course not, babe."

"Good." Picking up my fork, I resumed eating. "I'm going to follow a strict triple-S routine for the next three days."

"A what?"

"Triple-S." I counted off on my fingers. "First, I'm going to catch up on my sleep. Second, I'm going to study up on the Recognition ceremony."

When I didn't continue, Drake asked, "What's the third S?"

I propped my chin in one hand and fluttered my eyelashes at him. "Take your time and think it through, husband. I'm sure you'll figure it out."

Drake grinned in sudden comprehension. "I fully support this program of yours—*especially* the third S!"

Three days later, fully rested and just starting to feel boredom setting in, Drake and I transformed one more time into back-world bumpkins. As a show of our supposed disfavor with Lady Evelyn, we rode in a separate—and much less grand—car.

The palace attendants, obviously acting on orders, helped Drake and me from our car before doing the same for Evelyn. He and I stared all around with slack jaws and wide eyes, embellishing our bumpkin image. We tagged along behind a stone-faced Lady Evelyn, whipping our heads back and forth as if afraid of missing something.

And then we were there. A herald announced us—Lady Evelyn first, this time—and we descended the sweeping staircase to the vast chamber below. The Star Stone stood in the center of the room, its pulsing crimson radiance casting everyone in red.

It reminded me of all the blood spilled so I could reach the palace. The friends and family who gave so much so I could be here today appeared in my mind. In a fierce whisper, I made one last promise to them.

"I will not fail you."

Lady Evelyn chose our arrival time with great care though not without some resistance from Drake and me.

"We'll arrive a tad beyond fashionably late, something that will irritate Olivia quite a bit," Evelyn told us two days before the wedding. She had smiled at our confusion. "This wedding is *the* social event of the decade. Unimportant nobles will arrive ridiculously early in the hopes of currying favor with the royal family. Minor nobles arrive next, also hoping for favor while showing their superiority to those already there. Members of the great houses arrive last, ensuring everyone else is present to observe their entrance. The goal for them is to arrive as late as possible without being so late you insult the royal family."

Drake massaged his temples. "Ouch. That's so convoluted it actually hurts my head."

I considered my step-mother's explanation. "Wouldn't you want to show up very early so no one notices your embarrassing relatives? Then you could shove us into a hidden corner somewhere and go about your business? In your place that's what I would do."

"That's exactly what Olivia expects me to do, Jeanine. The

nobles would accept my choice and ignore you entirely throughout the ceremony. But that choice is also a very public admission that Olivia bested me at my own party. That is why we'll arrive so late we *do* insult the royal family."

"Is it a good idea to piss off the most powerful family in the galaxy?" Drake asked.

"Dear, this little stunt is nothing compared to what you and Jeanine are planning."

Drake had shrugged, conceding the point.

And here we were, two days later, descending the grand staircase in the Star Stone Chamber. "Come along, dears, we mustn't keep the kingdom's most vicious twits waiting. Expect the worst from them and pretend as if you don't comprehend the malice beneath their words."

While pretending to gawk at the chamber below us, Drake murmured, "I doubt I'll have to pretend."

I patted his arm. "Don't worry, I'll explain it all to you after the ceremony."

"You're sure no one will attack us outright, Evelyn?" Drake's voice held a hopeful tone. "At least, then I'll know I'm under attack."

Then we reached the floor below and the nobles surged around us like a pack of wild dogs fighting over meager prey. Like the predators they were, the nobles tried to cut Drake and me away from Lady Evelyn's protection. Like a mother protecting her young, Evelyn kept us close, blocking as many barbs as possible.

The initial attacks were subtle, even clever in a nasty way. In response to each thrust, Drake and I just smiled and responded in our false capital accents. In the beginning, we faced hidden smiles at our naïvety. With each undeflected barb, the smiles were more open. Then the smiles transformed into titters, and finally into outright laughter.

At last, certain there was no insult we were too stupid to recognize, one cocksure young noble smirked at Drake and drawled, "Why did you marry *her*? Was your sister already taken?"

Drake's innocent and uncomprehending smile vanished. Grabbing a handful of shirt, he yanked the noble close and cocked his fist. "Do you want to say that again you little snot?"

People backed away hastily, giving us our first bit of breathing room since we reached the floor. Evelyn quickly intervened, gently loosening Drake's hands from the young man's shirt.

"Now, dear, pay no attention to little Freddy." She turned a cruel smile on the man. "No one *ever* pays attention to little Freddy. That's because no one is less important than little Freddy. Am I right, little Freddy?"

As Freddy beat a hasty retreat, Evelyn's gaze swept around those watching. "My cousin is not as stupid as you all believe and I won't stop him the next time one of you pushes him too far."

Suddenly, everyone around us found something more interesting to do. Our peace lasted for no more than two minutes before the royal fanfare sounded.

The herald banged his staff on the floor several times and every voice within the room fell silent. "His Royal Majesty, King Bernard the Second, and Her Royal Majesty, Queen Charlotte."

Everyone dropped to one knee and bowed their heads. Arm-in-arm, the royal pair entered the chamber and ascended to their thrones. Only then did the herald announce, "All may rise."

As we stood, a priest and the prince entered and stood beside the Star Stone. The priest nodded and the bridal fanfare sounded. High above us, Sir Phillip escorted Lady Olivia down the staircase. Like many nearby, I drew a breath of involuntary wonder.

Olivia's gown was magnificent, flattering her form and enhancing her already considerable beauty. Those responsible for Olivia's makeup and hair also outdid themselves. The Duchess of Gaunner looked every inch the fairytale princess as she gracefully descended the stairs. Her gaze sought Prince William and, as it alighted upon him, Olivia's face transformed. She smiled in true joy and dabbed at her cheeks as a few tears escaped her glistening eyes.

"Good God, she truly loves him." I said it under my breath, so only Evelyn and Drake heard me. "This really is the happiest day of her life and I'm going to ruin it."

Evelyn turned a hard stare on me and whispered, "She does. It is. You are. Stay strong, dear. Olivia has earned what's coming dozens of times over."

Drake squeezed my hand. "It's your call, babe. We can just walk away if you want."

I squeezed back. "No. Evelyn is right. We're going to bring the bitch's happiest day crashing down around her."

The red glow of the Star Stone accentuated Olivia's beauty, giving her an almost supernatural glow. The priest led the pair through the ceremony with practiced ease. Before the vows, Prince William took one of Olivia's hands and placed his free hand on the Star Stone. Olivia followed his lead. A deep crimson glow enveloped them as they promised themselves to each other.

"Let God, the Star Stone, and all of your subjects bear witness to your promise. Your matrimonial bond is Recognized and stands for all eternity." The priest gently closed the book he never once referred to. "Prince William, you may kiss your princess."

Cheers filled the chamber as the prince did just that. After an appropriate time, the herald again banged his staff.

"The prince and princess will present themselves to the king and queen!"

Prince William took Princess Olivia's arm, and the pair walked toward the dais where his proud parents waited. At a respectful distance, the crowd of nobles followed the newlyweds. This was the moment I had been waiting for.

Drake and I hung back, letting the crowd flow around us. No one gave us a second thought, anxious as they were to stay near the center of attention. Oh, if only they knew!

A moment later, Drake and I stood next to the Star Stone as the herald once again banged his staff. I placed my hand upon the Star Stone.

Silence fell as those present waited for the herald to announce the prince and princess. So everyone in the chamber heard me speak.

"I, Jeanine Langston, bastard offspring of Arthur, the late Duke of Neert, his last surviving heir, and loyal vassal of His Royal Majesty Bernard the Second, request Recognition as the new Lady of Neert."

The silence in the Star Stone chamber was absolute. I heard Drake's quick, shallow breathing. I heard gasps from the nobles closest to me. I heard the pop of the king's knees as he jumped to his feet. I heard the soft rustle of the queen's gown as she rose gracefully to stand beside her husband. I heard the Star Stone hum gently.

Crimson light flowed up my arm and wrapped itself around me. I shut my eyes as the glow intensified.

Princess Olivia's voice broke the silence. "Burn, you bitch. Burn like my brother did!"

Then the crimson light flowed back to the Star Stone, leaving me whole and unharmed. Removing my hand from the Star Stone, I pulled off my wig. Shaking out my hair, I met Olivia's glare. "Sorry, princess, the Star Stone obviously likes me more than it did your murderous brother."

The king and the prince looked back and forth between Olivia and me, both struggling to figure out what was going on. The queen and the princess stared at me, no doubt wishing for some way to remove me from their lives.

Never breaking eye contact with me, Olivia spoke in her most commanding voice. "Sir Phillip, defend House Kahn. Kill the Wilkinson Bastard!"

The knight never hesitated, drawing his sword as he strode toward me. In a flash, Drake stood between the advancing knight and me.

Still twenty meters away from us, Sir Phillip said, "Move aside, Captain Haral. I have no wish to kill you."

"Too bad," Drake snarled. "You'll have to go through me to get to Jeanine."

The knight gave a slight nod. "So be it."

Drake looked over his shoulder at me. "Run. I'll hold him off as long as I can."

"My days of running are over, dear. But don't worry, I have this."

I think I do. I *hope* I do.

"What do you—"

I laid my hand on the Star Stone again.

"I, Jeanine Langston, Lady of Neert and loyal vassal of His Royal Majesty Bernard the Second, request Recognition as the new Lady of Gaunner."

As crimson ascended my arm for the second time in as many minutes, Princess Olivia screamed in fury. Seconds later, the glow receded.

Drake tried to block me as I stepped around him. I gently pushed his arm aside. Meeting the advancing knight's gaze, I felt my mouth spread into a predatory smile.

"That's enough, Sir Phillip. Sheathe your sword."

The knight's confident stride faltered, then stopped. His eyes widened as he slid his sword back into its scabbard. Dropping to one knee, he said, "As you command, my lady."

Pandemonium erupted from the gathered nobles. Ignoring it, I took Drake's arm and walked toward the staircase. A smiling Lady Evelyn joined us. Without a backward glance at Olivia, Sir Phillip fell in behind us. We were halfway up the stairs before the herald's banging staff brought order to the chamber below.

The king's voice cut through the quiet murmuring. "Lady Jeanine, this is a most irregular display."

Lady Evelyn spoke softly from behind me. "He used your title, dear. Well done. Well done, indeed."

And *that* was when I knew I had won. I let that knowledge illuminate my expression as I stopped and faced the king. "It was a most irregular situation, Your Majesty."

"Was it truly, my lady?"

"I believe so, Sire."

The king waved a hand, dismissing me. "Do not leave the planet, my lady. We may have further questions."

I curtsied as best I could on the stairs. "As you command, Your Majesty."

Without another word, we left the royal palace and returned to Lady Evelyn's—no, *my*—estate.

The minute we entered the palace, Drake caught my arm and pulled me toward an empty sitting room. "We have to talk. *Now.*"

Sir Phillip immediately drew his sword and leveled it at Drake. "Unhand Lady Jeanine this instant!"

Drake whirled on the knight, his eyes flashing. Before he could speak, I said, "Drake is my husband, Sir Phillip. You will *never* threaten him again."

Without a hint of embarrassment, Sir Phillip sheathed his sword. "I hear and obey, my lady."

Drake and I retired to the sitting room. He waited until the door clicked shut before speaking. "Was it always your plan to request Recognition as the Duchess of Gaunner?"

I shook my head. "No. I decided to do it two days ago though only if necessary."

"And what made you think it would be granted? Or was that just a lucky guess?"

"Jana found something interesting while searching the royal archives for information on the Recognition ceremony—the record of the last time a sitting lord married into the royal family." Suddenly exhausted, I dropped into a chair. "It was over three hundred years ago, that is why hardly anyone remembers anything about it. The wedding was followed by the Recognition of a new lord to replace the one who married the princess."

"Based on that little account, you assumed you could claim Gaunner?" Drake began pacing back and forth before me. "What if you had been wrong?"

"First, I wasn't wrong." I met Drake's glare with one of my own. "Second, Jana searched the entire archive for more information on the ceremony. She found several more such weddings, each with a simple notation of the Recognition of a new lord. But she didn't stop there. She investigated every lord's Recognition ceremony for the last two thousand years. Each time, the account included either a sitting lord voluntarily stepping aside or dying."

Drake stopped pacing and dropped in a chair opposite me. "And the two of you decided that was proof enough to take such a risk?"

"Yes, but only in dire need. I couldn't let Sir Phillip kill you."

"Do you honestly believe the king would have allowed that, Jeanine?"

"With all my heart, Drake. Did you hear the king gainsay his new daughter-in-law's order?"

Drake shook his head. "No."

"Neither did I. Perhaps he was simply testing our resolve and ingenuity. Or maybe he was just pissed off because we stole the spotlight from his only child. But I firmly believe he would have let us die if we couldn't save ourselves."

"You could have told me, you know." Drake came over and squeezed into the chair with me. With a deft move, he lifted me onto his lap and pulled me close.

"I will from now on, dear." I kissed him gently. "No more secrets."

When we emerged from the room, I immediately summoned Sir Phillip. "His Majesty ordered me to stay here. You were not included in that order, Sir Phillip."

"Where would you have me go, my lady?" the knight asked.

"Return to Gaunner with all haste," I said. "Several friends were captured rescuing me from the palace. Find them. Free them. Bring them to Neert. Until you hear otherwise from me, you will give them the same respect and protection you give me."

"As you command, my lady."

The king sent a minor reprimand when news of Sir Phillip's departure reached him. I sent an apologetic non-apology—worded by Evelyn since I had no idea what to say—in response. That was the end of the matter.

We remained on Xapreathea for another six days. Every noble who attended the wedding remained, also. The gossip flew fast and furious. Speculation on my fate ranged from execution to exile. The end, when it came, was anticlimactic. The king never summoned me. Instead, he gave me leave to depart.

Evelyn offered the most likely explanation. "The king gave Olivia all the time she needed to have Gaunner's files scrubbed. Rest assured, you'll never find anything tying Olivia to Sir Phillip's actions against you nor will you find evidence her elder brother murdered my husband and our children."

"Who needs that when we have Sir Phillip?" Drake asked. "Jeanine can simply order him to testify against the princess."

I shook my head. "Just as a Recognized knight cannot attack his Duke or Duchess, he also cannot disobey a direct order from them. If I ordered him to, Sir Phillip would accuse anyone, from a commoner on the street all the way up to the king, of treason. For that reason, Recognized knights cannot testify in court."

"Well, at least we've gained one ally from all of this," Drake said. "I rather doubt a single Recognized knight offsets having the royal family as enemies, but I guess he's better than nothing."

On that ambivalent note, we left for Neert.

As our spaceship approached Neert, Evelyn laid a hand on my shoulder. "Welcome home, dear."

Home.

A strange word that never had much meaning to me. Other people had homes. I had an apartment. Or a house. Sometimes even just a tent in the woods. Simply a place to live. A place to put what little I owned. But never a *home.*

I wished Grandfather—Sir Jared—was alive to share this moment with me. I would happily trade all of this—the title, the wealth, the power, and the responsibility—to simply have him by my side again.

Drake, his arm wrapped around me, gave me a gentle squeeze.

I suddenly realized having Grandfather by my side would almost certainly mean not having Drake there. It would mean the man I now love would still be out among the stars, playing the part of the carefree womanizer while slowly dying inside. It would mean me returning to my life as a timid-but-deadly wallflower. If you believe in spirits—which I do—it would mean leaving Heather and Candi restless and worried Drake would simply give up and join them in death.

"He's happy for you, you know," Drake said.

I roused from my reverie, knowing my husband had spoken but nothing more. "Hm? What was that, dear?"

"Your grandfather. Wherever he is, he's happy for you and proud of all you've done."

Thank you, Grandfather, for selecting Drake to deliver that message.

I wrapped both arms around Drake and rested my head against his shoulder. "Heather and Candi are proud of you, too, Drake. No doubt, Grandfather and Heather are together and swapping stories about us right now."

We held each other until the pilot told us to strap in for the landing. The view screens switched to canned images of Neert during the ship's entry into the atmosphere. I was so busy discussing policies with Evelyn and Drake, I didn't even glance at them again. So I was completely surprised by the welcome I received when we emerged from the ship.

As I blinked, temporarily blinded by the bright light, a band struck up the Neert anthem. Then Drake stepped to the side, letting me see the thousands gathered across the landing field. It also let the multitude see me. A roar rose, drowning out the band completely.

I just stood there, baffled by the crowd's reaction. To my right, Drake beamed in pleasure. To my left, Evelyn wore her usual, gentle smile.

Sensing my confusion at the crowd's welcome, she leaned close to my ear. "They've spent years waiting for one of the other duchies—most particularly Gaunner—to annex them and turn them all into second class citizens. You took what should have been their ancient enemy's greatest triumph—Olivia marrying into the royal family—and turned it into Neert's ultimate victory. You are their hero, Jeanine, and the people of Neert have always adored heroes."

Belatedly, I raised both arms and waved at my people. The roar swelled. It was so loud I almost missed Evelyn's next words.

"Just remember, as much as the people of Neert revere you, the people of Gaunner will revile you. It will not be easy to sway them to your side."

We descended the ship's ramp and passed between the ranks of my honor guard. Captain Pennington barked an order, and they saluted as one. Beyond my honor guard, the planet's officials all went to one knee. Only then did I realize they were blocking our view of Sir Phillip and, arrayed uncomfortably next to the knight, Drake's old crew. All except Tanner that is.

As I motioned for the officials to rise, Drake ran to embrace his friends. They laughed and hugged and drew me into their reunion. Only when Evelyn tapped me on the shoulder did I pull back from the tangle of arms.

My stepmother motioned to a raised platform just beyond our friends. On it stood a simple podium arrayed with audio receptors and cams. I was tired and didn't want to make a speech. But the wants and needs of my people were now a major consideration for me.

As I ascended into sight of the crowd, the cheers intensified yet again. All around the landing field, huge vid screens sprang to life. Ten-meter tall images of my head looked out from those screens. I let the cheering carry on for a few more seconds before raising my hands in a call for silence.

"My people..." I paused as the crowd roared another time. This time, I simply smiled and let the noise trail off on its own. Shaking my head, I said, "That's going to take some getting used to. Never in my life have I had people to call my own. Never have I had a home. Now, I have both. Thank you for your welcome. Thank you for letting me join you as a citizen of Neert."

I dabbed my suddenly damp eyes, drawing forth another round of cheering. I found myself laughing and crying, which only made the people cheer more loudly than before. Once again, I raised my arms, requesting silence.

"Gaining Recognition as your duchess wasn't easy, but it may be the easiest part of our journey together. Many of the nobles are not happy with me. They believe I overstepped by requesting Recognition as the new Duchess of Gaunner. And I can only imagine what the royal family thinks of me!" Though I wasn't making a joke, the crowd laughed. "But most pressing and most concerning, I cannot imagine what the people of Gaunner think of me."

A man close to the podium shouted, "Who cares?"

His question was picked up and shouted by many in the crowd. Cheering sounded every time someone repeated the question.

I stopped smiling and let my gaze sweep over the crowd. "*I* care! And so should all of you. Did you want to fall under the rule of Gaunner?"

No one shouted. No one cheered.

"Exactly." I gave one firm nod. "Do you think the people of Gaunner feel any differently? Do you think they aren't worried that I'll punish them for the actions of House Kahn? Of course, they are."

Now the crowd was completely silent, every eye watching me. "*We* must convince them otherwise. *We* must show them compassion! *We* must dispel their fear! *We* must welcome them into our fold."

I pointed at myself. "Not me."

I pointed out into the crowd. "Not you."

I swept my arm in an all-encompassing arch. "*We.*"

I took a deep breath. "It won't be easy. There is a lot of mistrust between Neert and Gaunner. But I think we can do it. Who's with me?"

The answering cheers were so loud the platform vibrated. I let the noise wash over me for a few seconds, hoping the crowd's enthusiasm would carry on beyond this welcoming ceremony. Finally, I waved and let Captain Pennington escort me to my ground car. Drake and Evelyn climbed in behind me, both of them smiling broadly.

"You were magnificent, babe!" my husband said. "It's too bad you don't want to be queen because you'd make a damned good one."

I punched him in the shoulder. Hard.

"Ouch!" Drake rubbed his shoulder with one hand and held the other out in mock surrender. Still smiling, he said, "Got it. You still don't want to be queen. I swear I'll never bring it up again."

"See that you don't." My glare didn't make him wipe the smile from his face. I gave up and smiled back at him. "I've got at least half of the galaxy's nobles arrayed against me, have two duchies to unite, a rebellion to support, and a kingdom to topple. I don't have time to be queen, too."

I leaned against Drake. "But if you ask nicely, perhaps we can find time to start that family we've been talking about."

Drake looped an arm around my shoulder. "I like that idea. I like it a whole lot."

MAGNIFICENT ENEMIES

Olivia

I was in a black mood and, from the way the servants and William did their best to avoid me, I wasn't hiding it well. Or at all.

The vid was playing again—the one the newsies couldn't get enough of. I'd expected one particular vid would dominate the news cycle, but I thought the vid would feature William and me. Instead, it was all about *her*—the Wilkinson bitch. The newsies skirted around the enmity between the new Duchess of both Neert and Gaunner and the new princess of the realm, but they jumped all over the rest of the story.

They told of the bitch's escape from the attack that claimed Sir Jared's life.

They recounted her desperate flight from 'unnamed' authorities.

They described her secret wedding as if it was the romance of the century.

And they talked incessantly of her 'courageous' and 'surprising' Recognition in the middle of *my* wedding.

Oh, yes, the beautiful bitch and her dashing husband were the darlings of the vids. Their popularity among the viewing public easily dwarfed the previous vid sensation—the romance between Prince William and me.

I was so wrapped up in my seething hatred for all things associated with *that* woman that I didn't even notice the door to our suite open. Glaring single-mindedly at the vid, I didn't hear the soft tread of footsteps coming my way. I only noticed the intruder when she sat down next to me.

"She's very photogenic and quite a beautiful woman," Queen Charlotte said, her tone almost dispassionate. "I don't believe she can quite match your standard, Olivia, but the contrast between her red hair and pale skin is very striking."

"How can you be so nonchalant about this?" I asked, turning an incredulous look on my mother-in-law. "She *ruined* my wedding."

"Yes, she did," Charlotte mused. "Rather brilliantly, too."

"You're complimenting her? And in *my* presence?"

Charlotte met my glare with a steely gaze. "Yes, Olivia, I'm complimenting her and I'm daring to do so directly to you. I understand your feelings toward the woman but, unless you check and channel them properly, they will do you no good."

"My God, you admire the bitch!"

"Most definitely, my dear, as should you."

My face reddened in a fury I didn't think I could control. When my mouth opened to vent that rage at Charlotte, she placed a single finger over my lips.

"Shush, daughter-in-law, before you say something your queen cannot excuse."

That got my attention. Closing my eyes, I breathed deeply and fought for control of myself. The struggle took a full minute, but I finally opened my eyes and regarded Queen Charlotte with a calm expression.

Removing her finger, Charlotte said, "That's much better, Olivia. Now, use that lovely mind of yours and tell me *why* I admire Lady Jeanine."

I carefully ordered my thoughts and said, "She relied on

instinct when it was necessary and her instincts were very good. She improvised with both flare and ingenuity. She planned carefully but acted audaciously. And, most importantly, she bested both of us at our own game."

"Very good, dear, though you left out her ability to find and recruit talented followers—especially her husband. They are a formidable pair, made even more dangerous by their association with Evelyn Wilkinson. The three of them will make magnificent enemies."

"If you like them so much, why don't you invite them to tea?" I growled.

"That's a splendid idea, Olivia! Though, we'll wait until you've both settled into your new positions."

"I wasn't being serious, Charlotte."

"I was."

"Well, if I'm going to have to socialize with the woman—"

"Which you will, dear."

"Why don't William and I take the Royal Navy and 'socialize' the upstart off the face of her planet?"

"Oh, Olivia, you really have to rein in your temper. What do you think the other nobles would do if the royal family attacked one of their number without provocation?"

I sighed. As a former duchess, I knew exactly what they'd do. "They would rally to Lady Jeanine's defense."

"Exactly, dear. Our forces are stronger than any four of the great houses, but nowhere near strong enough to face the combined might of all twelve. May I assume you do not want to be executed after a bloody civil war?"

"You may. It's just so frustrating to see her like…" I waved my hand at the vid unit. "That."

"Happy, you mean."

I nodded.

Charlotte patted my hand. "Trust me, Olivia, her happiness will not last. Her generous nature will eventually lead her astray. That is why we must be vigilant and learn everything we can about our newest noble. We must be ready to act when she stumbles."

I felt my mouth stretch into a fierce grin. "And then we crush her?"

My mother-in-law smiled at me. "Yes, dear, then we crush her."

241

ABOUT THE AUTHOR

Henry Vogel began his writing career in comic books way back in the 1980s, with the indie titles *Southern Knights* and *X-Thieves*. When the bottom dropped out of the black & white comic book market, Henry went into IT, where he worked for the next thirty-three years. Henry took up professional storytelling in 2006, and has performed all across his home state of North Carolina.

As a lifetime fan of science fiction, Henry always wanted to write science fiction novels. He began writing *Scout's Honor* in 2012, and released it to the world in 2014. He hasn't stopped writing since.

Henry makes his home in Raleigh, NC, and is hard at work on his next novel.

www.henryvogelwrites.com

ALSO BY HENRY VOGEL

Travis & Trouble

Trouble in Twi-Town

Trouble on Mars

The Fortune Chronicles

Fortune's Fool

The Scales of Sin & Sorrow

The Scout Series

Scout's Honor

Scout's Oath

Scout's Duty

Scout's Law

Scout's Training

Scout's First Mission

Hart for Adventure

The Princess Scout

Scout: The Lost Colony Adventures

Non-series books

The Lost Planet

Heart of Dorkness & Other Stories

The Connaught Family Chronicles

The Fugitive Heir

The Fugitive Pair

The Fugitive Snare

The Hostage in Hiding

The Captain Nancy Martin

The Counterfeit Captain

The Undercover Captain

The Recognition Series

The Recognition Run

The Recognition Rejection

The Recognition Revelation

Comic Books

Aristocratic Xraterrestrial Time-Traveling Thieves Complete Collection

Southern Knights Almost Complete Collection

Southern Knights Color Edition

Southern Knights: The Morrigan Wars

Southern Knights: Leaving Atlanta (prose novella)

Missing Beings

Illustrated Children's Book

I'm in Charge! and Other Stories